DEATH IN WEST HARBOR

By

John Lundquist

Dedicated to my wonderful wife Nancy

1. Welcome to West Harbor

    The rains hit the tin roof with a solid beat, giving the illusion that there was a drummer in the sky providing a tempo for Luella Chambers, sitting in her favorite chair, overlooking the ocean in her two bedroom house, as she rocked back and thought of the letter. She had made the seventy foot walk through the rain to the post office, talked to the postmistresses, Bonnie Williams, chatted about the weather and the prices of food in Young Tom's store, and picked up the letter, then returned home to her sanctuary by the sea. She walked into her familiar house, with its comforting pictures atop the sideboard, alongside the jars of shells and driftwood, its overstuffed furniture filling the small space, and the warmth coming from the wood stove in the far corner. She made herself a cup of camomile tea, adding a taste of honey to the steaming mug, then left the spoon atop the faded yellow linoleum counter, crossed the room and sat in the chair. She sipped her tea and read the letter, tears rolling down her cheeks.

    Louella pushed back a wisp of short curly gray hair and thought about her life. Living in West Harbor for the past twenty years had little prepared her for the cruel twists of fate. She had done a good job of digging in, gaining weight and thick ankles along the way, and providing a home for herself, husband, Tony, and daughter, Margaret, and had done her best when Tony left. He had better things to do, he told her, than stay with a fat, ugly woman with poor eyesight and limited imagination, though both had helped her tolerate the abusive Tony and his wandering eyes. He left her alone to raise their daughter, and fend for herself in this little town that was twenty miles from the nearest big city. It was difficult at first, then she came to love her solitude, walking along the beach below her house, and up to the old school, now used as a community center, and interacting with residents of the tiny hamlet. Louella liked her neighbors, though Young Tom could be brusque, and Bill Seavers rarely gave her the time of day, but Bonnie was nice, and the hippie girl, Sunflower, always wished her a good morning, whether it was good or not. It was a quiet life along the northern California coast, where fog and rain were constant companions.

The wind and rain continued to beat against the window overlooking the water, giving her a fuzzy view of the churned up ocean a mere hundred feet away. The wood stove fought to keep the room warm, but it was a losing battle, as the wood burned rapidly. The temperature seemed to drop as she sat in her chair, re-reading the letter.

Louella sighed, putting the letter and steaming mug of tea on a nearby side table, then pushed her girth out of the chair. She was ready to reach down and grab another chunk of wood to add to the fire and discovered that the metal stand next to the wood stove was empty. She sighed, then stood up slowly, feeling the ache in her bones.

"Stupid," she muttered to herself. "Should have brought in more when I was out."

She crossed the room and walked out the front door, feeling the wind and rain hit her face, then entered the carport, empty since she was without a car, and to the pile of wood stacked alongside the house. Louella picked up a half dozen foot length pieces of wood, cradling them in her bulky arms, feeling the sharp edges cut into her forearms, and headed back into the rain and cold on her way back to the relative warmth of the house. Once inside, she kicked the door closed with one foot, then quickly crossed the room and dropped the wood into the stand.

She opened the grate of the wood stove with an oven mitt, and tossed in a piece, followed by another, the warmth of the fire burning her face. As she about to close the grate, she looked at the letter sitting on the table next to her rocking chair. Louella thought about it for about two seconds as the trapped water in the burning wood popped, sending a burning ember out the grate and onto the old Navajo rug she and Tony got in new Mexico. She let it burn for a second, slightly concerned about the house burning down, then the fire was out. The heat of the open wood stove burned her neck. She felt beads of perspiration build on her forehead. Then without further thought, she snatched up the letter and tossed it into the fire.

Louella watched the letter burn, the inked letters shriveling up, before turning to flames, then ash. She closed the grate and sat back in her rocking chair. Many years ago, she shared this house and now, she was alone. She and her memories. Louella picked up the still hot mug and set it down quickly to avoid the burn, then took it by the handle and sipped the hot steamy liquid. She glanced at where the burning letter was all but gone behind the grate and thought, if only it were that easy. Then she began to cry.

#

Bonnie Williams had been the postmistresses since her father passed away some twenty years ago. The post office wasn't a fancy affair. It had a small space in the front for the customers with a high counter splitting the room. A small filing card system for the residents sat atop a counter next to the cubby holes for the mail and a long shelve for the occasional package. In the rear of the working section of the building was a door that led to the tiny quarters occupied by the post mistresses. Unlike her father, who wore the official uniform of the postal service, Bonnie preferred wearing bib overalls on her petite frame, her long hair touching her shoulders and her eyes alert at the possibilities of life that surrounded her. She was in her mid-fifties and hadn't had a boyfriend since high school.

But Bonnie wasn't alone in the office.

Adam Franklin, the widower from katy-corner across the street was visiting, as he often did, trying to ingratiate himself to her, trying to win over the enigmatic woman for whom life had dealt a strange hand.

Once upon a time, as the fairy tales go, Bonnie was a young lady with dreams of moving to the big city to pursue an acting career. She was going to be on stage and in film, showing the world her charm and ingenuity, but something happened along the way that derailed her dream. Her parents got sick. First her mother, who needed constant care while her father ran the post office, then mother died and somebody had to take care of father, who was hopeless in the face of adversity. Bonnie began helping out, running both the home and the post office and when her father got sick and died, she naturally took over. Opportunity had come to the door and left her to watch over the small community where she had lived her entire life.

West Harbor had been a thriving community, with a half dozen streets paralleling the coast, a hotel and three stores. The town was in full swing as a fishing port, then came the storms, knocking out the docks that served the industry, and a depression that closed the warehouse, then the fires destroyed the hotel and the nearby hatchery, and slowly, the industry moved south to Rock Port, leaving West Harbor to wither away and die.

Bonnie had seen it all, weathered the storms, watched her parents die, along with the community, and now held the one position of authority over her home town. She looked at Franklin, with his gray crew cut, maroon cardigan and striped red and white bow tie, sitting on a tall stool across the counter from her. She knew that he was sweet on her, but didn't feel much in return. Her days of boyfriends were gone, along with any hope of marriage. Somehow, things just never worked out for her.

"So what was Lou so upset about?" asked Franklin.

"She got a letter."

"What kind of letter?"

"How would I know? She didn't open it here. One look at the thing and she nearly fainted. From her reaction, I'd say it was bad news."

"Where was it from?"

"I can't tell you that," said Bonnie. "That's official post office business. You want to go ask her, be my guest." Bonnie knew that the letter was from Louella's ex-husband, Tony, from the return address, but didn't know what was in the letter. "You go talk to her and let me know."

"Bad news, eh?" Franklin scratched his chin. "I wonder what's going on with Lou?"

"You got nothing better to do with your time but sit around here and gossip? I've got work to do. Some of us still have to work for a living."

Just at that moment, the bell above the door chimed and the hippie girl, Sunflower, came in from the rain, holding onto an umbrella that did little to keep the rain off her long red hair or paisley dress.

"Morning, Sunflower," said Bonnie. "Rains coming down pretty hard still?"

Sunflower left her umbrella at the door, setting it on a piece of cardboard, then joined the other two. "Cold and damp. The goats are hiding in the shed, for all the good it's doing them. I told Star about the leaky roof last week, but do you think he'd get off his lazy butt and fix it? Not a chance."

"How are your goats?" asked Bonnie.

"Sick," said Sunflower, crossing the room. "I think somebody's putting poison in their food."

"That's awful," said Franklin. "Are you sure?"

"They're pretty sick," said Sunflower.

"It's probably the rain," said Bonnie. She liked Sunflower, even if she was a hippie girl with a strange name. Why couldn't she have a normal name? Did her parents name her after a flower when she was born? Sunflower and her common law husband, Star, had moved to West Harbor ten years earlier, had a child they named Genesis, and had become a part of the community, but in Bonnie's opinion, they were odd.

"Poison," repeated Sunflower, "or maybe some goat disease. I have no idea. That's Star's department. So, any mail today, Miss Postmistresses?"

Bonnie turned around, faced the hundred slots behind her and reached up and took a small bundle from the cubby hole and handed it to Sunflower. "The usual. No lottery winner this week."

Sunflower tucked the bundle into a pocket in her dress and smiled. "Nothing bad I hope." She headed to the door and picked up her umbrella. Sunflower looked over at Bonnie. "Don't tell anybody I mentioned poison, okay? I don't want Bill Seavers thinking I'm accusing him of killing off our livestock."

"Mum's the word," said Bonnie.

"Thanks. Well, it's back to the rain for me."

Bonnie and Franklin watched Sunflower leave, and the cold rain filled the small cavity for a moment, then the chill was gone. The ticking of the clock was the only sound for a brief moment, then Bonnie sighed.

"She's not a very happy girl, you know."

"But what about you?" asked Franklin. "Are you a very happy girl?"

Bonnie shook her head. "Go home, Adam, and let me do my job."

#

Sunflower walked in the rain, letting the drops hit her umbrella and keep her from thinking too much. She walked down the lane from the post office, passing Adam

Franklins' bungalow on the left with the oh so perfect Seaver house straight ahead. Off to the north was the old school house, with its silent bell tower and faded white shingle siding, and to the east of that were the small cottages that the new comers occupied, then Old Tom's place. Sunflower could see the dirt of Mountain Road, leading up to the cemetery above the town, then disappearing into the thick woods higher up. Old Tom's wife was buried in that cemetery. Would Sunflower meet a similar fate?

     She had not always been Sunflower, and as Bonnie noted, she certainly wasn't happy. She was born Tracy Johnson, in San Bruno, to a working class house. Her father worked as a mechanic for a garage down the block, her mom stayed home and took care of Tracy and her brother, Todd, and sister, Terry. The three T's, they used to call themselves. Then their parents got divorced, her brother got heavily involved with drugs, and her older sister ran away from home to get away from the fighting, leaving Tracy with no one to count on, and no one to help her through the troubling days of youth. Since her family was such a mess, she adopted another one to replace it, joining the hippies that roamed the west coast. It was at a concert in Golden Gate Park that she met Star and it was love at first sight. He was everything her father wasn't. Sensitive, worldly, and completely into promoting a green earth. Their ten years together, producing one child, an eight year old boy named Genesis, had been harmonious, to a point, but lately, there was a nagging feeling in Sunflower's mind that there was more to life than avoiding the middle class existence that she ran away from those many years ago.

She glanced at the Seaver house, built of brick and wood in the nineties, with a two car garage, the door open and a busy Bill Seavers busy working on a wardrobe cabinet inside. Theirs was a three bedroom house, with two baths, a large fenced in yard, central heat and air conditioning. Sunflower was jealous of the luxury. She waved at Seavers, then continued north on Second Street to her house, and a major let down after the solidity of the Seaver House. Her house was a ramshackle affair with leaky roof, warped flooring, and unfinished just about everything. The structure had once been a barn, and converted into a home, without any of the finishing touches.

Sunflower left her umbrella at the door and entered her home. The sound of the wind could still be heard and felt through the holes in the walls and ceiling. A constant drip hitting the several pans scattered on every available surface provided a cacophony of noise, each pan giving a different pitch as the water dropped from various heights to hit the pans. Some missed and hit the floor and counter tops. The kitchen, with its scarred linoleum counter tops, was separated from the big room by a half wall, giving a good view of the large open space beyond. The cavernous room looked even bigger with the second hand furniture and large Green Peace flag tacked up on one wall, with leaky windows filling the opposite side.

She could see out the kitchen window at the back yard and the small shed where the goats lived, and the crappy fence that mostly kept the goats on the property. Sunflower had been at Star for most of the summer to fix the fence, but her husband always had something better to do. Same with the holes in the walls and ceiling. Same with the dirty dishes. The only thing Star was concerned about was protecting his precious stereo and hundreds of albums that lined the opposite wall. No rain hit this ensemble. There was no television, no DVD player, no blue ray, nothing other than music, for Star claimed that entertainment was achieved through music. He was an accomplished dulcimer player and often accompanied Sunflower on guitar on those cold rainy nights.

Sunflower looked at her husband, lounging in his wicker chair, listening to African music on the stereo and felt only disgust. His lanky six foot frame was crunched into the small chair, his long braided hair hung over one shoulder. He wore his usual: blue jeans and a blue plaid shirt over a Grateful Dead t-shirt.

"Any mail from our dear postmistress?" asked Star, looking up from the macrame he was knotting on his lap.

Sunflower reached into the pocket of her dress and pulled out the bundle and handed it to Star without as much as looking at the contents.

Star took the offered pile and began shifting through them. "Bills, bills, bills. And some junk from our illustrious cable television outlet. When will they learn that we will not be subject to the mindless drivel associated with that so called modern convenience? If people would simply turn off that waste of time and focused on more important things, this world would be a better place."

"Like fixing the holes in the roof?" asked Sunflower.

"I told you that the holes are natures way of joining the outer and inner worlds, sharing our space in the universe as the great One intended, and that the holes are mere reflections of the master plan."

"The master plan is forming puddles on the kitchen floor."

"As it should be," said Star. "You know that the ancient ones came to this backward planet to colonize the local population and that eventually, the wise ones will return the enlightened ones back to the Pleiades from whence we came, and that a few holes in the roof will not matter one whit in the larger scheme of things."

"It does when I have to live with it. I am sick and tired of living like pigs. Look around you, Star. We live like animals. The plumbing only works when it wants to, the heat is nearly non-existent. We sweat likes dogs all summer long, even when it's cold outside, then come winter we freeze. Do you realize that I have to put three sweaters on Genesis every night so he doesn't freeze in his sleep? I'm sick of this. I need more."

Star pushed his tall body from his chair and walked over to Sunflower and held her in his arms. "You know we've always lived like this. Why is this a problem now?"

She lifted her head and stared at the wispy goatee that adorned his chin. "Because it is."

"What do you want from me? That I should crawl up on that slick roof and pound a few nails and risk falling off and breaking my neck? I thought we were so much above all that. We are living in harmony with out the extraneous crap that saddles down most of our fellow man. But if you want, I'll risk life and limb for you, right now."

She pushed away from him. "I don't want you to hurt yourself, Star, I just want more."

He smiled. "Whatever you wish, it's yours. You want the moon? I'll bring it to you. The milky way? It's yours. What is it that you want most?"

She turned and looked at the kitchen, then back to Star. "I want you to wash the dishes."

He made an exaggerated bow, then stood up and smiled. "Your wish is my command."

#

Bill Seavers planed the wood with care, making sure that there were no divots and no blemishes, for this piece was going to be front and center for the wardrobe he was completing. It was a big piece, one that would bring a lot of money to the table, and that was good, for they needed the money. The refrigerator was on its last legs and the Christmas was just around the corner. Granted it was only October, but the fall rains were here and before he knew it, November and Thanksgiving were upon him, then the quick three weeks to Christmas and he was expected to come up with the money to make sure that it was a merry Christmas indeed. Fortunately, the wardrobe was nearly completed, and once done, it was on the truck to San Francisco and his vendor.

Seavers was of average size, with sandy brown hair, cold blue eyes, and a clipped moustache, but what he could do with his hands was remarkable. If it was mechanical, Seavers could fix it, whether it was a automobile, a generator, or garbage disposal. He was equally talented when it came to home repairs. There were no holes in the Seaver house, no leaks in the plumbing, no loose tile in the kitchen, and no missing links in the fence that encircled both the front and back yards. He was a busy man, spending most of his days maintaining the house and grounds, and doing what he actually got paid for: his woodwork.

His strong work ethic and boyish good looks attracted Mary, ex-high school cheerleader, and mate, the mother of his two children, eight year old Cindy, a small version of her mother and Bill, Jr., known as Billy, a six year old just starting in the first grade. Seavers met Mary in high school in Rock Port, got married, and moved to West Harbor right after graduating. With some help from both parents, they bought a fixer upper in this small hamlet and Seavers went to work, shoring up the floors, re-wiring the electrical and moving the plumbing around, putting down hardwood floors and tile, and making their home the envy of the town.

Seavers divided his two car garage into halves, with one side holding his big truck and the other his work area. Here he had his sawhorses, his saws, his power tools, his wood shaping tools, all neatly arranged either on the long work bench, or on the peg board behind the bench, or on the large shelves against the back wall. Everything in its place, easy to access, and put back in its proper location when finished. It was the way he was raised, by an ex-military father and stern mother.

He was busy, planing the wood that would give them a good Christmas, the radio blasting country western music to keep time with the rain falling outside the open doorway, and didn't notice when his wife came through the doorway leading to the kitchen.

Mary Seavers was a pretty petite blonde, with big blue eyes and light freckles across her nose, who had maintained her trim figure, working hard to put the pregnancy weight behind her. She wore form flattering jeans and a Save the Whales sweat shirt that did little to hide her assets. She had a steamy mug of coffee in her hand, passing it off to her husband.

"Thought you might like something warm to drink," she said.

He took the offered coffee and eyed her outfit. "You think you can wear something a little tighter? It looks like you painted that outfit on."

"I thought you liked my figure."

"I do, but that don't mean you have to advertise it to the rest of the town."

"Well aren't you just a grumpy Gus today."

He sipped his coffee, feeling the heat on his tongue, the aroma of french roast tickling his nostrils. "It's those damn goats. Kept me awake half the night with their noise. I'm surprised you didn't hear them. Lousy goats. Why do they have to have them anyway? They stink, they're noisy, and I'm pretty sure they're a health hazard. I should make a call to the county and see if it's legal to keep them in a residential neighborhood."

"You will do no such thing," said Mary. "That's how Star and Sunflower put food on their table. Where are they going to get money to feed Genesis without the goats?'

"He could get a job. Cut his hair, toe the line like everybody else."

"Here? Where is he going to get a job in West Harbor? The only jobs we have are the postmistresses position, already taken, and Young Tom's superette. You think Star could get a job pumping gas for Young Tom? That's something I'd like to see."

"I'm just saying the goats are a menace. Somebody's going to put something in their food someday and then we'll see what happens to those darn hippies."

"You leave the goats alone, Bill, if you know what's good for you."

"All I'm saying is that anything could happen to them, you see that fence he has around their pen? No wonder the goats get out. He's lucky there isn't much traffic on this street. They wander down to the highway and they're dead meat."

Mary looked at the wardrobe. "It's coming along nicely, Bill. You do nice work."

"Don't try to change the subject."

"Why? You want to bitch some more about the goats? Let it go. Why don't you take a break and let me make you a nice lunch. The kids won't be home for another couple of hours, maybe you'd like to put that time to good use."

"I've got to finish this piece," said Seavers, ignoring his wife's look. He knew what she was saying, without saying it. As much as he wanted to just give in and accept her offer, he was too stubborn to do more than pout. The goats got on his nerves and he had work to do. "Thanks just the same."

She waited for a full minute, staring at her husband as he set the coffee mug on the bench and picked up the plane and started to work, before heading toward the house. "I'll bring you a sandwich."

#

Thomas Jones was known in West Harbor as Young Tom, as opposed to Old Tom who had been in West Harbor the past fifty years. Jones owned and operated the lone gas pump and grocery store. He was a forty year old bachelor with a shaved head, bushy mustache and looked like a saloon keeper with white shirt, black slacks and a bolo tie. His store, the Super Saver, was located fifty feet north of the post office and a hundred feet from the ocean. His was a small town operation, just a little off the main road with room enough for two cars, one pumping gas and the other waiting, with a ten foot walk to the front of the store. The building itself was built in the forties, had faded white shingles, and small windows, recently covered with wire mesh to thwart thieves. Inside was a counter to the right and shelves of food to the left, stocked with the staples that keep a village alive. Canned food sat on a shelve opposite laundry supplies, with sodas and ice cream in a cooler along the back wall. A back door led to his living quarters, consisting of a large room that doubled as a stock room. Here was his bed, under the lone window, a back door, a chest of drawers, and boxes of goods stacked on shelves lining the remaining walls.

Jones came to West Harbor two years earlier, took over a failing business and turned it around, mostly by charging prices twenty percent higher than those in Rock Port. His theory was a captive audience will pay more for the convenience and so far, he had been correct in his assessment. He was originally from Los Angeles and had come north to get away from a lifestyle that was bound to kill him. In West Harbor, he was a respected, if not liked, businessman. He kept to himself and expected others to do the same. Unfortunately, a small town is full of gossip, and there were many rumors around the village about Jones. What had he done before West Harbor? Some thought he was an escaped felon, others believed he had run away from a failed marriage. Believe what they will, Jones reasoned, as long as they continued to buy their food and gas in his establishment.

The bell over the door rang as a customer came in. Jones looked up from the crossword puzzle he was doing and nodded at Old Tom, his back bent over like a question mark, his white hair sticking out from under a watchman's cap, his black suit spotted with cat hair.

"Wet enough out there for you?"

"Seen worse."

Making conversation with Old Tom was worse than pulling teeth.

Old Tom shuffled into the store and walked right down to the limited pet food section of the store, next to baking goods and greeting cards on a spindle at the end of the aisle. He picked up ten cans of cat food and moved slowly to the counter, where he dropped the cans.

Jones started ringing them up. For most of the residents in town, he felt no remorse charging what he did for his canned goods, on the justification that he had to bring those things to town himself. Gas costs and time used were his usual explanations. And for the most part, he felt okay with his policies, but with Old Tom, he felt bad. He knew that the old man didn't have much money, spending it mostly on his six cats.

"Nothing for you today, Tom?"

"I'm good."

Good indeed, thought Jones. Most likely, the cat food was for all six of the residents of the Hoffman household. It had been five years since Old Tom's wife died, buried up at the cemetery up Mountain Road, and probably five years since he ate decently. In a fit of unexpected generosity, Jones moved around the counter, grabbed a couple of cans of stew off the nearby shelf and returned to his spot behind the counter.

"I don't need that," said Old Tom.

"It's a special today," lied Jones. "Ten cans of cat food gets you a couple cans of stew."

"Don't need it," insisted Old Tom. "The pretty girl down the road gives me goats milk and cheese."

Jones rang up the rest of the cans and put them in a bag. "That'll be seven dollars."

While Old Tom reached into his pocket for his wallet and was distracted, Jones shoved the two cans of stew into the bag. A wrinkled ten dollar bill appeared in the old man's hand and the transaction was quickly completed, with three dollars in change returned.

The old man took his bag and shuffled out the door, just as the newest arrivals to West Harbor entered the store. Robert and Millie Peterson were twenty something's who looked more like brother and sister than husband and wife, both with shag hair cuts, wearing jeans and pea coats and rain hats covering their heads.

"Good morning, Mr. Jones," said Millie. "Isn't it just wonderful today?"

Jones nodded at them. "Wonderful."

The young people walked down the aisles, looking at the items for sale and though they tried to speak softly, their voices could be heard by Jones.

"Look at the prices," said Peterson. "I can buy this exact same can of beans for half the price in Rock Port."

"Can you believe how much he's asking for these marshmallows?" whispered Millie.

"You folks finding what you need?"

"We're good," said Peterson, from the back of the store.

Five minutes later, the two returned to the counter with a half dozen items cradled in their arms. In quick succession, they laid out eggs, milk, bread, peanut butter, a can of tuna, and a bag of chips. They watched the readout on the register as each item was rung up, then sighed as the final item was placed in the bag.

"How come you charge so much more than the stores in Rock Port?" asked Millie.

"Overhead," said Jones. "You think this stuff comes without shipping costs."

"But everything is so much more expensive," said Millie.

"Convenience has it's costs," said Jones. "You don't like my prices, don't shop here. That'll be nineteen, fifty-six."

Peterson handed over a twenty and took the change and the bag. "Thanks."

"You're welcome." Jones watched them leave the store and picked up his crossword puzzle. He wasn't bothered by the direct questions over pricing, all new comers asked the same things. He looked at the rain outside for a moment, then focused on the puzzle. All he needed was a five letter word for frugal, starting with a C.

#

Louella took a long nap, wishing that the day would get better and woke with the sound of someone pounding on her door. She opened her eyes, disoriented, looking at the familiar four poster bed, her pride and joy, the scarred chest of drawers with it's pictures of Louella's childhood and early days of marriage, and the picture of Jesus on the wall, giving her constant relief from the harsh realities of life. All was the same, except for the pounding. What could that be?

She pushed herself up from the bed, wiping the sleep from her eyes. She placed her feet on the floor, sliding her feet into the mules waiting for her, then stood up, trying hard to wake up. It was a bad dream, she told herself, pushing the image of the burning letter from her mind. Maybe she had imagined the whole thing.

A sharp knock on the window woke her completely. She spun her head around and saw him in the window and for a moment, her heart literally stopped.

"Open up the damn door," bellowed the man outside her window.

She ran from the room, into the front room, then quickly turned the lock and opened the front door to reveal a wet and angry Tony Chambers, her ex-husband, dripping wet on her doorstep. He was a thick man with dark hair, now matted with rain, big hands, and a permanent scowl.

"You trying to keep me out, Lou?"

"Hello, Tony."

He pushed by, nearly knocking her over in the process. "What have you got to drink? I need a beer."

"I've got some orange juice," said Louella, "Or coffee. Would you like me to make you some coffee?"

He spun around and waved his hands in her face, scaring her. "Do I look like I want a cup of freaking coffee? I want a beer. You got any beer? Wine? Hard stuff? You sure ain't got any brighter since I left you. It's a miracle that you're still breathing, but that don't take no talent, does it?"

Louella didn't know what to do. She was scared of what he might do to her. Would he hit her like he used to? Or would he just berate her for her stupidities? She couldn't move, blinking her eyes behind the thick glasses.

"What's the matter with you, woman? Are you too stupid to talk now?" He stared at her for a brief second. "You always was a stupid cow."

Chambers set his wet cap on the yellowed counter top, then walked across the kitchen floor-- leaving puddles of water with each step-- into the living room. He reached into the wood bin and pulled out a couple of pieces of wood and tossed them into the wood stove, slamming the door shut after he was done. He sat down in Louella's favorite rocker by the window and looked at the house like an appraiser.

"You kept this place up real nice, Lou."

Louella hadn't moved from her spot, willing him to leave, but knowing that it wasn't going to happen.

"You listening to me? Have you gone deaf as well as blind? What a sorry sack of bones you've turned out to be. It's a good thing I left you when I did, or I'd have gone crazy growing old with the likes of you."

"You're in my chair,"said Louella, rooted to her spot on the kitchen floor.

"What was that? You can speak? Hallelujah. It's a miracle. You're going to have to come a little closer if you want me to hear what stupid thing you have to say."

Louella moved into the living room and took up a position five feet away, just out of harms way if Chambers should get violent. "I said, you're in my chair."

Chambers looked at the rocker, patted the wooden arms and smiled. "You talking about this one here? Why it ain't your chair no more, Lou. Didn't you read my letter? Don't tell me you didn't get my letter. You did, didn't you?"

"I burned it. And I won't let you sell my home."

Chambers smiled, a sickly grin. "It ain't your home to keep, darlin'. I've got a buyer coming in next week who wants to buy the property. He's going to tear down this pile of crap and put up something bigger and better and there ain't nothing you can do about it. If you will recall, this house has always been in my name. It's mine. I've let you live here for all this time out of the goodness of my heart."

"You ain't got no heart," said Louella.

He smiled again. "Well there you go, criticizing when you ought to be complimenting me. I let you live her for free and that's the thanks I get? No sir, that won't do. You've had a free ride long enough, it's time to fend for yourself. Why don't you go move in with Margaret down in Rock Port? That worthless daughter of yours won't turn you away."

"You can't sell my home."

He pushed himself out of the chair and walked over to where she stood. "I can and will. It was going to happen sooner or later. It's your bad luck that I lost my job and need the money. But that's the way it goes, right? Win some, lose some."

Chambers pushed by her, and headed to the kitchen, where he did a quick inspection of Louella's food and spirits. Refrigerator door open and close, cupboards the same, then drawers.

"I can't believe you ain't got one drop of alcohol in this house. You don't even got no cooking sherry. Who don't have that crap in their kitchen? You are as worthless now as you were when I lived here." He grabbed his weather hat from the counter and jammed it on his head. "I saw a grocery store up the block. I'm going to get some beer, then I'm coming back. Don't do nothing stupid, Lou. This time, I've got the law on my side."

In a flash, he walked out the door.

Louella felt the rain coming down in sheets hit her face as she closed the door. Her mind was a tumbled mess of thoughts. Why now? How could he do this to her? What was she going to do? She shuffled back to her rocking chair and sat down onto the cold and wet wood and tried to think. How was she going to get rid of him so she could keep her house?

2. Things get nasty

Tony Chambers woke on a sunny Friday morning with a hangover, surrounded by the empty twelve pack of cans scattered on the spare bed floor. He had no idea how he got to the bed. The last thing he remembered was arguing with Louella about the house and ownership. He tried to shift though his foggy brain. Though he wasn't sure, he thought he might have gotten into an argument with the owner of the super saver up the block. Something about the price of beer. Chambers shook his massive head, trying to clear the cob webs that had taken up a home in his brain. Had he taken a swing at the bald headed loser? Chambers couldn't remember. But did it really matter? His contact would be in town in one weeks time and he would sell this house and move to someplace warm and dry.

The sun peeked through the flowery curtains, casting long shadows onto the area rug, and shining on the silver beer cans. The rain from the day before had left, leaving sun light, but for how long? On the coast, the weather was mercurial and could change within a half hour. Sun could turn back to fog and rain without notice.

He rolled onto his back, annoyed by a constant humming in his head. It couldn't be the beer. He regularly drank a twelve pack without much effect, not that he was born to be a great thinker, but he could still shake off a hangover, but the constant hum was getting to him. Chambers opened one eye and looked at the room that had once belonged to his daughter. There was still stuffed animals on the night stand and dresser bureau, along with a vanity, full of pictures of girls that looked gothic, with stringy purple hair and dark eye shadow.

Chambers slid out of bed, holding his head. He staggered to the door and flung it open. The humming noise turned into a roar. He spotted the culprit. Louella was vacuuming the living room rug, running the ancient machine up and down, as if in a daze. Chambers stood there for just long enough to get his bearings, then he marched into the room and pulled the plug on the cleaner. Suddenly the air was still and quiet.

"That's better," muttered Chambers.

"What'd you do that for? I was cleaning the house."

"You're killing me here, Lou."

"I wish it was that easy."

"Don't be getting any stupid thoughts," said Chambers. "You try and I'll beat you so bad you'll wish you was dead. You hear me?"

"I hear you."

"That's better. Now, make me something to eat, I'm hungry."

Louella stared at him for a brief moment. "I ain't cooking you no breakfast. You want food, go somewhere else."

Chambers moved quick. He pushed Louella in the shoulder, knocking her over, then kicked her in the side. "Get your lazy ass up and cook me some breakfast, before I kick you again."

Louella pushed herself to her feet, and glared at Chambers. "You worthless piece of crap."

Chambers backhanded her across the face, sending Louella back to the floor. "You want more?"

Louella once again got to her feet and headed to the kitchen, her head down in defeat.

"That's right," said Chambers. "I like my eggs over easy, my bacon crisp and fresh orange juice. And don't burn the toast."

Louella moved slow through the kitchen, pulling out the necessary ingredients for the requested breakfast, then took a pan from under the stove and placed it atop the burner and turned on the flame. She tossed four slices of bacon into the heated pan and soon the sound of sizzling bacon filled the air. Louella flipped the bacon, added two eggs, then crossed to the counter and dropped two slices of bread into the toaster.

Chambers made himself comfortable at the counter, sitting on a stool on the opposite side of the kitchen, and watched Louella cook.

"You hurry up, I've got a busy day ahead of me."

While she cooked, he thought of his encounters with the hicks of West Harbor. Running into the store keeper hadn't been his only entertainment. Along the way he ran into Star. Chambers had run into another hippie in Rock Port who knew all about Star, his real name and a little history. A couple of bucks and a few beers in a local pub and Chambers knew enough to maybe put the squeeze on Star and make a few bucks. Even if he sold the house, the card shark in him wouldn't let a patsy get away unscathed. So he spotted the hippie and called him by his real name. The look on Star's face was priceless, as would be the bounty for Chambers remaining quiet about Star's past.

Then there was the post mistresses. Chambers remembered her from his days living in town. Bonnie

Williams looked much the same, only older. He didn't need anything from the post office, but that didn't stop him from going there and having a good laugh at Bonnie and the milk toast guy hanging out with her. Old spinster, Chambers called her, laughing all the way out the door. There was just so much you could do in a dull burg like West Harbor.

Louella slapped the plate of hot food in front of Chambers. "I hope you choke on it."

He smiled at her. "Thanks, darlin', cooking was always something you was good at."

#

Star was up early, tending the goats, and worrying abut what Tony Chambers might know about him. It had been a long time since anyone had called him by his given name. How much did he know? Star truly thought that part of his life was behind him, but what if it wasn't? Were there still some warrants out for his arrest from his days of impetuous youth? He fretted about it, all during Genesis' breakfast and the walking out to the bus, then continued to worry as he returned to the house. He didn't sleep the previous night, worrying about what might happen to his life and reputation if the news leaked out about his past.

He thought about his past, digging deep into his recessed brain, looking at the offenses that led him to run away from Los Angeles. As far as his family was concerned, he was dead and gone and good riddance, and he couldn't really blame them. Star was raised in a middle class home in West Covina, with a father in the Insurance business and a mother who held tupperware parties. He had an older sister and younger brother and all was well as he grew up. While Annie mostly ignored him, his younger brother, Carl, idolized him. Carl was two years younger and wanted to do everything that he did. There were a dozen kids in the neighborhood available for baseball games and bike hikes, and football, and overnights.

All was moving well until Star caught up with an older crowd in high school. Suddenly, nothing that his family did interested him. No more did he play with the neighborhood kids, no more did he hang out on the block. His new group went out at night, smoked a lot of marijuana, stole what they could to support a drug habit. Star turned into a sullen child, keeping secrets from his family, spending more time with his druggie friends. When he graduated from high school, barely, he floated around, hanging with his friends, smoking a lot of pot, and cigarettes, and drinking stolen beers. Then came the arrest.

Star and two of his buddies were cruising a back alley at night when they came across a sweet convertible sitting in the driveway. It was Manny Ramile who had the idea of stealing the car for a joyride. Star and his other buddy, a young kid named Terry Mills, jumped in the back and Manny jump started the vehicle. They didn't know about the alarm system. No more than two blocks away, they were pulled over by a West Covina police car. Ramile did time, being behind the wheel, and the other two got a stint in Juvenile Hall.

This was a watershed moment. When Star returned home, he was faced with two paths. Straight and narrow, or fun and dangerous. He choose the later. Manny was replaced by Frankie Andrews, and Terry Mills came along. More cars were stolen, sold to a chop shop at the south side of town, giving the boys money for drugs and recreation that didn't require getting a job. Two more stints in Juvie didn't stop Star from pursuing a life of crime. He moved up the ladder and hooked up with a group hitting the houses in the hills above Hollywood. His parents kicked him out and he moved in with Terry Mills, and the two lived a fast paced life of drugs and parties.

Star would have stayed on this path if not for the ill-fated attempt to rob a house that belonged to a retired Los Angeles County Deputy Sheriff. The house was supposed to be empty. It was late. Midnight. And the house was dark. Star was guarding the exit, keeping his eyes peeled for the police, when he heard the shots. Star could see the explosions in the darkened room and imagined the worse. He took off, running through the darkened streets, looking for an escape from his past and his future. It wasn't until the next morning that he found out that Terry Mills was dead and the deputy sheriff wounded. Andrews was in custody.

It was over. Star knew that it was simply a matter of time before Andrews turned state witness and he'd be in jail. No more juvie. This time he'd go to prison. He panicked. What to do? He took Mills' VW bug and headed north. He landed in San Francisco, left the VW in long term parking at SFO, then took the airport shuttle bus into town, moved into a commune in the Haight, let his hair grow, and took on the name Star. Two years later, he met Sunflower at a concert in Golden Gate Park, and they common law married and moved to West Harbor, settling in to the old barn. Here he was safe. At least he thought so until Tony Chambers showed up and called him by his given name.

Star dumped food pellets into the goats trough and added water to the bowls scattered on the floor. The goats had eaten most of the grass in the back yard and with their insatiable appetites, nudged each other out of the way to get to the offered food. The sickness from the day before had gone, leaving hungry animals in its place. Star stared at the tops of their heads and wondered just how much Tony Chambers knew of Star's past. Would this be the end of Star's idyllic existence? Would the community turn on him if they knew what he had done? Would he be arrested for the bungled burglary so long ago? The uncertainly was eating him up.

He looked between his and the Seavers house at Louella Chambers small house on the other side of town. There was only one way to find out what Chambers knew. Star would confront him and get it out in the open. And if the news was bad, what would he do?

He dropped the feed sack and headed to the gate. Star needed to keep his secret life just that. So what if Chambers decided to tell all? Star would do everything within his power to keep that from happening. He closed the gate behind him and headed down the road.

#

Sunflower watched her husband out in the yard. She could see the confusion on his face as he went about his goat duties, but was there something else there? She wasn't sure, but he looked like he had just received a scare. When Star came in the previous evening, he snapped at her when she asked him what was wrong. Nothing, he told her. Mind your own business, he said. Now, here he was, out in the back yard, staring vacantly out at the open space between theirs and the Seavers house. What was he looking at?

It wasn't supposed to be this way, she thought. Husbands and wives aren't supposed to have secrets between them, yet it certainly looked as if Star was holding out on her. What was he hiding?

She washed the last of the breakfast dishes, setting the bowls in the dry rack and looked back out the window at her husband, but he was gone. Now what? She wondered. Sunflower hung the damp wash rag over the faucet, then dried her hands on the towel hanging from the door handle on the refrigerator.

Sunflower walked out the kitchen and back door into the warm sunshine. She could smell the fresh rain washed air, temporarily enjoyed the breeze tickling her face and pushing her hair into her eyes. She tucked the long orange locks behind her ears and looked around for Star. Where did he go? She looked east to the goat shed and out to the rear of the property, but could only see clipped grass inside the fence and long grass beyond, with the dark green and black of the forest up the slope. To the south she saw Mary Seavers hanging her laundry on the clotheslines in the back. To the north, she could see Old Tom, digging around in his side yard. Her final glance was to the west, the ocean and the main road. It was there she spotted Star. He was walking down the lane, heading toward the post office. That made no sense to Sunflower. Mail wasn't delivered until well after eleven and here it was only nine in the morning. What on earth could Star be up to?

She crossed the back yard and walked over to the broken down fence that separated their property from the Seavers.

"Hello," said Sunflower.

Mary Seavers looked up and waved. "Hello yourself."

"Doing a little laundry I see."

Mary hung a sheet, then walked over. "It's all I can do to dry the clothes in this place. Rain, then fog, then rain again, and even when it's not raining, it's cold and damp. It's a miracle we get any sun out here."

"Don't you have a dryer?"

"Of course, but it's old and needs to be replaced," said Mary. "I have to use it when necessary, but it isn't very efficient. You should see our electric bills. Out of this world."

Sunflower thought of their own washer and dryer, purchased second hand five years earlier. The washer rarely got the clothes clean and the dryer never did a good job, requiring Sunflower to drape their clothes over every available surface to air dry

"Our machines don't work very well either."

Mary looked at Sunflower. "Are you okay? You look a little sick."

Sunflower dropped her head. "It's Star. He's acting weird lately."

"Weirder than usual?"

Sunflower lifted her head. "Very strange."

Mary reached into the basket and grabbed the last of the laundry. "You want to talk about it?"

Sunflower looked at the oh so perfect Mary, who looked like every pretty nightmare that haunted Sunflowers' earlier days. Was this some sort of trick? Still, she needed to talk to someone.

"Sure."

"Let me hang these last couple of things and we can go inside. You drink coffee?"

"Love it."

Five minutes later, all the clothes were wafting in the breeze and the two women were comfortable in the warmth of the Seavers kitchen. Sunflower couldn't help but compare the granite counter tops, stainless steel sinks and burnished cabinets with her own home. Here, all was nice and modern. Sunflower felt a pang of jealousy, wishing she had all that was before her.

Mary took a couple of mugs off the mug rack on the counter, next to the microwave and coffee maker, poured the coffee and placed them on the kitchen table over looking the back yard.

"Cream?"

"Please, but only if it's not goat cream," said Sunflower. "You have any of those flavored ones?"

Mary smiled, walked over to the refrigerator and came back with two, Irish Cream and French Vanilla, and two spoons. She placed the containers and silverware on the table. "Will this do the job?"

Sunflower took the Irish Cream and added a generous dollop to her coffee. "This is a nice." She looked around at the kitchen and out into the great room with its thick carpeting, big screen television above the fireplace and comfortable furniture filling the interior. "You've got a great home here."

"We like it, but that's not what you wanted to talk about, was it?"

Sunflower looked at her mug of coffee. "No. There's something going on with Star and I don't know what it is. A husband isn't supposed to hide things from his wife is he? I'll bet your husband is just about perfect in every way. You house is beautiful and I know it's wrong to say, but I'm envious of what you've got. Your guy is handy and does everything for his family. Why can't Star do that?"

"You think Bill is perfect?"

"He sure looks like it." Sunflower missed the wistful look on Mary's face. "You don't have a thousand holes in your roof, and your house is nice and warm. You have plenty to eat. You're safe from the elements, and most importantly, I'll bet you and your husband don't have any secrets between you."

Mary sighed. "Well, you wouldn't think so, but sometimes I wonder."

Sunflower sipped her coffee. "You mean everything isn't perfect over here?"

There was a moment of silence while Mary debated what to say, then it came out in a torrent. "He won't touch me. I've tried everything I can think of to make it obvious that I want some affection, and all he does is work out in that garage all day, then it's the fences, then the roof, working right up to bed time, then he tells me that he's too tired to do anything."

"You're kidding, right? I mean, you're beautiful. No offense, but I hated girls like you in high school. So good looking that every guy wanted her."

Mary shrugged. "That's the way it started, but not much anymore. All I get from Bill are excuses. He's too tired. He needs to get some sleep. He's not interested in that right now. He's got a project to finish. I just don't know how much more of this I can take."

Sunflower looked at her neighbor. She had no idea the turmoil going on in this perfect little house. She was so focused on her own problems that she couldn't see that there might be something wrong elsewhere in this little village by the sea. Sunflower reached over and patted Mary's hand.

"Men can be so stupid, can't they?"

Mary fought the tears. 'But what can I do?"

"Have you talked him about your feelings?"

"What good would that do? I tried and all he did was clam up on me. How about you? Have you tried talking to Star?"

"I have and he did the same thing to me, but I can tell you this, things are going to change around here." She looked at the Seavers kitchen. "Starting with the way we live. He doesn't give me the right answers and he's going to be sorry."

#

Tony Chambers walked out the front door of the house and took in the fresh air. He forgot how refreshing the sea air could be. Since leaving West Harbor, he'd lived in a half dozen placed, all in the central valley, starting with a job in Redding, then down to Sacramento, then Fresno, then his last job in Merced, always landing jobs as a janitor or night watchman, but in the end getting fired for insubordination and having to move to another valley community, but after he sold this house, he would be fixed for life. He could move up the coast to Eureka or even Oregon, house prices being lower there, and if he lived sparingly, he wouldn't have to work another day in his life. He smiled. No more bosses, doing what he liked. A small dark cloud of doubt entered his brain, for the things that he liked doing, drinking and gambling, cost money, but he thought philosophically, he'd worry about that later. First things first. Sell the house and get out of this little waste by the sea.

He walked down the short sidewalk to the road and turned north. What he needed was a drink. He was no more than ten feet down the road when he spotted Star coming at from the opposite direction. What fun, he thought. Hippie boy looked angry. More fun.

"Hey Harold," said Chambers when he was within hailing distance. "How's it hanging?"

Star marched up to Chambers. "Nobody here knows me by that name. Who told you my name?"

Chambers pushed Star in the shoulder. "You got a problem with that, Harold? Or do you prefer Harry? Is that it?"

"Who told you about me?"

"Some waste of space I ran into down in Rock Port. Why? You got a problem with your real name? Or is it you don't want people around her to know about you. That's it, ain't it, Harry? That's funny. Harry the Hippie. What a laugh. Does your little hippie wife know what you were before you turned into Harry the Hippie? I'll bet she doesn't have a clue." Chambers paused, saw the look of concern on Stars' face. He stuck a finger in the others chest. "I'd bet that sort of information would be worth a lot to you wouldn't it. Say a grand to keep my mouth shut? What do you say, Harry? Is my silence worth some green backs to you?"

Star's face clouded over with anger, and his fists flew before he had a chance to think about what he was doing.

Chambers knocked aside the flying fist and popped Star on the chin, sending the tall man to the ground. "You want more, hippie boy? You're a pathetic loser. Stick to goats, hippie, that's all you're good at."

Chambers left Star on the ground and headed north. He enjoyed hitting the hippie. Never liked them, he thought. Bunch of losers. Get a job. Get a life. He laughed aloud. Chambers crossed the distance to the post office and noticed the old man and postmistress standing on the steps watching him as he approached.

"What are you looking at old man?" Chambers said when he was within ten feet. "You want a piece of me too?"

"You're a bully," said Franklin.

Chambers crossed to Franklin and pulled back a fist. "You want to make something of it, old man? You going to protect the spinster here?"

Franklin put himself between Chambers and Bonnie. "You leave her out of this."

Chambers laughed at him. "She your girlfriend or something, old man?" He eyed the two. "You know what's good for you, you'll go back inside and pretend you didn't see nothing."

"Bully!" said Franklin as he ushered Bonnie inside.

Chambers left the two. This day was turning out better than he thought. He loved intimidating people and this town was full of victims waiting for him to pick on them. What a wonderful day. He continued walking toward the Super Saver. Arguing with people left him thirsty. He entered the building, setting off the little bell over the door, and walked straight to the back to the coolers. He grabbed a twelve pack and headed to the front of the store and a waiting Jones.

"You got a lot of nerve asking this much for brewski's," said Chambers, setting the twelve pack on the counter.

"You don't have to buy it."

"And where else am I going to go for a brew in this loser town? You know that the problem with this place is? You ain't got a decent bar. Would it kill you to have a spot where a fellow could stop and grab a beer and maybe watch a ball game?"

"You want to open a bar, that's your business."

"I'm not saying I want to open a bar, I want you to open a bar. You got nothing going in this shitty little store. Why don't you put a bar in here?" He turned around and looked at the interior of the building. "You could put a bar along that back wall and shove a couple of tables here in the front and put a TV up in that back corner."

"Sounds like you've got it all figured out."

"Better than you, baldy. I don't know what wrong with you people. It's like your all retarded. No vision. No brains. Just a bunch of losers waiting for life to pass you by. Not me. I've got plans."

"Like getting drunk before ten in the morning?"

Chambers' short fuse exploded. "You calling me an alky? I ain't going to take that shit from you."

"Fine," said Jones, taking the twelve pack. "Get your beer somewhere else."

"You can't do that! I'm a paying customer."

"And I'm a businessman who has the right to refuse service to anybody I don't like. You've been nothing but a jerk to everybody in this town since you arrived. What you're looking for is someone to kick your ass out of here."

"You volunteering, baldy?"

For a big man, Chambers could move quick. He reached across and tagged Jones alongside the head with a right fist, then clapped his left hand hard against the others ear, knocking Jones off balance. To his credit, Jones didn't fall, but before he could react, Chambers snatched back the beer and dropped a twenty dollar bill on the counter.

"Keep the change, Baldy, and don't piss me off again, if you know what's good for you."

Minutes later, he was out the door, back into the sunshine, whistling off key. This was just a fabulous day. He got to do what he liked best: punch a hippie; threaten an old man; and piss off the store owner, all in a twenty minute span. What others goodies were in store for him? He wondered as he headed back to Louella's house.

He passed the post office, grinning at the two faces staring at him as he walked by, then on to Louella's house. Up the sidewalk and into the front door, with a twelve pack of beer under one arm. He spotted Louella sitting in the rocker across the room.

"Honey, I'm home," he said, with a big smile on his face.

#

Morning passed and the afternoon moved in to early evening with the tiny hamlet living their daily lives. Old Tom snoozed on his front porch, the Peterson's did home repairs, and the warm October sun moved slowly toward the horizon. The big yellow school bus rolled into town from Rock Port and deposited Cindy and Billy Seavers, along with Genesis, in front of the post office. The three kids, all mop heads, dressed in school clothes, ran down the lane, Cindy's blonde locks flying behind her as she led the three home. She was a miniature version of her mother, with long blonde hair, blue eyes and a button nose. Billy Seavers looked like his dad, smaller and tighter, but at six years old, he had the same look in his eye that his father had. Then there was Genesis, long brown hair and tie-dyed shirt, and a denim coat with a peace sign on the back. He and Cindy were in the same class, eight years old and definitely superior to little Billy.

"Wait for me," Billy hollered as they passed Adam Franklin's house. "You guys!"

Cindy looked over her shoulder at her younger brother and laughed. "Try and catch us, worm boy."

"Quit calling me that," said Billy. He stopped and put his hands on his knees and watched the other two tear off, leaving him on the pavement.

Cindy and Genesis reached the front of their respective houses at the same time.

"Tied," said Genesis.

"I beat you and you know it," said Cindy.

"Whatever. I let you win."

"You did not. Anyway, what are you doing after dinner?"

He shrugged. "Dunno. There's not much to do around my house. Can I come over and watch TV at your place?"

"Depends. Maybe there's a stupid ball game on or something that my dad wants to watch, but we can still hang out, maybe go exploring."

Little Billy reached the two at the tail end of the conversation. "Where are we going to explore? I love exploring."

Cindy shoved her little brother in the shoulder. "You're not coming with us, worm boy."

"I'm telling mom that you're mean."

"Go ahead, see if I care."

Billy ran to the house. "Mom!"

Cindy turned back to Genesis. "We can do something. We should have a couple of hours of light left." She looked at her neighbor. Even if he was a hippie boy, she liked him. And she knew a secret about Genesis that most adults in West Harbor didn't. He hated his name so much that he invented his own. She smiled. "See you after dinner, Mike."

"Bye." Genesis ran to his house and disappeared inside.

Cindy opened the gate on the front yard and walked up to the house. She was almost at the door when it opened and a unsmiling Mary Seavers, with little Billy behind her, stood glaring at her as she came up the walk.

"You are in trouble, young lady."

Cindy breezed by her mother. "Did worm boy rat me out?"

"You will not call your brother that, he has a name you know."

"He has lots of names," said Cindy, moving through the living room and heading toward her bedroom. "Worm boy, squeege, spit head, loser, dirt ball, take your pick."

"Young lady, I am not through with you."

Cindy stopped in the hallway, put one hand on her hip. "What do you want me to do, mom? He's always in the way. Why can't he find something to do that doesn't bother me."

"Be nice," said Mary. "He's the only brother you're going to have."

"Isn't that a relief." She turned and ran down the hall to her bedroom before her mother could say another word. She closed her door, then flopped on her bed. Her room was pink, with frilly lace curtains filling the window overlooking the back yard. The furniture was oak, built by her father, with a dresser and matching vanity, and a four poster bed with lots of stuffed animals and pillows. This was her sanctuary from her little brother. No boys allowed, the sign on the door said. And she meant it, except for maybe Mike next door. They could play cards, or monopoly, or watch movies on her little television set, when her mother allowed it.

Cindy worked on her diary at her vanity until dinner time, then joined the rest of the family for a meal of chicken Parmesan, noodles and asparagus, her least favorite vegetable, with the usual questions of how school was that day, as if anything new happened when you were in the third grade. Cindy ate quickly, while little Billy told one long story after the next about a science project his class was doing, something about weather, then about a fight that happened on the playground at lunch, then Billy started in about her calling him names, and Cindy decided that she could skip desert.

"Can I be excused?" asked Cindy.

"May I please be excused," corrected her mother.

"You sure can," said Cindy. "That was a great dinner, mom."

"Where are you going, young lady?"

"Genesis and me are going to play explorer."

"Can I go, please, mom, make her let me play with her and Genesis, they never let me do anything."

Mary Seaver looked to her husband for support. "Bill?"

Seaver looked up from his dinner and stared at the three of them as if seeing them for the first time. "What was the question?"

"Never mind," said Mary. "Cindy, if you want to play explorer, you have to take your brother. Otherwise you can stay inside tonight."

"That's not fair," said Cindy.

"Take it or leave it," said Mary.

So it was that the two Seaver children left the house, with a happy Billy and an unhappy Cindy heading over to pick up Genesis. The three children headed to the bluffs to see what might have washed up on shore, with Cindy and Genesis moving fast, leaving little Billy trying to catch up. They walked on the bluff, overlooking the ocean, with the sun setting to the west, casting a glow on the shimmering water. The sound of the surf rolling onto the sandy beach below mixed in with the call of the gulls, kept them company as they walked along the path atop the bluff.

They took the path down to the beach, keeping an eye open for anything cool washed up on shore. Once they had a trunk that came from a passing ship that was full of clothes, another time it was a tattered piece of main sail. The ocean was a mysterious thing, giving and taking when least expected.

Cindy rounded the bend first and spotted the lump of something at the far end of the next curved beach. What was it this time? She touched Genesis on the shoulder. "Race you to whatever that is?"

"You're on."

The two older children tore across the sand, leaving little Billy, once again, pulling up the tail end of the group.

"Wait for me," cried out Billy.

Cindy arrived first. Up close, she could see that the lump was a body. She moved in closer and inspected the face.

"Is he sleeping?" asked Genesis.

Cindy got a stick and prodded the man in the shoulder. "Wake up, mister." she leaned over and spotted the bloody scalp, then looked at the two boys. "I think he's dead. Billy. Go get dad."

Billy took off, screaming.

3. Let the Dead Begin

Detective Lieutenant Benjamin Steele raked the leaves from under the back flower beds of their house on Gull Street, enjoying the rare early sunny evening. There were many October days along the coast that gave up sunshine. Fog and rain were constant companions, turning the fallen leaves into mush, and requiring the heavy prong rake to ferret them from around the bushes in the back yard. Their house sat on the top of Rock Port, with the hillside of houses below leading down to the harbor itself. On a clear day, Steele could see the fishing trawlers coming back to port after a days hunt at sea. The yard was no more than postage stamp size, measuring thirty feet to the back fence and as wide as the house, but it was full, with a swing set along the north border and a jungle gym along the south, for the amusement of the two Steele children.

The Steele house was a sixties ranch, with light blue shake siding and white trim around the windows, which needed to be replaced with the storm windows currently stored in the garage. Winter on the coast brought one storm after another, and the heavy pane windows kept both the cold and wet outside. He needed a sunny day to put them up. Perhaps tomorrow, he thought as he raked the leaves into little piles between the bushes.

Bed Steele was a thin rangy man with reddish brown hair, brown eyes and a warm smile, the same silly grin that helped convince his wife Arly to marry him. He preferred brown suits and subdued ties, though he had switched to jeans and a heavy shirt to do the yard work.

He was humming an old Beatles tune, enjoying the crisp air, thinking of nothing more than getting the job at hand done so he could relax for the rest of the weekend. His job was demanding, but he was good at it and enjoyed solving mysteries. The College of the Redwoods in Eureka gave him two things: an associate of science degree in administrative justice and a wife. Both followed him to Rock Port, where he signed on as a rookie police office twelve years earlier. Promotions led him to the detective squad. Marriage to Arly gave him eight year old Devin and six year old Aaron. His was a good life. A happy life.

"Dinner's ready."

Steele looked at the back door and his pretty wife. Arly was a red head with blue eyes, a little plumper than when he married her, but twice as beautiful. He grinned. "Already? I'm almost done."

"Finish up and come inside," said Arly, "And wash your hands when you're done."

"Yes ma'am."

She smiled at him and went back inside.

Steele did as he was told. He bagged the small piles of leaves and placed the bags in the garbage cans alongside the south side of the two car garage, then entered the back door, straight into the kitchen and the smell of garlic and lemon tickling his nose. He lifted a lid from one of the pots atop the stove and was about to stick his finger in the thick tomato sauce when Arly walked into the kitchen.

"What do you think you're doing?"

He stopped in mid-act and looked over his shoulder at his wife. "I just wanted to take in the heavenly aroma of your fabulous cooking."

"You were going to stick your dirty finger into my marinara is what you were going to do. Now be a good little soldier and go wash your hands. Honestly, Ben, you're just like the kids. Shoo."

Steele gave his wife a hug and kiss, then headed out the kitchen door, bypassed the dining room table, and the kids stretched out atop the brown shag carpeting in the living room that his wife hated, their eyes glued to the cartoons on the big screen television.

"How's it going, fellows?" asked Steele.

"Great," said Devin.

"He's hogging the remote," complained Aaron.

"Shut up, you little dweeb," said Devin.

"Dad, he called me a dirty name."

"Truth hurts," said Devin.

Aaron attacked his older brother, hitting him in the shoulder and the game was on. The two boys wrestled and pulled each other's hair.

Steel reached in and separated the two. "You want to lose your television privileges again?"

As quick as it started, it was over. The two boys sat a little farther apart and directed their attention to the cartoon.

"That's better," said Steele. "And I don't want to hear any more of it, you hear me?"

"Yes sir," the two boys said in unison.

Steele left them on the floor, continued down the hall, sidestepping big wheeled trucks and rubber balls, and other toys that spilled out from the boys rooms, and onto the master bedroom at the end of the hall. Here was the one place in the house that the boys were not allowed. The king sized bed dominated the small master, with cherry wood dressers and vanity along the side next to the master bath. As far as bath's went, it was a little on the small side, but the requisite combo bath/shower, double sink and toilet were all there. He washed his hands, drying them on the good towels, then crossed back to the bedroom, where he replaced jeans and work shirt for his good slacks, a white shirt and tie. Even at home, he preferred to be dressed as if he were on a case. After years of jeans and t-shirts as a undergraduate, he liked the dressed up feel of a shirt and tie. He glanced at himself in the mirror, pushed a lock of hair behind his ear. Need a haircut, he told himself. He then left the bedroom and joined his family.

Everybody was in their seats when Steele returned to the front room, with the boys on either side and Arly at the far end of the table. Steele took his seat. They reached out and held hands, each boy holding one of their parents hands. Steele smiled at his family.

"Bow your heads," said Steele. He closed his eyes and recited the usual family prayer. "Bless this food to our bodies and watch over us as we do your biding. Amen."

"Amen," said the other three.

They drop their hands and Arly loaded food on the boys plates. First the ravioli's, then the sauce, then the green beans, then the garlic bread before placing the food in front of each boy, then dished up her husbands, then herself.

"It all smells just great," said Steele.

Soon all are eating.

"I had a wonderful thought today," said Arly, looking across the table at Steele. "I know we can't afford much right now, but I was on the internet and found that little place we stayed at up in Oregon for our honeymoon. Remember the cottage with the views? Anyway, I talked to my sister and she said she could come up and watch the kids and we could get away, just the two of us."

Steele smiled. "I remember that place. The pipes were rusted or something and the water came out red."

"But the views were nice. Just the fresh sea air, and the two of us. Wouldn't that be romantic?"

"That'd be nice," said Steele.

"Auntie Denise is coming to stay with us?" asked Aaron. "That's so cool. No offense, mom, but she's a lot cooler than you are."

"You mean you get away with more from her," said Arly.

"Cooler, right, Dev?" asked Aaron.

"Definitely," said Devin. "Where are you going and when?"

The phone rang, interrupting the conversation.

"Hold that thought," said Steele, wiping his mouth and standing up. He crossed to the phone in the kitchen and picked up the receiver. "Steele residence. What was that? I'll get right on it." He hung up the phone and looked at his wife.

"We're not going to Oregon this weekend are we?" she asked.

"Sorry, no. I've got a case."

#

Detective Sergeant Kevin Walker moved fast for a big man. He was twenty-seven years old, already forty pounds overweight, with thinning hair and a wispy moustache. The captain, Terry Lane, told him that ten more pounds and he was going on restricted duty, making Walker the first policeman in Rock Port history to eat himself off the force. Diets didn't work and exercise only made him hungry. That left smaller portions, but to date, this method had been less than successful.

He put the finishing touches on his dinner of meatloaf, mashed potatoes, with gravy, and fresh steamed string beans. Every pot and pan he owned was dirty, sitting on the stove top, or in the sink. His kitchen was a mess. He may have lived alone, but that didn't stop him from eating as if he were a family of four. The apartment was his to do as he pleased, and for Walker's tastes, the walls were decorated with framed prints from old 1930's movies. He had James Cagney on one wall, with William Powell on another. His furniture was vintage, the lamps Tiffany, the carpet, a Navajo that he got in a thrift store in downtown Rock Port. Louis Armstrong blew his horn on the stereo, Walker's concession to the modern era, along with his state of the art flat screen television and blue ray player. He may have preferred the thirties, but the electronics of the era were inadequate for his tastes.

Walker was a throw back. A man born out of time. He was ridiculed in high school for his obsession with everything from a time sixty years ago. His classmates made fun of him, dressed in his double breasted suits, wearing a fedora and sporting a wide tie with a picture of Betty Grable stretched from his neck to the cut of the coat. He loved the past. For Walker, the advent of color movies was the end of good cinema. His parents down in Long Beach sent him movie collections from the past. One year it was the Gary Cooper set, another it the James

Cagney, last year it was the thin man series starring William Powell and Myrna Loy. Walker enjoyed them all.

His fellow students at the police academy called him J. Edgar, a moniker he loved. Then it was on to Rock Port where he spent five years in uniform before joining Ben Steele in the elite detective squad. He admired Steele for the way he handled both the cases and the people associated with the crimes. Steele had a way of getting the most out of the interviews. When Walker tried to get information from a suspect, he often found himself at wits end trying to come up with the key question that would send the suspect over the edge.

He loaded up his plate, and set it on the table, with a good view of the television, picked up the stereo remote, hit the stop button and the jazz trumpet was silenced. He then picked up the DVD remote and started the movie. It was one of his favorites: After the Thin Man, a 1936 second round of thin man movies with Powell and Loy, and of course, Asta, the wonder dog.

Walker ate his dinner and laughed along with the action on the screen, and just reached the part where Nick and Nora are riding through the streets of San Francisco and everybody from the porter to the police are glad handing Nick, when a well dressed couple pass in another car and say hello to Nora.

"Who are they?" asked Nick.

"Oh, you wouldn't know them," said Nora, "they're respectable."

Then the phone rang. Walker put the movie on pause, crossed to the vintage rotary phone and picked up the receiver.

"Your dime," said Walker. "Oh hi, boss, what's that? Now? Where? Yes, boss. I'll be ready."

Walker looked at the frozen image on the screen and sighed. He wouldn't be watching the rest of the movie tonight. He shut down the player and television, ate a couple of bites of his food, then covered the food with clear wrap and put it in the refrigerator. He then put the rest in containers and stacked them along side his covered meal.

Fifteen minutes later, Walker was ready. He wore his favorite gray pin stripped double breasted suit, matching fedora and wing tip shoes. He locked up his apartment, took the elevator to the first floor, then walked out into the warm October early evening air. The smell of a nearby barbecue made him wish he had eaten more. He adjusted the flower in his lapel and waited, imagining himself on a stakeout.

#

Ben Steele picked up Walker standing outside his apartment building and smiled at his subordinates choice outfit. The uniforms in the department made fun of him, not that Walker would care if he knew.

They headed north out of Rock Port, with the setting sun keeping them company along their left flank. It was a warm evening and the two detectives rode with the windows down. Walker took off his fedora and set it on his lap.

"What I don't get, boss," said Walker, "is why we're on this case at all. Isn't West Harbor in county land?"

"It is," said Steele, "and the captain explained that the sheriff's department is strapped right now. Their investigator is in Elk Creek on a murder for hire deal right now and couldn't work both cases."

"But it should be their case, right?"

"Of course," said Steele. "But there isn't much we can do about it. We've been loaned to the county for this murder and we will do our best to solve it." Steele thought of the discussion he and his wife had over the case. "Not that my wife is happy about this. She planned on a getaway for the two of us that we'll have to do later."

"That's too bad," said Walker. "I like your wife, she's nice to me."

"She's nice to everybody."

"Yeah? Well, I don't get a lot of that myself."

"People like you, Kevin."

"Not that you'd notice. There's not a lot of people my age that like the old stuff like I do, but I can't help it. I should have lived in the forties. I'd have made a great g-man."

They rode the rest of the way in silence, along the windy asphalt, taking them past the small businesses that lined the trunk highway north of Rock Port. They passed gift shops, and a nursery, and a rock quarry, then reached open space, with nothing but scrub oaks, pines and rocks on either side of the road, with an occasional glimpse of the ocean as they crossed bridges over canyons and inlets.

The trunk highway headed inland and took them through a patch of forest, the road darkened in shadows, then back to the sunlight, the road headed due west and the setting sun, before turning north at a small beach. A

quick rise and they crested a bluff that led to West
Harbor.

From the top of the hill, Steele could see all of
West Harbor, from the twenty or so dwellings, to the
cemetery on the inland slope, to the steeple of the old
school house at the far end of town. He spotted a sheriff's
patrol car parked past a small store/gas station, with its
lights flashing in the waning light. A dark sedan was
parked ahead of the patrol car.

"Looks like Sheriff Martin sent some help," said
Steele.

"What do they need us for then?"

"We'll find out soon enough."

Steele drove into the hamlet, stopping behind the
squad car. They exited the vehicle and headed toward the
beach. There was a small bluff overlooking the sandy
expanse, and as soon as they reached the crest, they
spotted the scene below. Two deputies held back the
curious town residents, while a thick man with a
magnificent head of gray hair bent over and examined the
body.

"Eddie beat us to the punch," said Steele. "Come
on, Kevin, let's go see what he's found."

The two men half walked, half slid down the
sandy slope. They crossed the sand and joined the medical
examiner.

Edward Lawton was a heavy set man with thick
gray hair and eyebrows that fairly danced when he spoke.
He was dressed in jeans, a plaid work shirt, and a pair of
old sneakers. He looked up at the arrival of the detectives.

"So they brought you two in on this, eh?" asked
Lawton.

"What have you got for us, Eddie?" asked Steele.

Lawton stood up and stretched. "This is a classic case of blunt trauma to the back of the head. The victim didn't struggle, and my guess is that he didn't know the blow was coming. Time of death was fairly recent, maybe within the last couple of hours, but I won't know until I get him to the lab and do a work up."

"Any identification on him?" asked Steele.

"Wallet identifying him as one Anthony Chambers, address on his license listed a Modesto address."

"What was he doing in West Harbor?" asked Walker.

Lawton nodded toward the group of on lookers. "His ex-wife is over there in that group. Apparently, Mr. Chambers used to live in this town and moved away, just recently came back to town."

The three stared at the body.

"Looks like someone didn't want him here," said Steele. "Who found the body?"

"A couple of kids," said Lawton. "The deputy over there has the information. They came down after dinner to play and found Chambers lying on his side. The little girl poked him with a stick, thinking that maybe he was sleeping, but decided that maybe something was wrong and sent her little brother for her father. He called the police and here we are."

Steele bent over and inspected the wound on the back of the head. In the waning light, all he could see was mottled blood mixed in with the victims hair. "Any idea what killed him?"

"Too soon to tell," said Lawton. "Could be a rock, or a something else. I need to clean up the wound to see what's there. Can I call in my boys and have the body removed?"

Steele looked at the sand around the body, disappointed to see so many footprints. There would be no identifying prints left in this sand. "Sure."

"I didn't need this, Ben," said Lawton. "This close to retirement, I just wanted to coast until the big day."

Steele smiled at Lawton. "Eddie, you're seven years away from retirement, unless you know something I don't."

"You don't to have to rub it in," said Lawton. "I should have gone early retirement, like yesterday. Now, I have to work."

"Life's not fair," said Steele.

Lawton walked away, grumbling.

Steele could hear the examiner call in the ambulance crew. "Eddie's a good man."

"He doesn't like me," said Walker. "Did you see the way he ignored me?"

"That's just his way," said Steele.

"So what next?"

"Let's go talk to the kids that found the guy."

There was a moment of confusion as the detectives separated the three children from the pack of residents looking on, stopping far enough away from the parents to be overheard. Steele dropped to one knee so that he could be at the same height as the kids. The girl, identified as Cindy Seavers, was the first on the scene, along with Genesis, according to the notes given to him by the deputy. The third boy, Billy Seavers was the one sent to go get his father and call the police.

Steele looked at the three. "So who wants to tell me what happened?"

"I will," said Cindy. "We were playing pirates, looking for buried treasure and saw that guy laying on the beach. We thought he was sleeping, or maybe passed out, you never know. So we ran over to him and I asked him if he was okay, even if he didn't look so good to me, and then I poked him with a stick. I didn't want to touch him, you don't know what kind of diseases he has, right? So he doesn't do anything, then I see that he's got blood on the back of his head. That's when I sent my brother to get our dad. The rest you know."

Steele looked at the other two. "That sound right?"

Genesis nodded. "He looked like something out of a scary movie. I knew he was dead as soon as I saw him."

"No, you didn't," said Cindy. "I had to point out the blood to you and you almost hurled."

"Did not," said Genesis.

Steele put his hand up. "Enough. It doesn't matter who noticed the blood first. What time did this occur?"

"Right after dinner," said Cindy.

"What time do you eat dinner?" asked Steele.

"Five-thirty, every night," said Cindy. "Even if I'm watching my favorite show."

Dead by five-thirty, thought Steele. He looked at the three and thought of his own two at home. They had to be around the same ages.

"Where do you kids go to school?"

"Rock Port," said Cindy. "Me and Mike are in the third grade and my brother is in first. He's still a baby."

"I am not a baby," said Billy. "I'm telling mom on you."

"Who's Mike?" asked Steele, trying to keep out of the sibling rivalry.

Cindy pointed a thumb at Genesis. "Don't tell his parents, they'd have a cow if they knew he had a normal name."

"I won't tell a soul," said Steele. "Anything else you can tell me that might help?"

The three shook their heads.

"Can we go now?" asked Cindy.

"Sure," said Steele. "Thanks for your help."

He watched them run back to their parents clustered behind the deputy, then walked back and joined Walker.

"Anything useful?"

"Time of death before five-thirty," said Steele. "Let's see what the adults have to say."

#

The old schoolhouse hadn't seen much activity since it was de-activated in the late nineteen seventies, with an occasional community event, or funeral. There was a time when a local resident named Rose tried to use the building for a cultural arts center, hosting classes for the locals, in an attempt to raise the consciousness of the people who lived in West Harbor, but that was ten years ago. No one was interested in taking classes, nor dances, nor in forming a community orchestra. The town was too small to do anything that would justify the expense of keeping the building open at night. Incorporated didn't mean that there was much room for unnecessary outlay. So the building stayed quiet most of the time. Until tonight.

The police took over the building, turning on most of the lights and rearranging what furniture still existed inside. The old wooden desks had been stacked in one corner and folding chairs and tables in another. There was a stage at the back end of the building that was once used for school plays, the wood floors warped with age and changing humidity. The windows were shuttered, but the panes were in desperate need of a good scrubbing. The last rays of sunlight light provided little light from outside.

Voices echoed off the tall ceiling and empty walls as the detectives moved in and surveyed the interior. Steele and Walker took one of the long tables and brought it to a spot centered in front of the stage, opened and locked the legs in place, then retrieved several folding chairs, placing two behind the table and two in front of the table.

Steele looked around the room. "This will do. Is the deputy still out there with the locals?"

Walker walked over to the front entrance and looked outside. "Wally?"

Deputy Sheriff Wally McNeill stuck his head in the door way. "Ready for the interviews, Lieutenant?"

"Send them in one at a time," said Steele.

"They're getting antsy," said McNeill, "some haven't eaten dinner and want to know how long this is going to take."

"Send in the hungry ones first," said Steele.

The detectives settled in on the uncomfortable metal chairs behind the desk and waited for the first resident.

"I'm a little hungry myself," said Walker. "Any chance of picking up something to eat on the way home?"

"We'll see how it goes," said Steele.

Adam Franklin walked in and quickly sat down on the opposite folding chair.

Steele took in the slight old man with the bright bow tie and smiled. "I know that this has been an exciting evening and we won't keep you longer than necessary, but we do have to ask you a few questions if you're up to it."

"I'm more than up to it," said Franklin. "I can tell you all about Tony Chambers. A bully and a brute is what he was. I'm glad he's dead. You should see the way he treated people. Just like dirt, that's how it was with him. I've lived in West Harbor a long time and I can tell you that he was one of the bad ones. He and Louella Chambers moved here twenty five years ago and had a daughter, and even then he was a bully, pushing people around like he was better than anybody else."

"Tony Chambers lived here?" asked Steele, jotting down what Franklin said.

"He and Lou had a girl. Margaret was not a pretty girl and grew up to be a not pretty woman, she lives down in Rock Port. Anyway, Tony left his wife and child must be around ten or fifteen years, I can't recall exactly how long, and it was good riddance to bad rubbish as far as the town was concerned. Nobody liked the man, for there was no good in him."

"I gather you're not unhappy with his death," said Walker.

"Unhappy? I'm thrilled," said Franklin. "Nasty piece of work. Whoever killed Tony did the world a favor."

"Where were you this afternoon between three and six?" asked Steele.

"I was at home," said Franklin. "I'm sorry to say that I don't have anybody to verify that, but I was alone at the time. You see, my wife passed away five years ago, and there just isn't much for me to do anymore. So I was home, thinking of what I was going to make for dinner, then I heard the commotion and came out to see what was going on."

"Do you know anybody who might want Tony Chambers dead?" asked Walker.

"Only half the town," said Franklin. "I saw him get into a fisticuff with Star this afternoon. Me and Bonnie, that's the postmistress, were inside talking when we heard a loud argument going on outside and when we went out to the steps, we saw Chambers push Star to the ground and laugh at him. Then when Tony passed us, I almost died with the look he gave me. I called him a bully and he pulled back his fist like he was going to hit me, then laughed and insulted me and went on his merry way. He was a nasty man and one that we will do well without. Now, is there anything else? I'm very hungry and need to eat before I literally pass out."

Steele looked at Walker. "You get all that?"

Walker finished writing in his book and looked up. "Who is Star?"

"He's our local hippie," said Franklin. "He and Sunflower live up the hill. They raise goats. Lovely girl, Sunflower."

"Is Star his real name?" asked Steele.

"I have no idea," said Franklin. "You can ask him."

"Do you know what their argument was about?" asked Walker.

Franklin shrugged. "Ask Star. May I go now? I truly am growing faint."

"That should do it for now," said Steele. "Thank you for your time. We may need to talk to you more later."

Franklin stood up. "That would be most acceptable. I do wish you well with your investigation, but you will pardon me if I say he had it coming. Good evening, gentlemen."

The detectives watched Franklin walk away.

"What do you think, Kevin?"

"Sounds like this Chambers guy was a jerk. So who's next?"

Steele thought about Franklin's testimony. "Let's get this Star guy in and see what he knows."

They sent Deputy McNeill out to retrieve Star. Minutes passed before the deputy returned with the tall long haired man in tow.

Star plopped down in the chair and eyed the detectives warily. "I don't know nothing about this. And before you ask, I did have an argument with the guy this afternoon."

"First off, your name," said Steele.

"My name is Star."

"That's your given name? Just Star? No last name?"

"Just Star."

"Okay, so tell us about the argument," said Steele.

Star stared at Steele for a moment. "He insulted my wife."

"What did he say?" asked Walker.

"None of you business," said Star. "Look, I didn't kill the guy, alright? I was with my wife all day, you can ask her. I never met him until he came to town a couple of days ago."

"Why was he in town?" asked Steele.

"I've got no freakin' idea," said Star. "You want to know that one, ask his wife, or ex-wife I guess. I don't know. He wasn't a nice guy, alright? And even if I didn't do the deed, I sure can see how someone else might have done so."

"Any ideas who might have killed him?" asked Steele.

"Take a number," said Star. "The guy, like, totally pissed people off. You want my opinion. You should ask Young Tom."

"Young Tom?" asked Walker.

"The guy that owns the super saver here in town. From what I heard, the dude went all ballistic on Tom when he wouldn't sell him beer. The news is all over town, man. I heard Chambers clocked Tom upside the head. I wouldn't be surprised if Young Tom did the deed. He's only been in town a year or so, who knows what dark secrets are in that dude's past. I mean, think about it, why come to this little one horse town if not to hide out."

"What about you, Star? Are you from here? Or did you come from somewhere else too?" asked Steele.

"I see where you're going with this," said Star, "and you're barking up the wrong tree. Me and my old lady came up here ten years ago to start a new life. We were like drifting down in San Francisco, living in the Haight, and decided that we wanted to get back to nature. I heard about this cool little place and we settled in and are making a good life raising goats and our boy, Genesis."

"Your married to Sunflower?" asked Walker.

"Common law wife, dude," said Star.

Steele looked at Star. There was something that wasn't quite right about what he said, but Steele couldn't put his finger on it. It would come, but Steele couldn't force it.

"Thank you, Star," said Steele. "Stay in town, we may need to talk again."

Star got up and left the room, leaving the detectives alone.

"Who next?" asked Walker.

"Let's talk to the ex-wife and see what Tony Chambers was doing in town. Then we'll talk to Young Tom and see what his story is."

Deputy McNeill brought Louella Chambers in and sat her down in the chair, then returned to his post by the door.

Steele looked at the stout woman with the thick glasses and tried to imagine her and Tony Chambers as a couple. Strange bedfellows, he thought.

"Thank you for coming," said Steele. "I'm so sorry for your loss."

"Ain't no loss as far as I'm concerned," said Louella. "Tony was a worthless prick. Good riddance."

This wasn't the reaction Steele was expecting. "You didn't get along with your ex-husband?"

"He walked out on me and Peggy fifteen years ago and I was finally happy, then he comes back and makes my life miserable. Just like he was when we was married."

"Why did he come back?' asked Walker.

"He was gonna sell my house," said Louella. "That rotten bastard don't even call or say how do you do for fifteen years, then he blows into town and threatens to sell my house without a care about where I was going to live. I'm glad he's dead."

"You realize that you just gave us a pretty good motive for killing him, right?' asked Steele.

She turned her big eyed gaze at Steele. "I don't care. I didn't kill the son of a bitch, but I'm glad he's dead."

"Where were you this afternoon between three and six?" asked Walker.

"In my house, as long as it belongs to me."

"Any witnesses?" asked Steele.

"Nope. Any more questions? I've got a pot roast in the oven that's likely to burn if I don't attend to it pretty quick."

"That should do it for now," said Steele. "But stick around in case we need you again, okay?"

She pushed her weight out of the chair and stared at Steele. "Ain't got nowhere else to go, now do I?"

She shuffled out the door, leaving the two detectives stunned for a moment. Then Steele laughed.

"No alibi and a good reason to kill the guy. And happy he's dead. Who's our next contestant?"

"Wally? Can you bring in someone named Young Tom, please?" asked Walker.

Jones entered the room like a swaggering pirate, all attitude and anger. His bald head gleamed in the stark lighting of the interior. Four quick steps and he was in front of the desk.

"You have no right to do this," said Jones. "What kind of crap is this?"

"Sit down," said Steele.

"Why should I? So you can crucify me? Is that your plan? I know how you guys are. Take the newest guy in town and harass him, that's what you're thinking, isn't it?"

Steele stared at Jones, trying to get a handle on the anger coming off the man. Why was he acting this way? And more importantly, from a police perspective, what was he trying to hide?

"Your full name sir," said Steele, "and lose the attitude. We're investigating a murder here and we've got questions for you. Now, you can cooperate, and let us ask our questions, or we can take you to Rock Port and make it a little more personal. Is that what you want?"

Jones reluctantly sat down, but kept the glare. "My name is Thomas Jones, and before you make any cracks, I am not the famous singer. I've been getting that crap all my life."

"Why do they call you Young Tom?" asked Walker.

"Because there are two Tom's in town, one older and me. I became Young Tom."

"What can you tell us about your run in with the deceased?" asked Steele.

Jones exploded out of the chair. "I knew you were going to pin this on me. I didn't do it. I had no reason to kill the jerk. Sure, I refused to sell him beer and the smuck hit me, but that don't mean I killed him. You ask around, nobody liked him. Am I sorry he's dead? Not a chance, but that don't mean I did the dirty deed."

"You got a alibi for between three and six?" asked Steele.

"In my store. I stay open late."

"You store is on the bluff above the beach where Tony Chambers was found," said Walker.

"So what? Somebody killed him near where I work, does that make me the killer? Sure, I hated the guy, he was a bad seed, and I've spent my life dealing with guys like that, but that's all I was doing, dealing with another loser. Do you think I would jeopardize my life and living for a loser like that? Not a chance."

"What made you decide to move to West Harbor?" asked Steele.

"I came here for my health," said Jones. "Look, fellows, I didn't do it, can I go? I swear to you, it wasn't me. You want, I'll be available, but right now, that's all I've got to say."

"What are you hiding, Mr. Jones?" asked Steele.

The anger in Jones reached a boil. Bolts of lighting danced across his eyes and he reacted. In one quick motion he was out of his chair, knocking the folding chair across the room. He glared at the police. "You guys got no right to harass a honest citizen. I'm not going to take any more of your crap."

In an instant, Jones was out the door, leaving a gap of silence in the room.

Steele looked at Walker. "Interesting, don't you think?"

"He's definitely hiding something," said Walker. "I'll run a back ground check on him when we get back to the station."

After Jones, the detectives interviewed, in order, the Graves, the Peterson's, and the Duncan's. None had anything to do with the deceased, all fairly new to West Harbor, all were out of town, or had alibi's for their whereabouts during the time in question.

Then it was Sunflower's turn for an interview. Walker perked up at the arrival of the pretty redhead. Steele glanced over at his sergeant and smiled.

"Easy, there, Kevin, she's married."

"Common law," said Walker. "Not the same thing."

Sunflower sat down and smiled at the two detectives. "I wondered when you'd get around to me. We've been talking outside, waiting our turn, and were curious if you've found out anything yet."

"We're asking questions," said Steele. "Do you have any idea who might have killed Tony Chambers?"

She thought for a moment. "Well, he wasn't a very nice man, and I certainly can see why someone might want to kill him, but for the life of me, I can't figure out who. Sorry, I was never very good at mysteries."

"Where were you between three and six?" asked Walker.

"My alibi? Oh my, I hadn't thought of that. I was home alone, no wait, I went over to visit my neighbor, Mary, for awhile. We had coffee and talked until maybe two, then I went home and did the dishes and waited for Genesis to come home from school, then I made dinner, and was cleaning up when I heard the sirens."

"Was your husband home all that time?" asked Steele.

She stared at Steele. "Are you saying that Star might have had something to do with this killing? He wouldn't hurt a fly. As a matter of fact, he's about the last person on earth that I could think of that would do anything like that."

"Was he with you all afternoon?"

She paused for just a brief second. "Absolutely."

"Except for the time you were having coffee with your next door neighbor," said Walker.

"Not Star. He's not like that. Surely, you can't think that he'd have anything to do with that sort of thing?"

"You'd be surprised," said Steele. "Sometimes it's the least likely candidate that does the killing. Take you for instance. You seem nice, and probably wouldn't kill anybody, but there is a large gap in time that you have no alibi for. You could have easily met up with Chambers, got into a fight and killed him and made it back in time for dinner. You don't have an alibi any more than your husband."

"You're accusing me of murder?"

"Not at this time," said Steele. "But you see what I'm saying? Anybody can be pushed to the edge. From what I've heard so far, Tony Chambers made a lot of people mad, and for at least one individual, mad enough to kill him. Were you that someone?"

She looked worried. "Well, it wasn't me. Can I go now? I've got to get home."

Sunflower left the room, to be quickly replaced by an anxious Seavers. "How much longer is this going to take?"

Steele gauged the compact man standing on the opposite side of the table. He saw a competent looking fellow.

"You would be?" asked Steele.

"Bill Seavers. My little girl found Tony dead on the beach."

"Sit down, Mr. Seavers," said Steele.

Seavers did as he was told. "There isn't much I can tell you. I'm a master craftsman, working out of my garage, and spend most of my time here in town either in the garage or fixing up what's broke in the house. I never knew Tony Chambers, having moved here after he was gone, and didn't have anything to do with him during his short stay. I heard from others that you're interested in alibi's. I was in the garage from three to five, when my wife called me in for dinner, then I was with my wife until Cindy found Chambers on the beach. My son came and told me what they had found and I called the police. Simple."

"You had no reason to want him dead?"

"Nope," said Seavers. "From what I hear, he was a jerk and probably had it coming to him, but I didn't kill him. Any further questions?"

"Can anybody confirm you being in the garage that whole time?" asked Walker.

"What are you saying? That I snuck out and killed the guy and came back like nothing happened?"

"It's possible," said Steele.

Seavers shook his head. "You're grasping at straws. Sorry. I'm not your guy."

He stood up and walked out before the detectives could say another word.

Steele thought about the exchange for a brief moment, and that was all there was, because no sooner than Seavers left the building, a very pretty blonde walked in.

Walker sat up in his chair and smiled. "Have a seat, miss."

"Misses. I'm married. Please forgive my husband, he doesn't have much tolerance for this sort of thing. My name is Mary Seavers and I don't know how much I can tell you."

"Where were you between three and six?" asked Steele.

"At home. I was doing laundry and met up with my neighbor, Sunflower, and we had coffee and did some girl talk that lasted until maybe three, then I did some housework, then the kids came home and it was time to make dinner."

"Did you have any run-ins with Tony Chambers over the past couple of days?" asked Steele.

"I saw him down the lane, but you know, I really didn't have much reason to go up and talk to the man. From what I hear, he wasn't very nice, but to answer your question, I never talked to him. Why? Am I a suspect? Bill would just love that."

"Ma'am," said Steele, "everybody is a suspect."

She left and the two detectives went over their notes. Steele felt that there was something he was missing, but couldn't put his finger on it. The small town had a lively group of individuals, but aside from being colorful characters, one was a murderer. But which one? There were several good candidates, but were they the only possible guilty parties? Was there a dark horse in the running that he wasn't aware of? Walker had many opinions, mostly about how good looking Sunflower and Mary Seavers were, but had few ideas on who might have killed Tony Chambers.

The next to come in was the post mistress, Bonnie Williams. She wore her bibbed overalls and oversized glasses, making her look more like a gnome than anything else. Bonnie sat down in the recently vacated by Mary Seavers, crossed her hands in her lap and waited to be questioned.

Steele looked at the diminutive woman across the table from him. "And you would be?"

"Bonnie Williams. I've lived here all my life, and knew Tony when he and Louella were first married. A beast of a man. Even back when he lived here. The village was relieved when he left all those years ago. By the time he came back, most of the old town residents were gone, except of course for Lou, Adam, Old Tom and myself."

"Why did he return to West Harbor?" asked Steele, already knowing the reason, but wanting to hear what Bonnie had to say.

"Well," she said, leaning in closer, "the rumor was that the old goat was going to take Lou's house, kick her out in the street, and sell the place to an out of towner who planned on tearing down the house and build a bigger one in its place. An eyesore is what it would have been. We're a small village, not some fancy big city suburb, and the new house would not have fit our community."

"Did you have any run-ins with Chambers during his recent appearance?" asked Steele.

She snorted and shook her head. "He came into the post office just once, and that was to make fun of me. I would have bet the man couldn't write a letter, let alone receive one, except for the fact that Lou got a letter from him no more than two days before he showed up. I had no other dealing with the man, other than to see how he treated others, which wasn't very nice. After the way he acted, I was greatly surprised that someone hadn't done him in years ago, but I guess he had to pick my home town to die."

"You don't seem too broken up about it," said Steele.

"No more than I would to hear about a rabid dog being put down," said Bonnie.

"Where were you between three and six on Friday?" asked Walker, looking up from his note taking.

She laughed, a bright cheerful lilt. "Oh my, isn't that delightful. Am I a suspect? What a wonderful thought. All these years, I've been many things, but a murder suspect is definitely something new. Sorry, between three and six? I was working at the post office, sorting mail and putting circulars in the resident boxes. I closed up at five o'clock, as ususal, and was in the back, that's where I live, making dinner and getting ready for the Friday lineup on PBS. They have such nice shows, don't you think?"

"Did you hear anything on the beach?"

"You mean seagulls? No, I'm afraid I didn't. It was getting a little chilly for my tastes, so I closed up the windows and turned on the television set. I'm afraid I'm getting a little deaf in my older years and have the volume turned up quite loud to be heard in the kitchen where I was preparing my dinner."

"What did you eat?" asked Walker.

She looked at the sergeant. "Is it important? I guess everything is in a murder investigation, right? Well, as I recollect, I was boiling up a chicken breast, and some vegetables. You get to be my age and you don't need to eat as much as when you're young. Is this any help at all?"

"Did you have any personal reason to kill Tony Chambers?" asked Steele.

"None," said Bonnie. "But like most of the village, I despised the man and I have to say, though its very uncharitable of me, that I don't care that he's dead. Is there anything else I can help you with?"

Steele closed his notebook and looked at the elfin woman. "No, thank you for your time. We may need to talk to you again later."

She smiled. "Ask away. I live behind the post office and am available whenever you need my assistance." She stood up and bowed slightly. "Good day, gentlemen, I hope you find your killer soon."

With that said, she ambled out the door, leaving a open mouth Walker and a smiling Steele in her wake.

"What do you think of that, boss?"

Steele shook his head. "I'm not sure, but she sure has spunk."

"A suspect for us?"

"Probably not, but definitely entertaining."

The detectives were just about ready to call it a night when an old man shuffled in the open doorway.

"Is this where the inquisition is being held?"

Steele looked at the man, with his black suit and shock of white hair. "Can I help you?"

"You've talked to just about everybody in town," he said, "but not me. I got opinions too, you know."

"Sit down and tell us your name," said Steele, re-opening his notebook.

"My name is Thomas Hoffman. They call me Old Tom. I've lived in West Harbor since I was twenty-five. My wife is buried up Cemetery Road. Married a long time. Lived a long time. Seen a lot. This town used to be a busy port. Watched the docks built, watched the ocean take them away. It ain't what it used to be, but I like it just the same."

"About the murder?" asked Steele.

"Don't rush me," said Hoffman. "Everybody is in an all fire hurry to spill their guts. Like I was saying, West Harbor used to be a big deal. We had three hotels, over a thousand residents. You can see the remains of the foundations if you look through the grass. And we had our violence too. This was a fishing port, with sea men and lots of liquor, and many a fight. Had a few murders back in the day, but not so much now. After the last good storm took out the docks, all the fishing business went south to Rock Port, and the town just dried up. Last murder we had was over twenty years ago. Fellow named Trenton got in a fight with a man named Wills over a woman. Trenton had a knife; Wills had a gun. They buried Trenton up Cemetery Road, not too far from my wife. Haven't been much violence since."

"What do you know about the death of Tony Chambers?" asked Walker.

"Knew him when he moved here with Louella back twenty years ago. Arrogant man. Drank a lot. When he left fifteen years ago, he left a wife and daughter, who were better off without him. Why he came back, I don't know. But he sure made his presence known. Made a lot of people angry. I'm not saying I approve of killing, but sometimes I think it's justified."

"Do you know who killed Tony Chambers?" asked Steele.

Hoffman turned his head and stared at Steele. "All I'm saying is that sometimes the good Lord provides a way out, taking care of his children when the time is right."

"You didn't answer my question," said Steele.

"That's all I'm going to say. Thanks for listening. Young people don't listen to their elders no more."

The detectives watched the old man push himself out of his chair and shuffle out the door, leaving silence in his wake. Minutes passed before the deputy stuck his head in.

"That's the lot of them. Do you want me to stick around any longer?

Steele shook his head. "Go home, Wally. Thanks for your help. We'll lock up when we're done."

Then it was just the two detectives. Steele scanned what he had written in his notebook, flipping the pages, looking for something he might have missed. "What do you think, Kevin?"

"There are several likely candidates for the killing. This fellow Star must have a real name. I can't believe a mother would name her child Star, which makes me think he's got something to hide. And I didn't believe him when he told us that the dead guy insulted his wife. I think there is more to that than he's saying. Number two is Thomas Jones, no relation to the singer. He got awful angry just answering questions. What is he hiding? And could that anger have been enough to kill? Hard to say. Not done with him. Then there was the ex-wife, Louella. She was going to lose her house if he lived. That's plenty of good motive for me, and she had no alibi, leaving her with motivation and opportunity. I'm not sure about the means yet, but we'll know what killed Chambers soon enough. As for the rest of them. I can't really say. Nobody has a decent alibi. For all I know, it could be any of them. What do you think, boss?"

"I agree with your analysis," said Steele. "Any of them could have done it, including your numbers one through three, but what bugs me the most is what that old guy said when we asked if he knew who did the killing. The lord provides a way out when the time is right? He knows something."

"Maybe he's our killer."

"Possibly, but not likely. He can't weigh but a hundred pounds and Tony Chambers was a good two twenty. I can't see him overpowering Chambers, but he knows more than he saying." Steele closed his notebook. "Let's get back to town and see what Eddie's got for us."

They shut down the lights, and locked the door behind them, then headed through the moon lit night back to Rock Port.

4. The Aftermath

Saturday morning came with sun shining through the window panes of the post office, and the sounds of the surf hitting the beach outside the open doorway. Fresh sea air seemed to cleanse the tinge of murder from the day before. Now, all was good and new, as if Tony Chambers never came back to town.

Bonnie moved slowly and methodically, performing the same functions she had been doing for the past thirty years. After turning on the lights and opening the blinds, she opened the door, letting the fresh air in. She stood on the top step and took in the fresh air and looked at her town. There was little activity up the lanes. She could see the Seaver garage open and Bill Seaver doing something, but he was too far away to see much. To the south, Louella's house was quiet, with the curtains drawn. Still abed, Bonnie decided. To the north, there was a car gassing up at the Super Saver, one that she didn't recognize. There was a fine blue sky over the old school, making her think of her days long ago when she attended the West Harbor school. She sighed. Many days gone long ago.

She turned and headed back inside to finish her opening routine. She made sure the cubbyholes on the tables under the window were filled with the appropriate forms for shipping, domestic and international, and the shipping boxes in the bin next to the table were full, then checked the ink in the pens attached by chain worked, then went behind the counter and checked the register, making sure that she had plenty of change and low bills, just in case, then closed the till, and turned on the radio to an easy listening station from Rock Port.

The morning began with Bonnie sorting the mail. Bills for the Seavers, bills for the Duncan's, a post card to Louella from her daughter, just back from San Francisco, and the usual circulars for each and every resident in town. Bonnie slid each into the corresponding slot, double checking to make sure the right mail went to the right person.

She was just finishing when Adam Franklin walked in, the bell tinkling over his head, a cup of coffee in each hand. He looked worried as he approached her.

"Are you okay?" he asked, handing her a cup.

Bonnie took the coffee and smiled. "You worried someone might murder me next?"

"Don't even say that," said Franklin. "You know how much I care about you."

"How much do you care about me, Adam?"

He got flustered. "I'm very fond of you, Bonnie. I just don't know what I would do if something happened to you."

"What are you not saying?"

He reached over and took her hands in his. "I would absolutely die if something happened to you. There, I said it, now can we discuss this murder rationally?"

"Rationally? Oh my yes, let's do. Do you have any theories?"

"My bet is on Young Tom," said Franklin, "Or maybe Star. You saw how angry he was when Chambers shoved him to the ground yesterday, didn't you? I don't know if it was enough to make Star kill him, but you never know, and as far as Young Tom is concerned, we don't really know much about him, do we?"

"Not too much," agreed Bonnie. "But is he capable of murder? My bet is on Louella. Tony comes to town, and from what I hear, he was going to sell her house, leaving her on the streets. Where was she going to go? Live with her daughter down in Rock Port? As far as I know, she doesn't have any other relatives, not that there aren't any, but in all the years she's been here, she's gotten like two pieces of mail from someone other than her daughter, and they were from a brother somewhere in the middle of Iowa."

"Tony was a pretty big fellow," said Franklin. "Do you think Lou could have overpowered him?"

"Why not? It's all a matter of physics. All one would need is sufficient force on the right spot and Tony would go down like a ton of bricks. He wouldn't consider her a threat, and would be willing to turn his back on her. This is what I figured happened. The two had a fight and Lou followed him down to the beach. He'd been drinking, you know–I heard about the fight with Young Tom–and his reflexes were probably a little slow. So, she follows him down to the beach and they continue to argue. He laughs at her, and when he turns his head, she picked up a rock and smacks him on the back of the head. He drops dead. End of story. Then all she has to do is chuck the stone in the water and walk home. Simple. What do you think?"

He rubbed one hand along his chin. "It could have happened that way, though I still see Young Tom or Star being the more likely prospect. Either one of them could have got to him on the beach, using the same rock you mentioned. Both are stronger than Lou and both had a reason for wanting to hit him. Perhaps the murder was accidental. Maybe the killer was mad and only intended on giving Chambers a good lesson. Show him that being a bully wasn't getting him anywhere."

Bonnie smiled. "That's a lesson he won't easily forget. You may be right, but my money's on Lou. She had the motive, means and opportunity, as they say on those crime shows. Either way, he wasn't a nice man and in the end, he got what he deserved."

"No hard feelings for his death?"

"Not a whit. The way I see it, sooner or later, someone would give him what he'd been giving everybody else. It's all karma, you see. In the end, he made someone so angry that they did him in. Simple. But you mark my words, Adam, it was Lou. When all is said and done, the police will be driving away with her in the back seat."

#

Star was in a foul mood following the events of the previous day. While he normally enjoyed his quiet time on a sunny Saturday morning, this was no normal morning. He worried about what he didn't know. The police knew that he had an argument with Chambers on the day he died, but did they believe Star's excuse of Chambers insulting his wife? Or were there future questions coming Star's way? It was all maddening. All the years when he was able to float along, embracing the persona of Star were in jeopardy. Would he be exposed? Would he be shamed? Worse. Would he have to go back to Los Angeles and face criminal charges? Worse yet. Would he be charged with Chambers murder just because he was seen having a fight with the man on the day he died? This was turning out to be a major bummer. Why did Tony Chambers have to come to town? All was clicking nicely until then.

Then there was the fight he had with his wife after Genesis went to bed. It was obvious that he was hiding something, no matter how much he argued the point, she clearly didn't believe him, and that was enough to cause a restless night. He could feel the ice coming off her, sleeping next to him, and wished for the nightmare to end, but it didn't. Come morning, she was still chilly to him, and flatly ignored him when he tried to get her to talk to him. She hadn't forgiven him, but still he couldn't tell her the truth. What if she left him? Was his past so horrific that she would up and leave? It wasn't something he wanted to risk. Better to leave her in the dark, than have her find out and take off with Genesis. His life would be ruined.

So he said nothing and ate his granola and goats milk in silence, sipping on the organic range free coffee, hoping for a miracle to occur. Nothing of the sort was in his immediate future. She took his dirty dishes and walked away with out so much as a glance at him. It barely registered when Genesis asked if he could go next door and play, leaving him alone with Sunflower. He couldn't take it any more. He would go out and tend to the goats, at least they wouldn't give him the cold shoulder.

"Where are you going?"

Star looked over at Sunflower. "So you're talking to me now."

"I'm listening if you're willing to talk."

"What about? Are we going to fight again? I gotta tell you, I'm not up for another round of "what did you do?" It's getting old, Sunflower."

"I'll tell you what's getting old," she said. "It's having a husband who lies to his wife. We're supposed to be a team, you and I, and honestly, you're letting me down. Why can't you just tell me what's going on with you? What's the worse thing that can happen?"

Other than you leave me and I go to jail? He thought, but didn't say. Instead, he was evasive. "Let's not argue anymore, okay?"

"What are you hiding, Star?"

"I'm not hiding anything," he lied. "Why can't you believe me?'

She stared at him for a moment, then said. "My god, you killed him, didn't you?"

"How could you think such a thing?"

She backed up against the kitchen counter and gripped the peeling linoleum. "It was you."

He reached out to hold her and she moved away, sliding under his arms and running into the next room. When he followed her, she ran to the corner, picking up a poker from the fireplace along the way.

"Don't you touch me," she said. "I swear, I'll defend myself."

Star stopped in the middle of the room and smiled at her, hurting his face in the process. "Sunflower, you're being ridiculous. Look at you, hiding in the corner. What are you going to do? Stay in that corner for the rest of your life?"

He moved toward her only to have her point the poker at him. He walked up until the poker was touching his chest. "If you really think that I killed Tony Chambers, you might as well just stick that poker into my heart. I would die and that would be the end of it. I promise you, I did not kill him."

She held onto the poker, the tip wavering under the pressure. A moment passed, then another while husband and wife stared at each other. Finally, she dropped the poker.

He tired to embrace her, but was denied. She side-stepped his open arms and walked back to the kitchen. He followed, attempting to grab her along the way.

Sunflower knocked his arms away, then looked up at him. "You may or may not be a killer, but I do know you are a liar. And I don't want to be with a liar. You've got a big decision to make here, Star. You can tell me the truth and see where that gets you, or keep up the silence and make the decision for me. Your choice."

She walked over to the bedroom, went inside and closed the door behind her.

Star felt awful. This was no way to start the day. The nightmare from hours ago remained, leaving him empty and angry. How was this his fault? He tired to change. Wasn't that what he was supposed to do? Move on and make a better life? He left his life of crime and became a peace and love guy, and for what? To have his past come back to haunt him? It just wasn't fair. He took one last look at the closed door, wondering if that was a sign. Was this the end of his marriage? What would become of him? He knew that he certainly couldn't go back to his parents, they had disowned him years ago, so where did that leave him? He headed out the door to take care of the goats. At least they wouldn't hate him.

#

Louella sat in her chair, overlooking the ocean, and watched the sea gulls swoop down and pull at the fish heads on the beach below her house. Her cup of camomile tea sat on the small table next to her, with the steam rising off the hot liquid, the scent of fresh lemons mixed with the tea, soothing her jangled nerves. Was it really yesterday that Tony was harassing her about selling the house? He was such an animal. And now he was dead. She smiled, in spite of herself. It wasn't a good Christian attitude to take murder so lightly, but he was so deserving. How could that be a bad thing?

She reached over and took hold of her cup of tea and sipped, burning her lips in the process. Louella blew on the tea, sending ripples across the surface. Now that Tony was gone, she could go back to the way things were before his untimely arrival, and death. Good riddance, she thought, watching the gulls tear apart the carcass of some fish. Tony was a good for nothing husband who brought nothing but misery to everybody and everything he encountered, and for once, it appeared that the just overcame the evil. He was gone, and she wouldn't be losing her house.

A knock at the door brought her out of her reverie, and before she could get up and answer, the door opened to reveal a dumpy girl, with a chopped page boy hair cut, thick nose and lips, and body to match. She wore an unflattering top that pinched the fat folds around her middle, making her appear more corpulent than she was. Margaret Chambers had come home.

Louella crossed the room. "Peggy. How good of you to come."

"Don't you be all nice to me," said Margaret. "Why didn't you tell me what happened? I can't believe you, mother. Daddy comes to town and you don't tell me and then what do I see when I open the paper this morning? He was murdered! Murdered! I can't believe you didn't think to pick up the phone and call me." she began to cry. "Daddy's dead and I didn't even get to say good-bye, and you knew he was here. I saw him in town last week and he was so nice to me, now he's gone."

Margaret ran out of steam. She stumbled over to the couch and collapsed.

Louella helped her sit down. "Let me get you a nice cup of tea, that'll make you feel better."

Margaret looked up with tears in her eyes. "How can that make it better? Daddy's dead! What am I going to do now? He never said he loved me. I always figured we have the time to work it out and now we don't. It's not fair." She wiped away a tear and looked at her mother. "So what happened here?"

"Your father came to town a couple of days ago and told me that he was going to sell our house. My house. He hasn't lived here fifteen years. He was going to throw me out in the streets. Not so much as a how do you do. I pleaded with him, but he didn't care. He laughed at me. Honey, your daddy wasn't a very nice man."

"I knew that. Then what happened?"

"He drank a lot. Your daddy always was a drinker. On the morning of his, you know what, I made him breakfast, then he went out to do who knows what. He came back a hour later with more beer, drank all he could, then passed out on your old bed."

"And."

"I lay down to take a nap and when I got up he was gone. I didn't know where he went, but to be honest, I was glad he was gone. He was mean to me. I was scared, honey. I never told you about it, but your daddy used to hit me sometimes when he got mad."

"Why didn't you tell me?"

"I didn't want to worry you. Anyway, he up and left when you were a little girl and I didn't see much reason to disrespect your father when he wasn't around to defend himself."

"So he left and that was the last time you saw him alive?"

"That's the honest truth, honey. I woke up and he was gone, then come dinner time, I heard the sirens and went out to see what the ruckus was about and there he was, dead on the beach."

"How awful." Margaret sat up and dried her face with the backs of her hands. "I can't believe it. Daddy's dead. And you swear you had nothing to do with it?"

"I'll admit it, I wished he was gone and then he was, but I didn't kill him. I couldn't do that. You've seen him. He was a big man, a powerful man. Do you think I could have gotten the jump on him and killed him? You think that little of me? Once upon a time, I loved your daddy, but that was a long time ago."

"You swear you didn't kill him."

Louella crossed her heart with one finger. "Double swear."

"What happens now? I mean once the police are done with him, daddy deserves a decent burial."

Louella hadn't thought of that. "I don't have no extra money for that, honey. Maybe we can put our heads together and figure out what we should do. Can you stay over a couple of days and help your old mom? Your bedroom is just the same as when you left."

"The bed daddy last slept in? That's gross and disgusting."

"I can wash the sheets," said Louella. "Please stay with me. You never come visit me no more, not since you've got your big job down in the city."

"I'm a waitress, mom," said Margaret. "But I guess I can call work and take a couple of days off. Don't worry, mom, we'll get through this together."

Louella hugged her daughter so tight that the young woman gasped.

"Jeez, mom. You trying to kill me?"

The two looked at each other and both began to cry.

#

Mary Seavers put the laundry away, then began dusting the knick-knacks in the living room, trying to erase the dirt from her existence. The previous day seemed like a some sort of dream to her. She had never seen a dead body and was little prepared for the coldness she felt looking at the still face. Yesterday afternoon, Tony Chambers was a loud noisy intrusion on their quiet lives, now he was dead. And the worst of it all, there was a killer in their midst. But who? She considered the possible suspects while she dusted, clicking them off mentally as she ran down their confrontations with the man. Louella seemed likely, being that she was about to lose her house, but could she kill in cold blood? Then there was Young Tom. She heard about the fight between he and Chambers. Could he be the killer? They really didn't know much about Young Tom. Perhaps he had been hiding out in West Harbor this past year and Tony Chambers said the wrong thing and set Young Tom off. Who knew? Then there was Star, her long time next door neighbor. Mary had heard of his little set to with Chambers. Was he too hiding something? According to Sunflower, Star had been acting strange ever since Chambers came to town. Was there enough between the two men that it pushed Star over the edge? Mary found it hard to believe that her hippie neighbor could be a killer, but stranger things had happened. She then thought of her husband. Had something happened during the past two days that caused him to kill? That wasn't likely, she decided, but she wanted to be sure.

The kids, plus Genesis from next door, were sprawled out in front of the television, watching cartoons, when she passed them.

"Can we have some popcorn, mom?" asked Billy.

"Yes, but don't make too big a mess," said Mary, continuing through the kitchen and the door leading to the garage. She could hear the kids scrambling behind her as she reached for the door.

"Let me make it this time," said Billy.

"Get out of my way, squirt," said Cindy. "I'm oldest, I get to do it."

Mary shook her head at the sibling rivalry, then opened the door and crossed into her husbands domain. She spotted him measuring out planks of wood, running his hands along the grain.

Seavers looked up at her approach. "Lunch time already?"

"Not yet," said Mary, trying to come up with a good way of accusing her husband of murder.

"Then what are you doing out here?"

That threw her off. "I just wanted to talk to you, is that a crime?"

"You're keeping me from my work," he said. "I'd like to get started on another piece before the next rain comes. So what do you want?"

"I was thinking about the poor Tony Chambers and the way he was killed," said Mary.

"Look, there wasn't anything poor about Tony Chambers. The guy was a jerk. He ran into a bigger jerk. End of story. Is that what you wanted to talk about? If so, I've got nothing to say. Now, can I get back to my work?"

"Well, I was thinking that, you know, that someone in our little town murdered that man."

"Your point being?"

"That one of us is a murderer. Doesn't that worry you? Having a killer on the loose?"

He sighed, put down his measuring tape and pencil and walked over to his wife. "The guy had it coming to him. Plain and simple. The rest of us have been around for years and no one has tried to kill us, right? I think we're safe from the killer."

"But he or she is probably one of us," said Mary. "One of us. Maybe a neighbor, maybe someone we're close to."

Seavers stared at his wife for a moment, trying to read the look on her face, then nodded. "I get it now. You think, maybe I killed the guy, right? Is that what this is all about? You think I might be the killer?"

"I didn't say that."

"You don't have to. It's written all over your face. That's why you came out here. I'm right, aren't I? You got to thinking about the murder, and correct me if I'm wrong, you ran down the list of all the possible killers here in town, and lo and behold, along comes my name. Is that what you were thinking?"

Now that the issue was out on the table, Mary shied away from the discussion. What was she thinking? Just because her husband wasn't interested in her sexually, didn't automatically put him in the killer category, did it? And from the look on his face, she could see that she had made a big mistake coming out here. For a brief moment, she wished that she could come up with something, anything, that could get her out of this situation and save face.

"That's not true," said Mary, lying. "You were absolutely correct in that I was thinking about possible suspects, but I wasn't thinking of you. I was curious if you had an opinion on the matter. You know the people here in town. I just wondered if you considered who might have done the killing, that's all. How could you think that I'd put you on the list of killers?"

He softened his glare, and smiled. "Sorry. I'm a little tense lately. Trying to finish off enough work to give us a good Christmas and buy a new refrigerator has left me a little edgy. I guess I was reading too much into your look. As far as a killer goes. You never know who might be pushed over the edge and kill. But you can rest assured. It wasn't me. Now, can I get back to work?"

She left him in the garage, unsatisfied with his response, but could she expect otherwise? If he had killed Chambers, would he admit it? She returned to her cleaning, more worried than she was before she talked to her husband.

#

Sunflower stared out the window at her husband, doing busy work with the goats in the back yard. She could see that his heart wasn't in it by the way he stared off in the distance every five seconds. It was as if the goats were only a distraction. What was he hiding? It bothered her, not knowing what was going on. Following her parents divorce, she had no idea what she was doing, or where she was going, then she met Star and everything seemed to click. It was as if she had found her calling, and for the past ten years, it had been a good one, but lately, she wondered if maybe she had made a bad decision all those years ago. Becoming Sunflower had made it easy for her to forget her upbringing and her past life, but somehow, the past was creeping back into her present, making it difficult for her to decide what to do about her future. Would she stay Sunflower forever? Would she live the hippie life until she was old and withered, brewing her sun tea, making goat cheese, and shunning all things modern? Seeing the modern conveniences of the Seaver house had awoken a part of her that she had thought long gone. The sad fact of the matter was, she yearned to be Tracy Johnson once more. Maybe not live with her dysfunctional family, for she hadn't really kept in touch with her parents or her brother, but to embrace the normal life of middle class America. Why couldn't she have all those things that Mary Seavers had?

She gazed out the window at Star. Would he be able to provide those things? At this time, it didn't seem likely. Not only didn't it seem possible that Star could turn their existence around and become the Seavers, he wasn't even being true to himself. He was lying about something and Sunflower was determined to find out what it was. Then she thought of their time together. What did she really know about Star, other than what he had told her. Live in the present, he told her, the past was behind you. He never wanted to talk of the past, but everybody had one, what was he hiding in his? She was amazed on how little she knew her husband. Where was he from? What about his parents? Family? What was he like as a kid? How could she have gone so long without answers to these questions?

Sunflower put away the dishes and set about to clean up her domain, thinking about her relationship the whole time. Suddenly, everything around her looked suspect. How had she let herself get talked into this existence? She liked nice things, why had she settled for less? A quick walk into the bedroom only depressed her. She flopped on the mattress on the floor, no headboard, no frame, and eyed the posters on the wall and the shelves made of bricks and boards. This was how she lived back in her college days, and now ten years later, she still lived like a poor student. Why?

Living like a pauper was more of a prison sentence than she realized. There was no chance for change, unless she made it happen. Star was happy the way things were, why wasn't she? Could it be that there was more Tracy Johnson in her than she knew? She got off the bed and headed out to the back yard.

She could see Star shoving goat feed into the troff, not seeing her until she was nigh upon him.

"Star, we need to talk."

He looked up, rested the shovel on the ground and stared at her. "More questions?"

"I was just in the house doing dishes and realized that I don't know much about my own husband."

"You've been with me for ten years, isn't that enough?"

She thought about that for a moment, then shook her head. "I know you only from what you've given me. Face value. I don't know who you were before I came along. I don't know where you grew up. Whether you have a family out there somewhere who's missing you. Face it, Star, I don't know much about you at all."

"I don't talk about my past."

"Why not? I've told you about my crappy upbringing, yours can't be much worse than mine. Why don't you want me to know about you?"

"I've blocked out most of my childhood. You want the honest truth, talking about my past depresses the hell out of me. Okay? Why can't you just let it go and accept me for what you know to be the real me."

"That's the problem, Star, I don't know the real you. Don't you trust me? Isn't that what a marriage is built on? Trust?"

"And the fact that you don't trust me. You're the one that accused me of murder, I'd never do that to you."

Sunflower saw how the conversation was going. He was going to stonewall her until she gave up, but why? She looked at their back yard, with its sad broken down fence, and the holes in the goat shed, then back to her husband.

"Why can't you be like Bill Seavers and keep this up? If you're going to make a living out of goats, the least you can do is provide for them."

"Whoa! Where's this coming from? Honestly, Sunflower, I think you're losing it. One minute you accuse me of murder, the next you want my family history, and now you're bugging me about becoming an automaton like our next door neighbor? What's wrong with you?"

"I'm tired of my life, and for your information, my name is Tracy. I don't want to be called Sunflower anymore."

#

Thomas Jones looked over his crossword puzzle and thought about his current situation. All had been good, up until Tony Chambers had arrived. Jones was able to blend into a new community, leaving his troubled past behind him. But the murder of Chambers would bring more scrutiny, much more than Jones would like. This had been a good spot for him, but was it over? Was his time in West Harbor coming to an end?

There was a time when Jones knew all the answers, at least he thought he did. He was a young kid coming out of Los Angeles and had worked a scheme or two, primarily selling real estate that either didn't exist, or was situated on the bottom of the ocean. Money rolled in and he stayed two steps ahead of the law, then came a time when a man with a gun confronted him in an alley in the Hollywood Hills. A fight ensued and the pistol was fired. Seconds later, the other man lay dying on the dirty pavement. As soon as he could, Jones left southern California and didn't look back. He emptied his bank account and moved north, working scams along the way, padding his accounts, until he arrived in West Harbor. This was to be his last stop. Or was it?

He picked up his puzzle and tried to come up with a seven letter word for defiance. The fresh air came in through the open window next to his register and Jones could smell the ocean, almost taste the salt filling the air. It looked to be another stellar day on the coast, except for the pervasive gloom that permeated the air. A murder could do that to a town.

The bell over the door rang as Old Tom lumbered in. He walked over to the cat food section and pulled a couple of cans off the shelf, then shuffled up to the counter.

"You ought to buy a case of that stuff, the way you go through it."

Old Tom pulled crumpled ones from an inside pocket and dropped them on the counter. "Emergency food. Two more cats showed up on my doorstep this morning. Got to take care of God's creatures, don't we?"

Jones rang up the purchases and bagged the two cans, handing the other the change. "We sure had a lot of excitement around here yesterday, didn't we?"

"Just nature taking care of business. Never cared much for the man. Can't say I'm sorry he's dead."

"It doesn't bother you that there's a murderer out there?"

"Nope. Justice was done. The lord giveth and the lord taketh away." He pocked the change and headed for the door. "Wouldn't hurt locking your doors at night. See you around."

And he was gone, leaving Jones alone in the store. The silence was ominous, but not something that bothered him. He was used to the quiet. Having a murderer for a neighbor was another thing altogether. He picked up his puzzle and looked at his down clues for help on defiance. Started with a C and ended with a T. He thought for a moment, then penciled in contempt. It fit perfectly.

5. The Police Investigate

      The Public Safety building in Rock Port sits in the flats at the bottom of the hill, facing the ocean. It is a brick building, two stories tall, built in the sixties, with a parking lot in the rear that separates it from the morgue and jail. The city administration offices are on the first floor, with a majestic wide stairway leading to the police department, and fire safety, and public safety all located on the second floor. There is a open space at the top, with three doorways, leading to each of the sub-departments. The police to the rear, public safety to the right and fire to the left. Inside the police department is a entry with a few chairs facing a counter, manned by a person in uniform, the first line of defense handling the public. Behind this section are a half dozen desks, occupied by the clerks and staff members dealing with the daily operation of the department, then a line of office behind this section. The uniformed officers operate out of the bull pen, a large room to the far right of the department, with the junior officers, and detectives in the offices in the middle and to the far left, the office of the Captain of Police.

      Detective Ben Steele's desk sits behind a glass wall separating the clerks from the detectives, sharing the space with four others, Sergeant Kevin Walker, Public Safety officer Wallace Sand, and Education officer Henry Cray. Of the four, only Cray and Steele had windows overlooking the back parking lot and a view of the morgue, along with a line of apartment buildings and the back of several businesses lining Oak Street to the east. At the moment, only Steele and Walker were in the room.

Steele was wearing his blue suit today, with a red tie and black shoes. Walker was adorned in his other thirties outfit, a dark gray pinstripe with wide labels, a light gray shirt and a checked tie. His fedora was on the coat rack behind him.

Steele looked through his notebook. There were too many people in West Harbor that were available and had a reason to kill Tony Chambers. Alibi's were a scarce commodity for these people, and there wasn't any sorrow on the death of Chambers. Nobody cared, and worse, most were happy that he was dead. What kind of town was this that tolerated such behavior? He flipped though each page, carefully reading what he had jotted down about the interviewees. So much angst. So much hatred for one man.

"There's a lot of folks that could have done the crime," said Walker from his desk next to Steele's. "I've been thinking about it all night. This guy comes to town and manages to irritate just about everybody in that little town and within twenty four hours is found dead on the beach. So who did the deed? My bet is on either Star, if that is his real name and Tom Jones, not the singer."

"Either could have done it," said Steele. "Neither has a decent alibi, and both had run-ins with Chambers on the day he died. But what about Louella, the ex-wife? She was going to lose her house and from what I got, Tony Chambers was plenty mean to her. She has no alibi, with plenty of opportunity and motive for the killing."

"I don't feel it," said Walker. "She didn't look much like a killer to me."

"How does a killer look?"

"You know what I mean. She seems more like someone's grandmother to me. And look at the size of the dead guy. He was huge. Can you see that little old lady coming up from behind and beating him to death? I mean really? So that leave Star and Jones. And just who is this Star guy anyway? Who names their kid Star? Got to be hiding something."

"Maybe he's just another hippie who dropped out of the human race. He doesn't have to be hiding something just because he chooses an unusual name. You've got to be a little more open minded, Kevin."

"I'm sure you're right." Walker thought for a moment. "He's sure got a hot wife though. Man, what a looker. I sure could go for a girl like that."

"Settle down, boy. She's taken, and as far as we're concerned, she could still be a suspect."

"Her? Are you kidding me? She looked too good to be a killer."

Steele flipped through his notebook until he found the page with Sunflower's interview. "No alibi for the time of death. She could have done it. Say she heard about the run-in between Star and Chambers, got mad, then ran into Chambers on the beach and killed him."

Walker was shaking his head as Steele explained. "I just can't see it, boss. Again, look at her and look at Chambers. He was huge. She's pretty petite. Do you think she could come up with enough power to kill him?"

"Anything's possible. Don't discount any of them due to size. Just because the victim was bigger than the rest doesn't mean a smaller person couldn't have done the killing. All you need is the right position and the right amount of force to get the job done. Any of those people could have killed Chambers and its up to us to figure out who."

"Anything on him when he died?" asked Walker.

Steele opened a folder on his desk, then flipped through the papers until he got to the one he was looking for. "A set of keys, a comb, a wallet, twenty-four dollars, a licence with a Modesto address, and a lucky rabbit's foot."

"Not for him," said Walker.

"No," agreed Steele.

The ringing of the phone interrupted their conversation. Steele picked up the receiver and hit the blinking line. "Steele. Oh hi, Eddie. What's that? Sure, we'll be right down." He hung up the phone and looked over at Walker. "Eddie's ready for us. Let's go."

Walker blanched. "I don't like seeing dead bodies much. They make me kind of sick."

Steele stood up and clapped Walker on the shoulder. "It's a good thing you're a homicide man. No chance of dead bodies in this job."

Walker joined him at the door. "All I'm saying is that they make me a little queasy, that's all. You don't have to make federal case about it. I can handle it." He paused. "You don't mind if I stand in the back, do you?"

"Come on, Kevin," said Steele. "This is what we do. Take an antacid if it makes you feel better."

#

The walk from the Public Safety building was no more than a hundred feet from the back of the building to the morgue, but it was a step back in time. The structure holding the jail and morgue had been built in the thirties with WPA money. The halls were yellowed tile, the walls a sickly green, and the odors from seventy years of stress and death permeated the place. The Morgue occupied the left side of the building with the jail housed in the right.

Steele opened the door for the morgue for Walker and let his subordinate enter first. There was a small entry with a open window facing the lone chair in the lobby. Normally, Shirley Withers would be behind the window, as she had for the past twenty years, but the spot was vacant at this time. Steele poked his head through the window.

"Anybody home?"

"Back here. Come on through."

The detectives opened the glass door to the left of the window and entered a long hallway, passing the office to the right, then on to the morgue itself. The floor of the room was gray linoleum, slanted to the center from all sides, with a huge drain in the center. There was two autopsy tables of stainless steel. White cabinets were bolted to the green tile walls. The lighting was supplied by two long fluorescent lights.

Laying on one of the two tables was Tony Chambers, face up, his face ashen in death, his eyes closed. A sheet pulled up to his chin. Even with the covering, it was apparent that Chambers had been a large man in life.

Eddie Lawton, dressed in pale green scrubs, with a long, not so white, apron stood by one side of the body and looked up at the arrival of the detectives.

"Howdy boys," said Lawton. "Glad you could spare a few minutes of my time."

"What've you got, Eddie?" asked Steele.

"The usual fun and mayhem. I tell you, Ben, if I had given notice last week, I'd be chasing senoritas down Mexico way, hooking marlins by the pound. Instead, I get the pleasure of digging around the skull of this galoot."

"And what did you find?" asked Steele.

"No remorse for my soon to be retired state of mind? I'm surprised, Ben."

"Give it up, Eddie. What did you call us down here for?"

"Fine, be that way. I don't get a lot of live company down here, you know." He looked over at Walker, pressed up against the opposite wall. "What's wrong with Sam Spade over there?"

"He doesn't like dead bodies," said Steele.

"They don't hurt anybody. Pretty quiet most of the time. Unless they weren't totally dead when they came in. I had this case one time where the officers on the scene tagged and bagged a body and had him brought to me and guess what? Surprise. He wasn't dead. Mostly dead, yes. Totally dead? Not a chance. He got up off the table and started swinging at me. I swear. Must of been knocked unconscious and came to on my table. Can you imagine what was going through his mind."

"You didn't check him at the scene?" asked Steele.

"Didn't see the point. The victim was a MVA and a DOA. No point in my going out to the scene. Anyway, he came off the table and boy howdy was he mad."

Steele listened to the story, again, for he had heard it many times, and only played along because he knew that Lawton wasn't going to tell him what he wanted until he played his little game. All for Walker's benefit. Steele turned and looked at his junior partner, sweating and pale against the wall.

"If you're going to faint," said Steele, "just back up against the wall and slide down. I don't want to have to catch you if you fall on your face."

"I'm good," said Walker. "How much longer?"

Lawton laughed. "Homicide detective? You're in the wrong field, Spade. Maybe you should transfer to school safety. I'll bet you'd do real good making sure the little kiddies cross the street without getting hit."

"Leave him alone, Eddie."

"What? I can't have any fun anymore?"

"What about those precious minutes of your time that you were willing to give up for us?"

"Fine, be that way." Lawton moved to the head of the table and leaned over. "See this?"

Steele bent over and inspected the nasty gouge on the back of Chamber's skull. "Yep."

"Blunt trauma with enough force to kill the man."

"Could a rock have done the job?" asked Steele.

"Not likely. Something metal would be my guess. A rock would have crushed in the skull with one focal point. You can see that this one covers a length of maybe four or five inches. If I were you, I'd be looking for a lead pipe, or piece of rebar, or something like that. And I've narrowed down the time of death for you. Lividity and body temperature puts the time of death between maybe four and six."

"Anything else you can tell us?"

"He was a smoker. His lungs were full of tar and precancerous cells. If he hadn't been clubbed on the head, he was heading toward COPD and emphysema. His liver was in the beginning stages of cirrhosis, and he had an ulcer that was tearing up the lining in his stomach and may have advanced into the small bowl tissue. He may have developed lung cancer, but the blow on the head put an end to that possibility."

"Thanks for getting this done so quickly," said Steele.

"No problem. What else do I have to do with my time?"

"Dream of senoritas and marlins?"

"There is that," said Lawton. "I'll call you if I find out more."

Steele headed toward the door, nodding at Walker as he passed. "Fresh air?"

Walker pushed himself away from the wall and headed out ahead of Steele. Minutes later the two were outside.

"That place gives me the creeps," said Walker. "I don't know how you can stand it in there."

"Practice," said Steele.

#

Margaret Chambers lived in a small cottage on the flats down by the hatcheries and warehouses, where living was cheap and life dangerous. At night, the streets were dark and unattended, and during the day, the roads were filled with trucks going to and from the docks. This was the oldest section of Rock Port, dating back to the early nineteen hundreds. What houses still remained from those days were dilapidated, mixed with the businesses that catered to the waterfront. Margaret's house was one of four on the block, wedged between a security office to the north and a fishing supply shop to the south. The sidewalk in front of the house was cracked, as was the walk way up to the single story bungalow. The house itself was in dire need of a good paint job, along with a few repairs. The windows looked forlorn from the street, the porch sagged, the roof was missing shingles, the tap paper exposed in places.

Steele pulled the car in front of the house and glanced up and down the street. "Hard living down here."

"You got that right," said Walker. "I've never been down here before."

"Old town," said Steele. "When I first joined the police here I was patrolling down this way. There's a lot of activity down here in the flats, especially at night. Right now, it all looks pretty calm, but wait until the ships are in port. There's a half dozen bars just down the block. See that bar down on the corner?"

Walker squinted, staring toward the sea side of the block. "The Rusty Anchor?"

"Three people were stabbed there my first night on watch. One died, the other two ended up in the hospital. Sailors, drinking, and loose money make for a bad combination."

Walker turned and looked at Margaret's house. "Yet people live down here."

"Rents cheap. Come on, let's see if our little lady is home."

They walked up the cracked sidewalk, passing the unkempt lawn and foot high weeds in the small yard. The front porch was a half dozen steps above the lawn, with a old couch against the splintered wood and under a picture window. There were a few scattered pots on the edges of the wood, with dead and withered plants drooped over the sides of the clay pots.

Steele knocked on the door, then stood back a step and waited. Seconds passed and he knocked again.

"Maybe nobody's home," said Walker.

Just as they were ready to give up, the door opened. Inside the doorway was a chubby blonde, with a pug nose and bangs that threatened to cover her eyes. She was wearing worn jeans and a pink sweatshirt that said "GO GIRL" on it.

"May I help you?"

"Are you Margaret Chambers?" asked Steele.

"No. I'm her roommate, Sheila Groves. Margaret's not here right now. Who are you?"

Steele reached into his top pocket and pulled out his badge. "Lieutenant Steele and this is Sergeant Walker from the Rock Port Police. Do you have any idea where she might be?"

"She could be at work. I haven't seen her today. Why? Is she in trouble?"

"Do you know where she was yesterday afternoon?" asked Steele.

"Is this about her father? Oh my god, I read about it in the paper. What an awful thing to happen. Not that he was that nice mind you."

"You met Tony Chambers?"

"Maybe you should come in," said Sheila. "I don't want my neighbors to hear all about it."

Even if there weren't any neighbors to hear, thought Steele, but he nodded and they followed Sheila into the worn interior. She led them to the living room, with its broken down, second hand furniture and scarred coffee table.

"Have a seat. I don't have much to offer, but I do have some soft drinks," said Sheila, "Or I could make some coffee. Would you like some coffee?"

"We're good, thank you," said Steele.

They all sat down, with Walker and Steele on the flowered couch that looked like it had sprung a spring, and Sheila on the opposite chair. There was a television in one corner with extended rabbit ears, indicating no cable. The walls were mostly bare, except for a couple of framed pictures of the two girls in a seaside setting.

Steele pulled out his notebook and held his pen in hand. "So what can you tell me about Tony Chambers?"

"Other than he was a creep? He came over a couple of days ago and barged in here like he owned the place, barking out orders for this and that. He wanted us to get him beer and food and then berated us when we brought the wrong kind, and when we tried to make him some food, he threw the plate against the wall and called our food slop. Said he couldn't eat it and where were the pigs that were missing their meals."

"Sounds like a real sweetheart," said Walker.

"That's not the worst of it," said Sheila. "He told Margaret that she was ugly and should have never been born, and that he was sorry that he ever hooked up with her mother. Said that if he had his way, he would have made Margaret's mom have an abortion and the world would be better off without the waste of space that his daughter turned out to be. Margaret ran off to her room and cried and he just laughed. And if that wasn't enough, then he came on to me. Gross. He tried to put his hands on my leg but I pushed him away. He called me a slut and said that he knew that I wanted it, but just to punish me, he wouldn't give me the pleasure of his company. What a pig!"

"How long did he stay?" asked Steele.

"Too long," said Sheila."But I guess it couldn't have been more than a hour, maybe a hour and a half."

"When was this?"

"Like I said, a couple of days ago. It must have been Thursday. He came over around eleven and stayed until maybe one at the latest. He was the most disgusting man I've ever encountered and I can't say that I'm surprised that somebody killed him. He was a disease that needed to be eradicated from this planet."

Steele faithfully jotted down what she said. "Anything to add?"

"That's all. Anyway, he left and Margaret didn't say much after he was gone and I haven't seen much of her since. To be honest, I'm not sure where she is at this moment, but if I had to guess, I'd say down at the Blue Grotto. That's where she works. She's been putting in a lot of time so she can save up and go back to school."

Steel closed his notebook. "Thank you for your time, Miss Groves."

"I hope I didn't get Margaret in trouble. She's a real nice girl and even if she's had some bad luck, she's always so cheerful."

"I'm sure everything will be fine," said Steele. "We'll see if we can find her at the Grotto. Is it near here?"

"Down on the wharf," said Sheila. "You can't miss it. "It's the only fish and chips place at the marina."

#

The marina was alive with activity at this mid-afternoon hour. There was a line of businesses facing the parking lot and the marina, with many a small yacht moored in the inlet cove on the rocky shore. Morning fisherman were returning to port to unload their catches, while the mid day fisherman headed out, joining the various pleasure craft dotting the inland channel leading to the open water. Sea gulls cried out in the air, swooping and diving for the entrails thrown overboard as the men gutted and filleted their catch. Tourists with cameras and bright shirts strolled up the board sidewalk, and everywhere was the smell of the salty sea air, mixed with diesel fuel closer to the water and with the aroma of garlic and onion, coming from the classier restaurants that lined the boardwalk.

The Blue Grotto was nestled among the business that catered to the fishing crowd, with a bait and tackle shop next door and a dive shop a couple of doors down. The Grotto was low rent, with laminate tables, plastic chairs and tiled floors, with posters of Greek temples tacked to the wood paneled walls. Greek music, consisting of guitars and tambourines greeted the customers, along with the heavy grease of deep fried foods. There was a long chest high display case along the back wall, full of octopuses, salmon and the fresh catch of the day. The tables were full of customers, with little kids wearing bibs, parents chattering, waitresses humming down the aisles with basketfuls of fresh cod and chips. The man behind the counter was a thick man with little hair but a magnificent mustache.

Steele and Walker made their way through the crowd, bypassing a couple of angry customers who vocally expresses their displeasure of line cutters. Steele flipped open his badge and showed those behind him.

"Sure, the police always get served first," said one fat man with a too tight blue shirt and baggy shorts. "Why don't you wait in line like the rest of us?"

"Police business," said Steele.

"Is that what you call getting your lunch?"

Steele stepped up close to the fat man. "I'm investigating a murder. Perhaps you have something to say about it?"

"Murder? Oh no, not me."

Steele turned and continued up the line, passing customers until he reached the counter. "I would like to talk to the manager here."

The thick man behind the counter turned and smiled. "That's me. I am Dimitri Popudopulous. How can I assist you?"

Steele showed his badge. "We're looking for a Margaret Chambers. We were told that she works here."

"She does. Whatever she did, I had no part of it. I am only her employer. It is hard enough to run a business without worrying about the employees. My wife told me that I should be in insurance, but I said, no, I was born to run a restaurant. We have the best fish on the coast, you ask anyone. No high prices like down the street. Here, you get good food for a reasonable price."

"Back to Margaret Chambers," said Steele.

Popudopulous eyed the policeman for a moment, then turned to look at a dark curly haired boy of sixteen. "Remi, run the counter for a moment, I'll be right back."

The young man stepped into the fray without hesitation, grabbing the order book and asking the next person in line for their order.

"Come with me," said Popudopulous.

The manager led the detectives past the counter and through a small hallway to an office in the back of the building. There was a screen door to the left of the office, open to let in the fresh air and to let out the steam from the kitchen directly between the office and the front. The three men entered the small office. The space was small, but everything was in its place. There was no clutter. The desk top was clean, the file cabinets were closed, the framed pictures of the man's wife and family were arranged neatly on the wall.

"Sit," said Popudopulous. "And I'll tell you everything I know about Margaret."

Soon all were settled in. Steele and Walker had pulled out notebooks and pens, ready to take the manager's statement.

"So," said Popudopulous. "Margaret came to work for us maybe seven months ago. I feel sorry for the girl. She's not Greek and has no beauty, but maybe she's a hard worker, I think, and for that I am not wrong. She works hard, but she is very slow. And clumsy. Many times she drops the baskets. And she is not very smart. But she is loyal and there is a lot of turnover for her job. Not many are willing to work for such a wage. What is wrong with this country that people would rather let the government take care of them than work a honest job? In my country it is different. Everybody works. Everybody has a place."

"Back to Margaret?" asked Steele.

"Yes. I am sorry. I get carried away sometimes. My wife, she tell me that I am having a heart attack from this place, but she is wrong. I love my job. Margaret, not so much. She hard worker, for that I keep her on, even if she costs me money."

"Is she working today?" asked Walker.

"No. She called. Family emergency, she tell me. Here I am, with one waitress short and what does she do? Calls in sick. Got to go see her mama, she says."

"When was this?"

"Yesterday. Friday is my busiest day of the week, and where is she? I don't know. She was supposed to work both days and she has family emergency. Who doesn't? I have emergency all the time, but do I neglect my job? My business would fall apart if I wasn't here to make sure that everything is working okay."

"She wasn't here yesterday afternoon?" asked Steele.

"That is what I am telling you. Family problems with her mama."

"Have you ever met her father?"

"No. Why? What happened?"

"He was murdered yesterday afternoon," said Steele.

"That is terrible. No wonder the girl has been absent. She needs her mama right now. I will forgive her for not giving me notice. Do you have any idea who might do such a thing? Not Margaret. She's not bright, but a killer she is not. I've seen killers, back in my village in Greece. Terrible men. You take one look at them, and you say, there is a killer. But Margaret? Like a lamb. Meek and quiet as can be."

Loud noises could be heard coming from the front of the restaurant.

"Sound's like Remi is having troubles. He is good boy, but he is only sixteen. My wife's nephew. He is a good Greek. I must go and help him."

With that said, the interview was over. The detectives followed Popudopulous out the door into the chaos out front. Minutes later the detectives were back on the board sidewalk.

Walker closed his notebook. "She doesn't have an alibi."

Steele shook his head. "It doesn't look like any of them do."

"So what next? Do we go back to West Harbor and shake a few trees?"

Steele looked at his watch. "It's getting late in the day, why don't we run some checks on what we've got and get the interviews typed up, then hit West Harbor tomorrow. I've got a feeling that we're going to be pretty busy."

#

The rest of the work day passed and soon Steele was driving home through the early evening traffic. Downtown was busy with cars and pedestrians, but as he rolled up the hill toward his home on Gull Street, the traffic thinned until it was barely a trickle. The one advantage of being at the top of the town. He pulled into his driveway, got out and waved at Mr. Jennings across the street, then headed into the chaos that was his home and hearth.

The boys were playing some sort of space ranger game, chasing each other down the halls and in and out of the bedrooms, with loud explosive sounds and dire death scenes, nearly running Steele down as he tried to navigate the treacherous waters of the living room. The floor was covered with toys, the television blaring and his wife was no where to be found.

"Daddy's home!" cried out Devin, running full tilt into his father's arm.

Aaron followed suit, crashing into the two of them, nearly knocking all three to the ground.

"Slow down there, little fella."

"Ben, is that you?"

Steele looked up to see his wife come out of the master bedroom at the end of the hall. She walked over and kissed her husband.

"Sorry about the mess," said Arly. "I tried to keep them quiet, but lost the battle."

"Why aren't they outside, wearing off a little of this energy?"

She shook her head. "They were. They found a mud hole down the block, came home full of dirt, tracked mud all over the place. After I cleaned up their mess and got them changed, they started playing space rangers, and I just lost all hope of keeping them quiet. Sorry."

Steele knelt down and looked at his sons. "You've been very busy boys, haven't you?"

They nodded in unison.

"Look at this mess you left in the living room. See all your toys scattered around on the rug? I will give you exactly ten minutes to get them picked up and put in their proper place or I'll do it myself. You don't want me to do that, right? What do I tell you about your toys?"

"If we don't keep them picked up, you'll give them to little children who need them more than us."

'That's right." Steele looked at his watch. "Ten minutes. Starting now."

The boys took off like they were shot out of a cannon, hurled into the living room. Each boy had a half dozen action figures in their hands as they scampered down the long hall to their bedrooms. For a moment, all was quiet.

Steele reached over and hugged his wife. "You want me to pick up something for dinner? Maybe taco's or something?"

She snuggled in closer. "Aaron decided that he doesn't like taco's anymore, how about Chinese? I'll call, if you pick it up."

Such it was that one half hour later, the family was sitting down to dinner, eating chow mein, kung Poa chicken, pork fried rice, sweet and sour pork, and egg noodles. Arly had taken the food out of the containers and placed them in serving dishes, then helped scoop the food onto the boys plates to avoid them dribbling the food onto the table. The boys were excited, talking about their days adventure. Everything was new to their young minds, and each and every detail needed to be related to their parents, on the off chance that the older generation had never encountered frogs, mud, rope swings, ponds with algae, and the joys of a sunny afternoon with nothing to do and all day to do it.

As the boys wound down on their activities, Steele reached for another helping of sweet and sour pork.

"Devin," said Steele, "do you know the kids that come in from West Harbor? They go to your school don't they?"

"You bet," said Devin, shoveling rice into his mouth. "That Cindy is the prettiest girl in my class, but don't mess with her. She's mean. I heard that Billy Swanson tried to kiss her and she punched him so hard he had to go to the nurses office."

"What about Genesis?"

"He's weird," said Devin. "He isn't good at sports, sucks bad at kick ball, can't throw, can't catch, and wears really strange clothes."

"Do you ever talk to him?"

"No way. I'm not going to been seen with that weirdo, but Cindy Seavers does. I've seen her fight a boy who was giving Genesis a hard time. And he likes to be called Mike, but the teacher always calls him Genesis which makes the class laugh. I don't see the big deal if he wants to be called something different."

Steele looked at Aaron. "What about Billy Seavers, is he weird too?"

Aaron shook his head. "We get along okay on account of we both have to put up with somebody older who won't let us play with them."

"What's that supposed to mean?" asked Devin from across the table. "I play with you."

"Only if there isn't somebody better around," said Aaron.

Steele let his children argue for a moment, then stopped them with one hand. "That's enough of that. So what else did you two do today?"

The boys told of their space rangers and the cartoons, and with playing with Trevor next door who had the coolest motorized airplane that they flew down at the school yard, and could they have one and how they never get anything cool to play with, and on through the end of the meal.

Later, when the family was settled down to watching a movie about a dog that saved his family, Arly cuddled up on the couch next to Steele, with the kids sprawled out on the rug with their eyes glued to the set.

"So how's the investigation going?" asked Arly. "Any chances of finishing up quickly? I could chance the reservation for next weekend. Denise said she'd come up and stay with the kids."

"How come we never get to go with you?" asked Devin.

"Watch the movie, Dev," said Steele. He kissed the top of his wife's head. "As far as the investigation, we've got a lot of suspects and very few alibi's."

"You'll figure it out," said Arly. "You always do."

After the movie, the boys got ready for bed, leaving the parents with a precious few hours to spend together. They watched some television while Steele reviewed the typed up transcripts of the interviews, then they went to bed, happy to be together, content in their lives.

6. Back to the blackboard.

     Ben Steele took his family to church bright and early on this Sunday morning. The Steele family attended the First Presbyterian Church located four blocks down Gull Street. They walked as a family, with the two boys in the middle and the two adults on the outsides. It was a warm October morning with just a hint of chill for the upcoming winter. Steele was dressed in his brown suit, fresh shave, white shirt and tan tie. Arly wore a summer dress with a white sweater to cover her shoulders, her auburn hair done up in curls that bounced with each step. The boys wore matching gray slacks and white pull over sweaters. The Steele family joined others on the walk, all enjoying the sunshine.

     The church was old, built at the turn of the century, with white slate siding, and a steeple that rose above the street. The entry was a majestic two dozen steps up through double doors. The chancel music from the sanctuary floated out the door and onto the worshipers as they rose to the occasion. Inside, stain glass windows adorned one wall with large banners proclaiming "He is Risen" filled the opposite. The pews, split with the center aisle, slanted down to the pulpit.

     The pews filled up, the choir sang and Pastor Dave gave a rousing sermon on being a good steward to ones fellow man. There was coffee and cookies after in the rectory behind the church, giving the adults fellowship time and the children a chance to run around and wear off some pent up energy from sitting during the long service.

After church, the Steele family returned home and had a nice ham dinner, with scalloped potatoes and a green bean casserole. The kids changed to jeans and headed out to play with their friends, Arly settled in on the living room sofa with the Sunday papers, and Ben Steele prepared to go to work.

Steele picked up Walker on the way out of town. Steele, still in his favorite brown suit, Walker back to his double breasted blue pin stripe, and the ever present fedora, this one blue to match the suit.

"Cagney this morning?"

"I wish," said Walker. "I can't help what I like, boss. Sue me. Where are we going first?"

"See if we can't find the missing Margaret."

They drove in silence out the north end of town, passing the small businesses that lined the trunk highway. It was a Sunday and most of the businesses were closed, but the hamburger stand and bowling alley were open, as were the tourist shops that catered to the stop by traffic. Soon, Rock Port was behind them, leaving them only the rolling hills and bright blue ocean for company. It was a pleasant drive along the coast, with the windows down and the cool air coming in the interior of the car.

Fifteen minutes later, they rode the rise up to crest, then on top they could see all of West Harbor below. All was quiet on this Sunday afternoon. The roads were empty, and only a few residents could be seen out in their yards. From the distance, the town looked like a picture postcard.

Steele parked in front of Louella Chambers house and the detectives exited the car, and walked up to the front door. Steele knocked and the two waited.

Seconds later, the door opened, to reveal a homely woman in her low twenties, wearing bib overalls over a purple sweater.

"Who are you and what do you want?"

Steele reached into his pocket and pulled his badge. "Detective Steele of the Rock Port police and this is Sergeant Walker. You wouldn't be Margaret Chambers, would you?"

"Peggy dear, who is it?'

The woman in the door turned and talked to someone inside. "Nobody important, mother." She turned and looked at the two, still holding onto the door to prevent them from getting inside. "What is this all about?"

"We'd like a few minutes of your time, Miss Chambers," said Steele. "You are Margaret Chambers, aren't you."

She opened the door and stood aside. "You might as well come in, you're going to anyway, aren't you?"

The detectives followed Margaret into the interior of the house where they noticed Louella sitting on a couch drinking tea. Margaret walked over and sat beside her mother. The only sound coming from inside the room was the ticking of a cuckoo clock on the wall by the wood stove. It was cozy warm inside with the wood stove kicking out heat enough to fill the room.

"Please sit down," said Louella, staring at the two men through her thick glasses. "You might as well get this over with."

"Sorry to bother you both on Sunday," said Steele, settling down in a comfy chair opposite the couch. "But we've got a few more questions of you, Mrs. Chambers, and some for your daughter as well."

"Why me?" asked Margaret. "I didn't do nothing. What did I do that you gotta come and bother me at my mother's at a time like this?"

Steele looked at the younger woman, noticing the resemblance between mother and daughter. Margaret had the same nose, face and body build as her mother and would most likely end up looking like her in another twenty years.

"We're investigating the murder of your father," said Steele. "And during the course of the investigation, we ask a lot of questions, trying to sift through what we hear and see to find the perpetrator of this terrible crime. First, Mrs. Chambers, where were you between four and six P.M. last Friday?"

"Here, cooking a pot roast," said Louella. "It takes a lot of time to cook a pot roast. You have to cut up the potatoes, and the carrots, and the celery, and pre-heat the oven."

"Nobody to verify it?" asked Steele.

"I'm sorry no," said Louella. "Maybe there's a peeping tom in town who saw me, lord knows why anybody would want to do that, but as far as company, no. I live alone and spend most of my time by myself. I'm used to the silence, but others find it a bit off putting, if you know what I mean."

"So, no alibi," said Steele.

"Can't help you there. I did not in fact kill my husband, if that makes you feel any better."

Steele directed his gaze to Margaret. "How about you, Miss Chambers? Where were you between four and six on Friday evening?"

"I was at home," said Margaret.

"Not according to your roommate," said Walker, leaning up against the wall.

Margaret turned and looked at Walker. "I'm sorry, I meant to say I was at work. Yeah, that's were I was."

Steele shook his head. "Your boss said you called in sick on Friday, then asked for a couple days off for a family emergency. So where were you between four and six Friday evening?"

Margaret waved her hands in the air. "Are you accusing me of killing my own father? You've got to be kidding. I loved my father. How could you say such a thing?'

"Even after he told you that he never wanted you?"

"Who told you that? Did Sheila blab? I swear, you can't trust nobody no more. Sure, my father could say some hurtful things, that's the way he was, but that don't mean that I wanted to kill him."

"Then where were you during the time in question?" asked Steele.

Margaret sat silent for a moment, then blurted out. "I went for a drive, okay? I didn't want to tell anybody, 'cause it's nobody's business."

"Where did you go?" asked Walker.

Margaret flew off the couch. "Why is this so important? I just told you that I went for a drive. Are you deaf? How do I know where I went? I have a lot on my mind right now and the very last thing I need is for you guys to come up here and harass me and my mom. My daddy's dead and all you care about is where I went for drive? Are you kidding me? Will it make you happy if I come up with an answer? Okay, I went driving to the mall in Rock Port. Satisfied?"

"What stores did you go to?" asked Steele. "Look, Miss Chambers, we're not trying to be jerks about this. We're just doing our jobs. Now, I understand that you're upset at the loss of your father, but don't you want us to find the killer? So you drove out to the mall and stopped in some shops. All we need to know is where so we can verify your presence other than here in West Harbor."

Margaret crossed the room and looked out the window at the ocean. "I never went to the mall. Okay?" She turned and faced the three in the room. "Look, I've been seeing a guy. He's married, okay? And his wife works late on Friday afternoons. We were together during that time, but don't ask me his name. I can't give it to you, I just can't. You'll talk to him and ruin his life and ruin mine"

"We can be discreet," said Steele. "We're just putting alibi's together."

"I can't. Sorry," said Margaret, with tears rolling down her fat cheeks. "You'll just have to trust me."

Louella got off the couch, walked over to her daughter and gave her a hug. "There, there, honey. It's going to be alright."

The detectives watched this display for a moment, then Steele closed his notebook. They weren't going to get anymore from these two.

"Thank you for your time," said Steele, standing up.

They left mother and daughter and headed back out to the sunshine of the day. The tension of the inside was gone, replaced with a gentle breeze, blowing salty sea air into their faces.

Steele looked back at the house and shook his head. "There's something not right about those two."

"Like her having an affair with a married man?"

"No, that I could believe, if it weren't for the way she came around to telling us about it. First she's at home, then at home, then gone for a drive, to no where specific, then to the mall, then finally to a tryst with a married man. She's lying to cover up something, I just don't know what."

"We could take her to the station and sweat her," said Walker.

"Need to charge her with something first. No, let's let it lie for now, but we'll get back to her and try again."

Walker looked around the village. "So who's our next contestant?"

"I'd like to talk to Star again. See what we can shake out of that tree."

"Drive or walk?'

Steele inhaled the wonderful sea air. "Walk. The exercise will do us both some good."

Walker sighed. "I should have known."

"What?"

"You're trying to get me to lose weight, aren't you, boss?'

"I said we, didn't I?"

"Yeah, but you meant me," said Walker. "I know what the captain says about me. I can't help it if I'm big boned. I swear, I just look at food and it sticks to me."

Steele clapped Walker on the shoulder. "Come on, Kevin, a little walk won't hurt you."

#

They left the car parked in front of Louella's house, walked past the post office and turned up the lane, passing Adam Franklin's bungalow with its fenced in trim yard, lovely flowers and a big picture window overlooking the street. As they passed, Franklin caught their eye and waved. The detectives waved back.

"Should we talk to him?" asked Walker, nodding at the man in the window.

"Why not."

The door opened and Franklin stood in the open doorway. "Would you gentlemen care for a cup of coffee?"

"That would be wonderful," said Steele, stopping to open the gate at the sidewalk. "You have a nice home here, Mr. Franklin."

"Thank you. My dear departed wife loved this place. Come in."

The detectives walked up the sidewalk and entered the home. After the bright sunshine, the interior seemed dark, until they adjusted to the change in lighting. The front half of the home was filled with overstuffed furniture, with plenty of dark antique sideboards lining the back and side walls, the surfaces covered with framed pictures of Franklin and his late wife covering a span of fifty years of married life. On the walls above the sideboards were tasteful oil paintings of pastoral settings.

"Please, make yourself at home," said Franklin. "I've got a pot of coffee on, but if you prefer, I can make you some tea. I've got some orange pekoe and oolong if you'd rather."

"Coffee please," said Steele.

Walker shook his head. "Nothing for me, thanks."

"It's no trouble," said Franklin. "Perhaps a soda instead? I believe I have some Cream Soda or Ginger Ale if you don't want the caffeine."

"I'm good," said Walker, "but thanks just the same."

Franklin looked at Steele. "Cream and sugar?"

"Black please."

Minutes passed while Franklin left the room via the arched doorway leading to the kitchen in the rear of the house. "I was wondering if you might stop by. I saw you parked outside Lou's house and figured that you were here to talk to us again."

"Just trying to nail down the alibi's, sir," said Steele.

Franklin returned with a tray, two mugs of coffee, a small container for cream and another for sugar and a plate of cookies. "Very understandable. Terrible thing to occur to our little village." He sat down, picking up his mug along the way. "So what can I do for you gentlemen?"

"We're trying to firm up the chain of events on Friday last," said Steele, "and were hoping that you might be able to shed some light on what happened."

Franklin sat back in his chair and sipped his coffee. "Let me see. Friday was like any other day. I told you about Star arguing with Tony early in the day, that must have been around eleven in the morning, but don't quote me on that. I'm not very good with time. Bonnie and I had our chat time–we do most days–and then I left the post office and came home. I heard that Tony got into a fight with Young Tom, that must have been around noon, but I have no way of knowing. For all I know, it could have been earlier or later. I came home after talking to Bonnie and stayed in the rest of the day. There isn't much for a widower to do around here, so I mostly putter around the house. The time goes pretty quick, considering how little I actually do. Not much happened for me, until I heard the sirens. I was trying to decide what to eat and my curiosity got the better of me. I went out to see what happened and you know the rest. Sorry if I can't be more helpful for your time line."

Steele jotted down his testimony as best he could, then looked up when Franklin stopped talking. "Any ideas on who might have killed Chambers?"

"Like I told you the other night, Tony Chambers was not a liked man. He stayed away from town for years, then comes back and instantly makes people dislike him. I've never seen a man so instantly hated in all my days. As far as possible suspects? If I were you, I'd spend my time looking at Star and Young Tom. They're the ones that got into it with Tony on the day he died."

"What can you tell us about them?" asked Walker.

"What do you mean?"

"Does Star have a real name? What do you know about him? Is he a good neighbor? That sort of thing."

Franklin looked at Walker. "I only know what he's been like since coming to West Harbor. I don't know if Star is his real name, though I doubt any respectable mother would name their child Star, but I truly don't know. Times change. When I was a boy, people named their children reasonable names, but like I said, times change. As far as Star as a neighbor, he's always been very polite, but I don't approve of the long hair and the atrocious clothes. Have you seen their boy Genesis? Terrible. Little boys shouldn't have pony tails. But I can't say that I've ever seen any violence out of Star, if that's what you're looking for. He tends his goats and I suppose he makes a living out of it. Not like my day when a man went to work in the morning and came home in the evening, but this is a different time, isn't it?"

"It is," said Steele, "What about Young Tom. What can you tell us about him?"

Franklin seemed to think for a moment, sipping his coffee before speaking. "Young Tom came to town maybe a year ago, though it might have been two, time goes so fast the older you get, anyway, he came to town and turned the old Esso Station into that super saver thing, and other than charging outrageous amounts for his goods, has been a pretty good addition to the village. The Esso station closed twenty years ago and we've had to drive to Rock Port to gas up our automobiles and groceries were only available out of town. He's provided a valuable service, even if he's a bit surly at times, at least he's doing something good for our community."

"Do you know anything about his past?" asked Walker.

"Not at thing. Now that you mention it, it was as if he was dropped from outer space with no past whatsoever. He doesn't talk about himself and keeps his cards pretty close to the vest, if you know what I mean.

For all we know, he could have been a mass murderer somewhere else and only came to West Harbor to hide out. My lord, do you think he's the one? I must tell Bonnie to lock her doors."

"Has he given cause for you to be concerned?" asked Steele.

"Not really. Like I said, he can be surly. I can tell you this, do not go into his business and tell him how much cheaper something he sells is down in Rock Port. You'll be lucky if he sells you anything. I've calculated that he has a thirty percent mark-up on all goods he sells. Price of location, I suppose, but to your question. I haven't seen anything that would prohibit me from shopping in his establishment, though a little variety wouldn't hurt. There are more mustards than french yellow, you know."

Steele let the man ramble, hoping for a tidbit that would give a clue to the murder, possibly point them in the correct direction, but so far, all he was getting was gossip. That's the way it went sometimes.

"Is there anything else you can think of that might help us?"

"Well, like I said, I believe that Star and Young Tom are your best candidates for the killing, but if I were you, I'd take a close look at Bill Seavers up the road. He spends most of his time in his garage making cabinets, but he has a mighty pretty wife and I remember Tony used to like his ladies. I wouldn't be surprised if Tony didn't make a pass at Mary Seavers. He may look innocent, but who truly is innocent nowadays? Is there anything else I can do for you gentlemen?"

Steele closed his book, then reached into his pocket and pulled out his business card. He handed it to Franklin. "If you can think of anything else, just give me a call. Thanks for your time, Mr. Franklin."

Franklin walked them to the door. "I sure hope you find the killer soon. I worry about Bonnie with a killer on the loose."

They shook hands and left the old man in his open doorway, stepping back into the warm sunshine. Steele heard the door close as they reached the gate.

"Where to, boss?"

Steele nodded up the lane. "Star can wait a few more minutes, let's talk to Bill Seavers and see what he has to say."

#

They found Bill Seavers working in his shop, the noise of the planer splitting the air and the dust from the wood dancing in the splintered light. Seavers had his back to the open doorway and didn't hear or see the detectives until they were right upon him. He was busy working on the long boards of a hutch, with pieces stacked neatly against the opposite wall, ready for planing. The dust filled the air, along with the smell of burnt wood. Seavers shut off the planer and turned and faced the detectives.

"Come back for more questions?" he asked.

"If you don't mind," said Steele, opening his notebook. "We've narrowed down the time of death between four and six."

"Like I told you fellows on Friday, I was here, working in my shop between noon and five, then I went in to dinner and had a nice meal with my family."

"Nobody to confirm you being out here between four and five?" asked Walker.

Seaver held his planer like a weapon, staring at the two detectives. "Am I a suspect?"

"At the point in time," said Steele, "everybody is a suspect. You want the truth? We heard that Tony Chambers considered himself a bit of a ladies man and you have a very pretty wife."

"You saying that my wife had anything to do with that guy? That's nuts. My wife is not a cheater. I do not appreciate you making insinuations about her or me for that matter. If you have nothing better to do that go around spreading idle gossip, then you can do if off my property."

"Take it easy, Mr. Seavers," said Walker. "We're only trying to get to the bottom of this."

"And slander my wife along the way," said Seaver. "Get out of here before I call your boss and tell him what you're doing up here. I'm sure he wouldn't approve."

"Mr. Seavers, we're only doing our job," said Steele. "You have a killer on the loose up here, doesn't that bother you?"

"For what? The death of one worthless piece of garbage? I told you the other night, I didn't know the guy, but from what I hear, he wasn't worth wasting a tear for, so who cares. It sounds like whoever did that guy in did the world a favor. So, unless you want to slander me or my wife some more, I suggest you get the hell off my property."

And just like that, the detectives were dismissed. They walked away from the garage and seconds later the planer started up again, filling the air with the high pitched whine of sander against wood. They walked down the long driveway, turned north and headed to the next house in line, that of Star and Sunflower.

#

All was quiet as they headed up the walk leading to the house, but as they neared, they could hear raised voices inside. It appeared that they were about to step into the middle of an argument. Walker looked over at Steele.

"Should we come back later?"

Steele shook his head. "Maybe we'll find out more than they were willing to give us the other night."

They walked up to the door in time to hear a woman's voice, yelling, "Don't you walk away from me. I'm talking to you."

Steele knocked firmly on the wood door and waited.

All became quiet inside. A full minute passed before the door opened, revealing an angry Sunflower. "What do you want? Sorry, that was rude. How may I help you?"

"We're back talking to you and your fellow residents about the murder," said Steele. "May we come in?"

"You might as well," said Sunflower. She stood back and let the detectives enter her home.

Steele looked around as they crossed the threshold. He took it all in, the cracked linoleum, the sparse furniture, the bare floor, the Green Peace flag, and the equally angry Star sitting on his bean bag chair with a pair of headphones on. His expression said it all. He was royally upset.

"Is there someplace we can sit and talk?" asked Steele.

Sunflower guided them to a broken down wooden table in an area between the kitchen and living room. "I can offer you some sun tea, if you're interested."

"No thank you," said Steele. "Can your husband join us?"

Sunflower looked at the inert form of her husband, staring off in the distance. She walked over and kicked him in the foot.

Star pulled off his headphones. "What did you do that for?'

"The police want to talk to both of us."

"I've got nothing to say," said Star. He stared at the detectives, then made a big show of pushing himself out of his chair and ambling over to the kitchen. He stared at Steele. "I told you everything last time."

"Sit down, Star," said Steele. "You too, Sunflower."

"My name is Tracy," she said, sitting down. "Tracy Johnson. That was my maiden name and that's what I'm going with, since Star won't tell me his real name. Married or not, I can't see calling myself Tracy Star, can you?"

The four sat down, with Star and Tracy sitting on two sides and the detectives on the other.

"Where's your little boy?" asked Steele.

"He's next door," spat Star, "pretending he's normal. Isn't that what you want to be, Tracy?"

"Don't start with me," said Tracy.

"You're the traitors. I'm still holding to my values. Remember them, Tracy? I'm not the one that wants to be a stepford wife. I'm not the one who's changing."

"That's right," said Tracy. "You're the good one, except that you hide the truth." She stopped talking for moment, then looked at the detectives. "Sorry, you stepped into the middle of our discussion. You said you had some questions for us?"

"We're narrowed down the time of death," said Steele. "Where were you two between four and six, last Friday?"

"I was with my wife, all day, right honey?"

She stared at him. "Don't lie, Star, or whoever you really are. I didn't see you at all for a couple of hours. Where did you go? What did you do?"

"I was home, Tracy," said Star. "Don't give me a hard time, here, okay." he looked at the detectives. "Okay, I had a fight with the dude early in the day, but that was it. I hung out with the goats, trying to get my mantra back, okay? It was like all messed up, my aura was off, and I, like, needed some peace and quiet. So I wasn't with my wife all day, sue me, I didn't kill the dude, even if he, like, had it coming to him."

Steele looked up from his notebook. "What's your given name, Star? And where are you from?"

"Whoa. Dude, where is this coming from? I'm just a peaceful hippie trying to make it a harsh world, why you dragging all that negativity into this scene?"

Tracy stared at him while he talked, then looked at the detectives. "I've been asking him the same thing for the past two days. Good luck getting him to talk."

"We can solve that pretty easy," said Walker. "A trip to the station and fingerprints and we'll know his real name. If he's in the system, we'll know."

Star hung his head in sorrow, lifting it to look first at Tracy, then at the detectives. "I'm beaten. You dudes and my old lady all want to know about me? Fine, I'll tell you, but it ain't pretty." He paused for breath, then started in, talking fast. "My real name is Harold Gaithers, I was born and raised in West Covina. My old man was an insurance dude and my old lady did the tupperware thing. I got a little bro and a big sister, neither of whom I've seen or talked to in like ten years. I'm sorry to say, I hung with some bad dudes down in LA and got out to save myself. Call me a chicken if you want, but dude, the life was, like, killing me. If I stayed down there, I'd be a dead man for sure. So I split from LA, moved to San Fran where I hooked up with Sunflower, I mean, Tracy, and we moved up here. That's the truth."

"What did you do down in LA that sent you running?" asked Steele.

"Who said anything about running? I didn't like the way I was living and had to get out of town, that's all. It's no big deal."

"Then why wouldn't you tell me who you really were?" asked Tracy. "I'd have understood that you had issues, we all have those, but you've been lying to me ever since that guy came to town."

Steele leaned in closer. "Is that right, Harold?"

Star looked uncomfortable. "I never liked that name."

"Is Harry better?"

Star shook his head. "I didn't like that one either. Could you just call me Star?"

"Okay, Star, what else aren't you telling us?" asked Steele.

"That's it, okay? I didn't have nothing to do with the dude getting killed, is there anything more? I've got goats to feed."

Steele flipped back through his notes, then looked at Star. "You said that you got into a fight with Chambers because he insulted your wife, would you care to elaborate on that?"

"You didn't say anything about that," said Tracy. "You should have said something."

"I didn't want you to worry about it." Star looked at the detectives. "Are we good here? The goats need their food. They're just like kids you know. Dudes go without food, they can make some righteous noise."

The interview was over. Steele thanked them for their time and left the hippie house. They headed back to the sunshine. The crisp air filled their lungs and the sounds of gulls filled the air. Steele thought of what he had heard and wasn't sure about the truthfulness of Star's testimony. He had an uneasy feeling during their first interview and it only continued through the second. The man was definitely hiding something. But what? Time would tell. Still, it bothered him that he didn't know, but that happened a lot when murder was involved. It was his job to sift through the information and ferret out the killer and he would do that to the best of his ability. Star could lie all he wanted, Steele knew that in the end, the truth would come out.

#

The next in line, walking north down the lane, was the residence of Thomas Hoffman. His was a ramshackle affair, with many additions to the original four room box, with a mix of shingles and sidings that made the house look odd. There was no fancy fence like that of Adam Franklin's, instead, the long grass grew naturally, waving in the wind, and buffeting the foundation of the old structure. The first thing a visitor noticed was the number of cats that sat around on available surfaces. There was a tabby sitting on a old barrel by the door, a black with white paws perched on the windowsill, a pair of tiger stripes were chasing each other around a spindly tree, and a tan and white kitten sat perfectly still on the doorstep.

Steele moved between the animal kingdom to the front door, knocking on the splintered door. Many minutes passed before Hoffman opened the door. Bent over as he was, it was an effort for him to straighten up and look at the detectives.

"Figured you'd come see me. Come in."

They followed him into his living room where they were greeted by another couple of cats perched on top of the old dusty furniture. Everything in the room was dark, starting with the deep brown carpets, three that didn't match under the dark furniture, to the dark framed pictures of sea landscapes, to the dark walls, unwashed for many years, and the dark cabinet that held the television.

"Sit down where you can," said Hoffman. "I'd offer you coffee, but I don't got none."

"That's okay," said Steele. "We don't need anything."

"Got water, if you're thirsty."

Steele sat down lightly on the nearest couch, avoiding the loose springs, and looked around. It was apparent that Hoffman didn't employ a housekeeper. There were layers of dust on every available surface. The air was stale with the odors of a man who has lost his sense of smell, with a lingering stench that filled the air.

Walker chose not to sit, standing by the front window and the fresh air. He pulled out his notebook and pen.

"So what can I do for you, gentlemen?" asked Hoffman.

"We wanted to review your testimony from the other night," said Steele. He pulled out his notebook, flipped through the pages until he got to the one he wanted, then looked up at Hoffman. "You were a little vague about knowledge of who might have killed Tony Chambers, saying, and I quote, "the good lord provides a way out, taking care of his children when the time is right", unquote. What exactly did you mean by that?"

Hoffman stared at Steele. Minutes passed, and Steele wondered if the old man was going to respond, then he did.

"Sometimes there is a higher power involved. The lord knows what's best. He takes care of things. Fellow like Chambers was a disease. A blight on society. Someone has to remove the blight. The lords' tool. Making things right."

"That doesn't answer my original question, Mr. Hoffman," said Steele. "Do you know who killed Tony Chambers?"

Hoffman sat back in his chair, leaning back enough for Steele to see his eyes under the shock of white hair. "I know many things. Some good. Some bad. Been here a long time. Seen a lot. Men have been killed for as little as a shot of whiskey. All things even out in the end. Good and bad. Sometimes bad wins. Sometimes, bad loses. This time, the good lord took care of business, removing the stain."

"By a very human hand," said Steele. "If you know something, Mr. Hoffman, it is your duty to tell us so that we can punish the guilty. Killing Tony Chambers might have been morally right, but that doesn't make it legally right. Someone needs to be punished for the crime."

Hoffman sat and thought about that for a moment, then smiled. "I'll let the good lord sort that one out. That's all I've got to say to you. Mind the cats on your way out, they're all the family I've got left."

Minutes later, they were back on the lane, staring at the closed door.

"He knows who did it," said Walker.

"I think he does."

"So how do we get him to talk?"

"Not sure, but we've got the time. Old Tom isn't going anywhere."

144

\#

The detectives talked to the newest couples in West Harbor, with little results. That left them with the Super Saver and the post office before leaving town. While Steele enjoyed the exercise, the work out was taking its toll on young Walker. The junior detective was sweating, holding his hat in one hand while he held his other to his chest.

"You okay, Kevin?"

"Sure thing, boss," said Walker, stopping to get his breath. "It's not like I hate exercise or anything, it's the suit. I got this out of a vintage clothing store down in the bay area, made of one hundred percent wool. There just isn't any breathing room in this. Looks good, doesn't breath."

"Why do you wear it?"

"Because I look good, don't you think? A man has to make a statement once in a while, I prefer to make mine in the clothes I wear."

Steele waited until Walker caught his breath, then continued on to the Super Saver. "Come on, Kevin, we'll be done shortly and you can sit down."

Walker stuffed his hat back on his head. "Yes, boss."

They entered the Super Saver and found Thomas Jones behind the counter working a crossword puzzle. He looked up at the sound of the bell over the door announcing their arrival.

"What can I do for you gentlemen? Some refreshments for your trip south perhaps?"

"Just looking for a little more information," said Steele, walking over to the counter. "We've narrowed Chamber's time of death to be between four and six on last Friday. Where were you during that time?"

"Like I told you before, I was here in the store. I don't have much of a social life, but look around you, there isn't much to do around here, except stare at the sky. And it was a Friday night, sometimes I get folks coming in to buy stuff for dinner."

"Anybody come in during that time to vouch for your presence?"

"Sorry, can't help you there. I was alone the whole time. You're going to have to come up with someone other than me for this. I can't help it if I don't have an alibi. Sue me, I stay close to my shop. I've got a lot invested in this business, I can't just piss it all away and run around and play in the ocean like the little kiddies do around here."

"We did some checking up on your, Mr. Jones," said Walker. "If that is your real name."

Jones smiled. "You want to see my drivers license? It's made out to Thomas Jones, you can call the DMV and see."

"That's the thing, Mr. Jones," said Steele. "We did. We tried to find you on our data bases, but you weren't listed. No crimes, no misdemeanors, no jay walking, no over due library books. In short, you don't exist."

"Sure I do, I'm sitting right here talking to you."

"And the DMV has about ten thousand Thomas Jones' around the state of California."

Jones thumped his chest. "And I'm one of them."

"How about we take you down to the station and get some fingerprints on you," said Steele. "Maybe that will solve our little mystery."

"Not without just cause," said Jones. "Look fellows, I'm a peaceful, law abiding man, and I wouldn't have a problem complying with your request, but I'll loose business and you'll end up with egg all over your face. I didn't kill the guy, how many times do I have to tell you? And no, I will not go down to your fascist station and put up with who knows what. You want to charge me, fine, I'll find a lawyer and slap a wrongful arrest suit on you. I've got the time and don't mind sticking it to you, but why don't you just take my word for it and let it go?"

Steele leaned in close. "I don't believe you, Mr. Jones. I think you're hiding something and don't want us to find out what it is."

Jones put the paper down and eyed Steele. "I don't give a rat's ass what you believe, pal. So, what's it going to be? Charge me and face a law suit? Or get the hell out of my shop?"

Steele pushed off from the counter. "We're not through with you, Mr. Jones."

Jones picked up his crossword and smiled. "Hit the skids, boys, you're stinking up the place."

They left the man behind the counter and walked back to the sunshine.

"What do you think, boss?"

"He's hiding something big. Did you see the sweat on his forehead when we talked about bringing him in?"

"What about the lawyer he mentioned?"

"It'll probably come down to that either way," said Steele. "I'd bet dollars to donuts that guy has a record somewhere. Maybe not here in California, but somewhere, and we will get to the bottom of it. He thinks he smart, but he's not. We'll get him to talk."

#

The last stop for the day was the post office. Being a Sunday, the post office was closed tight. Steele peered in the pane glassed door at the darkened interior, then back to Walker.

"There must be a separate entrance for her residence, let's look around the back."

It didn't take long to find the door, it was down along the right side of the structure, facing the back of the Super Saver and the beach below. What was immediately of interest to Steele was the four windows that faced the beach. He reached over and knocked on the door, then stood back and waited. Minutes passed before the door opened.

"You're back for more?" asked Bonnie, wearing jeans and a dark blue sweater. "I heard you were in town."

"We have a few more questions to ask," said Steele. "May we come in?"

Bonnie stood back and ushered the detectives into her home. "Most certainly. Don't mind the mess, I've been in a lazy mood and haven't gotten around to cleaning up today."

They followed her through a small entry way, up two steps into the living area, with a kitchen to the left, and a great room to the right. The furniture was Danish modern, with lots of blonde wood and patterned cushions with mementoes from around the world on every available flat surface. There were masks from Africa on the walls, clocks from Switzerland, and a three curio cabinets in the corners of the room full of china dolls.

"As you can see, I do like my travels. I never moved from West Harbor, but I have seen the world, and I've got to say, there truly is no place like home. Sit. Please. And tell me what you need. Coffee? Cookies? I don't get many guest back here."

Steele sat on the couch, while Walker eased his large frame into what looked like a Swedish version of an Adirondack chair. Both detectives pulled out there notebooks and pens, at the ready.

"Nothing for me, thank you," said Steele.

"I'm good," said Walker.

"Well, if you change you minds, just say the word." She sat down on the other end of the couch, opposite Steele, crossed her hands on her lap and looked expectantly at the detectives. "How may I help you?"

"We've narrowed the time of death between four and six last Friday," said Steele, "and we're hoping that someone around here might have seen something that will help us solve this mystery."

She shook her head. "Dinner time for me, like I told you fellows the other night. I was in the kitchen or here in the living room the whole time you mentioned."

"Coming up to your door, I saw four windows facing the beach. You didn't happen to look out any of those windows during the time in question, did you?"

"Sorry, no. There was a fascinating program about Nebula's on the television that kept my attention during that hour. Did I go back to the bedroom during that time? I might have, but I honestly can't remember doing so. I'm sorry I can't be of more help."

Steele nodded. It was worth a try. "Is there anything you can add to your earlier testimony?"

She sat for a moment, the smiled. "I wish I could tell you that I did."

"Does it bother you that one of your neighbors is a killer?" asked Walker.

She turned to look at the sergeant. "Not really. I've been living here nicely all my life and know my fellow residents pretty well–you get that way when you deal with their mail–and if one of my neighbors did kill that man, why, he probably had it coming. So no, I don't worry about that. Of course it's your job to figure it out and I wish you luck with that. However, I must say, as far as I'm concerned, justice was done and we can all move on from this unfortunate situation."

The interview was over. She sat quietly, waiting for more questions, then got up with the detectives and walked them to the door.

"Good luck with your sleuthing, boys," she said as she guided them out.

#

Steele pulled in behind the wheel while a sweating Walker plopped down in the passenger seat. Steele looked at the bucolic setting outside the window. It looked nice and clean, yet there was a killer hiding out in this place.

Walker took off his hat, then reached into the inside pocket of his suit and pulled out a handkerchief. He wiped the sweat off his face, then rolled down the window.

"I still put my money on Mr. Jones," said Walker. "He's got the opportunity, and the motive, and sooner or later, we'll find the means, right boss?"

"Could be," said Steele. "This is a strange case. We've got three good suspects and maybe a fourth. Louella Chambers was going to lose her house, giving her a good reason to kill Tony. Remove Tony, remove the threat. She has a good motive, but nobody can put her at the scene. No alibi. Star, aka Harold Gaithers, gets into a fight with Chambers on the day he died, maybe he was angry enough to drop the hammer on Chambers, but who knows. No alibi except for goats. Then there's Bill Seavers. He's an angry man who might have killed Chambers for no good reason. Maybe Chambers made a play for the man's wife. Who knows."

Walker sat back in the seat and closed his eyes. "My money is on baldy back there. I don't buy his story and I don't buy him. The way I figure it, Chambers had something on Mr. Jones, and baldy killed him to keep the information quiet. You'll see, boss, in the end, our Mr. Jones will be going down for this murder."

Steele started the car and turned them around, heading back to Rock Port. "You may be right. Sooner or later, one of them will make a mistake, then we'll get them."

7. New Developments.

      Monday morning came to West Harbor, bringing
in a few high clouds and a strong cold wind. Bonnie
Williams could see the yellow school bus come down the
hill and stop at the bottom of the lane, with little Cindy
Seavers, bundled up in a pink hoodie lead her brother, and
Genesis to the waiting door. With the windows and door
shut, she couldn't hear the screaming children on the bus,
but she could see the exuberant faces and waving arms as
the three locals joined the bus crowd. Then the bus door
closed and the yellow bus headed north to pick up the
kids in Monroe, ten miles up the road. Bonnie watched
the bus leave, then resumed her work. There wasn't much
mail to distribute, but that didn't stop her from making the
most of the forty pieces of mail to be stuck in slots for the
residents. She wasn't a nosy person, or so she told herself,
but she did inspect each and every letter, circular and ad
that made its way to her capable hands. She remembered
the times she sat on a stool and watched her father do
these very tasks. As a child, she was interested in where
the mail came from, more than what was in the letters, but
as she got older, her interest was reversed. After years of
world travel, she was more interested in the human aspect
of the mail. Who was saying what? What news was being
imparted? She knew when Louella got the letter from her
ex that there was bad news inside, instinctively, knowing
full well that Louella rarely got letters, and when she did,
it was something from her sister down in Tucson, or once
in awhile a post card from a long lost nephew in
Nebraska.

Bonnie tucked the mail into the correct slots with a letter to Robert Peterson from his brother in Sacramento, along with a letter from an attorney, then a post card for Mary Seavers from her mother in Portland, then a congratulations on new baby card for the Duncan's, then the usual gas and electric bills for everybody in town, along with cable bills for the families that had televisions, finished up with the circulars for the Red Roost Grocery store down in Rock Port for all the residents. The entire sack of mail took one half hour to distribute.

Her ritual done, Bonnie walked around the counter and flipped over the closed sign and unlocked the door. She had barely done this task when she noticed Adam Franklin ambling down the lane with two covered cups of coffee in his hands. He smiled and lifted the cups when he spotted her in the window. Bonnie waved and waited. She wasn't sure exactly how she felt about Franklin, at least in the romantic category. As a friend, she was more than happy to have the company, but in truth, she saw him more like a maiden aunt than a potential boyfriend, but as they say, friends first, lovers second. She opened the door and felt the cold air hit her face.

"You took long enough to get here," she said.

He half jogged to the door, his cheeks rosy from the effort. "I timed it pretty close, didn't I?"

She let him in and headed back around the counter to her stool. "Not bad. You're getting better at it. What kind of coffee did you bring today?"

He set the cups on the counter and pulled up the stool on the opposite side of the counter. "French Roast. Perfect for a windy day, don't you think?"

She took the hot cup and opened the lid, inhaling the deep aroma of coffee. "Perfect. And before you ask, you didn't get any mail except bills. Would you like them now or later?"

"Later would be better," said Franklin. "Why spoil a perfectly good cup of coffee with bad news."

They drank their coffee in silence, enjoying the heady brew. This had become a semi-regular morning ritual just as real as the sorting of the mail for Bonnie. She had come to expect it, even enjoyed the company. Being the postmistress left her little time for much else, and truth be told, there weren't many people her age in the village. As she liked to say, she was older, but not dead. At least not yet. Perhaps Franklin was her only hope for a relationship, but was he what she wanted?

"So," said Bonnie. "You want to talk about the murder?"

Franklin waved on hand. "Old news, I'd say. No, I'd like to broach an entirely new topic for today's discussion."

A minute passed without him continuing.

"So what is this new subject?" asked Bonnie.

"Love."

"Are you proposing to me, Adam Franklin?"

"No, no, nothing like that," said a stammering Franklin. "What I wanted to know was why you never married. Didn't you have boyfriends who longed for your company?"

She sighed. Over the past year, Franklin had skirted the subject. Bonnie thought it was out of respect for his deceased wife, but sooner or later, she knew that this subject would arise, and so it had.

"When I was a young girl, this town was hopping crazy with ships coming and going and a processing plant operating twenty four hours a day, and I had many boys chasing after me. There was on particular boy who liked me more than most. His name was Jack Miller. He was a wonderful boy. Blonde hair, blue eyes, strong enough to fight off entire crews of rival ships. Jack and I went out for an entire summer and talked of marriage, but come fall, he shipped out to warmer waters and never returned."

"That's so sad. Did he write?"

"Jack was never much for writing letters. He was more a man of action. During the summer, I was the envy of every girl in town, but I guess it wasn't meant to last. Maybe love is like that."

"Surely you had other boyfriends."

"I went out with other boys, then the fishing industry moved down to Rock Port and my options dwindled. Families moved out and businesses closed up."

"You could have moved with them. Why didn't you?"

"Because Rock Port is my home. I was considering it, then mother got sick and father needed someone to take care of her. Being the only child, the job fell on me, then after she died, father got sick and I continued taking care of things. He died and I took over the post office and never looked back."

"So no great loves other than Jack Miller the sailor?"

"Sometimes I think it's all timing and unfortunately for me, the timing was always off. Maybe I was destined to live alone all my days."

"You can't mean that. Bonnie, you're an attractive woman with a lot going for you. Why not love for you?"

She thought for a moment, then smiled at Franklin. "It's not in the cards, Adam. At least not for me. Something always happened to keep it at bay, making me think that I wasn't meant to have love in my life. Now, enough of that. Do you want your mail?"

"I suppose so," said Franklin.

The chiming of the door interrupted their conversation. The two turned and watched Sunflower enter the post office.

"Good morning, Sunflower," said Bonnie. She got off the stool. "Looking for you mail?"

"Yes and something else." Sunflower glanced at the counter under the window at the forms. "You have something I can fill out that adds a name to my mailing address?"

"It's on the change of address form," said Bonnie. "Is someone moving in with you? If so, they need to fill out the form, not you."

Sunflower found the appropriate form and walked over to the counter. "No, it's me. I've decided to go back to my original name. I'm letting people know, so that if I get any mail, it'll get to me." she searched the form for the right box to fill in. "Where do I put my new name?"

Bonnie leaned over and pointed out the small box of residents listed at the address. "There. So what would you like to be called?"

Sunflower lifted her head and smiled. "Before I moved away from home, I was Tracy Johnson, and that's what I would like to be called."

"No more Sunflower?"

"Call me Tracy."

"Are you having a mid life crisis?" asked Franklin.

She looked at him and smiled. "No, I'm just waking up from a long dream." She filled out the form and handed it to Bonnie. "Did I do this right?"

Bonnie took the piece of paper and scanned it. "Perfect. So, Tracy, would you like your mail?"

"I would, thank you."

She took her mail and left the building, with a bounce in her step.

Franklin watched her leave, then turned back to Bonnie. "What do you make of that?"

"I'd say that Star better watch himself. Big changes are coming his way."

#

Margaret Chambers slammed the cabinets open and shut, searching for pancake mix and syrup. Why didn't her mother stock such items? It wasn't just a lack of food that got her upset. Thinking of the interaction with the police had her in a dither. Why couldn't she have kept her cool when they asked their questions. Other people lie easily, why was it so difficult for her? And it wasn't as if she had that much to hide, but it just wasn't their business. So what if she looked guilty. That wasn't her problem. She leaned over and glanced under the sink, on the hope that there was a box of mix there, but was disappointed. She pushed up the sleeves of her purple sweatshirt and started again, methodically opening each cabinet in turn, starting with the top left, can goods, then the next to the left of that, cups and saucers, then the one over the sink, vases and jars, then on to the last one nearest the door, glasses and plates, then turned and faced the interior of the house and worked on the cabinets over the counter that separated the two room. Top right had dry goods, and the natural location for the pancake mix, then left of that, she found empty pickle jars, then to the left of that, pots and pans. Why were the pans on top when they should be below the sink? Nothing in her mother's kitchen made any sense to Margaret.

"What are you looking for dear?"

Margaret leaned over and glanced between the bottom of the cabinets and the counter at her mother. "Do you or do you not have pancake mix? I've been looking for the past ten minutes."

Louella shuffled into the kitchen, wearing her tattered gray robe over her pink pajamas, with her feet stuffed in a pair of worn mule slippers. "I must have run out when you father was here. He loves his pancakes. Loved. I'm sorry, dear. I should have gotten more when I was at the store. Would you like me to make you some bacon and eggs. I've got those."

"No, Mother, I wanted pancakes. And I noticed that you're out of sugar, and creamers and a bunch of other stuff. What's the matter with you?"

Louella looked confused. "I've had a lot on my mind, dear. And don't you use that tone with me, young lady. I'm still your mother."

Margaret sighed. "Am I going to have to move up here and take care of you? I can't believe how you've let the place go. I go away for a couple of years and you let the place fall apart."

"I'm doing the best I can, and you don't have to stay here if you don't want to. I didn't ask you to come home."

Margaret looked at her mother and shook her head. "I'm sorry, Mom. I'm just a little on edge. I wanted pancakes and there wasn't any mix and you're out of syrup and I, . . . , well, I'm just sorry. Anyway, I'll run over to that little store up the block and get some mix, and then I'll make us some pancakes, would you like that?"

Louella poured herself a cup of coffee and wandered back to the living room. "That would be nice dear."

Margaret watched her mother walk away, momentarily worried about her welfare, then scrounged in the junk drawer by the sink for paper and pencil. Soon she had her list. She glanced out at the sunny day and decided that her sweatshirt and jeans would be enough, then headed for the door.

"I'll be right back, Mom."

Margaret left the house and headed up the lane, passing the post office and all the memories of her childhood. It wasn't easy being born and raised in a place so small that she had to be bused to Rock Port for her education. The big city kids, she called them, made fun of the country kids. In her day, there were only a half dozen kids, all grown and moved away by now, but then, it was a fight for survival with the big city kids who had nicer clothes and cliques that didn't include the kids from West Harbor.

She noticed the cold wind as she passed by the post office, and ducked her head to keep the pin needles from attacking her bare cheeks. Margaret kept her head down and shuffled quickly to the Super Saver, grateful when she reached the door. She should have worn a coat. Margaret entered the warmth of the store. The first thing she noticed was the quiet. After the buffeting wind outside, all inside was calm.

"Can I help you, miss?"

She turned her head and noticed Thomas Jones behind the counter, with the ever present crossword puzzle in his hand. "I'm picking up some things for my mother."

"Let me know if I can help you find anything," said Jones, staring at her. "Why haven't I seen you here before? I know most everybody in town."

Margaret walked over to the counter. "I don't live here anymore. I moved away from here when I turned eighteen. Couldn't wait to get out of here. Small towns aren't for me."

"Really, I love them," said Jones. "So where do you live now?"

"Rock Port." Margaret wasn't used to being flirted with, but she recognized the signs, and she wasn't sure she liked it. This bald man across the counter had to be nearly twice her age, and she didn't like the look in his eye. "I'd better do my shopping. Mom will get worried if I stay out too long."

"Rock Port is pretty close," said Jones. "What do you do down there?"

"I've got a job, you know how it is, got to work for a living," she said, backing away from the counter.

Jones put down his paper and followed her down the aisles. "A pretty girl like you, I bet you've got a lot of boyfriends. Am I right?"

"I have some male friends."

There was one thing that Margaret was certain of, she was no pretty girl. On a good day, she could fix herself up to look pleasant, but pretty was a stretch. Why was this man bothering her? She reached up and grabbed hold of the box of pancake mix and almost died when she saw how much it cost, but she was too embarrassed to do anything but take it and move on down the aisle with Jones near on her heels.

Up and down the aisles the two went, with Margaret wincing at the prices and Jones asking her personal questions. Finally, her shopping done, Margaret dropped the items on the counter and wished for the whole experience to be over.

"I could go for a pretty girl like you," said Jones, ringing up the items. "I know, I'm a lot older than you, but age doesn't matter if you're with the right person."

"I'm not interested," said Margaret, pulling a couple of twenties out of her pocket, "but thanks all the same." She grabbed the bag of groceries and headed toward the door.

"I never got your name," said Jones.

She turned at the doorway. "That's because I never gave it to you. Good bye."

Margaret didn't notice the wind on the way back, nor think of her mother's ineptitude, nor her father's murder, only the unwanted attention of Mr. Thomas Jones. It wasn't everyday that she was given the full press, actually, she had never been given such attention, and it was nice, even if unwanted. She clutched her bag of groceries to her chest and wondered. Was it such a bad thing? She reached her mother's house and opened the door.

"Mother, you would not believe what just happened to me!"

#

Tracy washed dishes and thought about her future, while her husband rattled on about the murder and possible suspects in the heinous crime, his words. She stared out the window at the familiar goat shed and tall grass, blowing in the wind, and wondered how long it had been since she was totally aware of her surroundings. She took her existence for granted, never questioning and never thinking that there might be an alternative to what she had chosen. She was a flower child named Sunflower who wore sweeping dresses and ribbons in her hair and her husband was a hippie man who raised goats. This was her life. Until the veil had been lifted. Suddenly, she saw things through different eyes, more critical than she had in the past ten years. She was coming alive, and what she saw didn't please her. Her house wasn't nearly as nice as the Seaver home next door, with its modern conveniences and upgrades. Why couldn't she have such a house? It wasn't as if she wished she lived in a mansion in Bel Air, all she wanted was a nice house with a roof that didn't leak, solid walls that kept out the elements, and the creature comforts of middle class America. Was that too much too ask?

Then there was her little boy, Genesis, who wanted nothing more than to be a normal kid like the two Seaver children. Tracy heard them talk when they thought they were alone. Genesis wanted nothing more than to eat hamburger and fries, not tofu and sprouts, wear jeans and t-shirts, play baseball, and live a life like all the other little boys at his school.

She had bundled him up for the bus ride that morning, walking him to the door and holding onto his little hand, feeling the sorrow coming from him. He must of heard the discussion going on between his parents the night before. She had watched him walk down the lane, join the Seaver children, then down to the bus and on their way to school. She felt the sadness in her home fill her up, blotting out any happiness that might have seeped in.

Tracy used the two sinks, washing in one and rinsing in the other, then setting the drying dishes in a rack to her far left, a task she had done countless times, and never questioned it, until today. Why didn't she have a dishwasher? She could simply rinse off the plates and put them in a machine and let it do the work. Why was she a slave to this? She dried her hands on the towel hanging on the refrigerator and turned to Star.

"And another thing that really bothers me," said Star. "Why aren't the police looking at our intrepid store keeper a little closer? I mean, where did he come from? We don't really know that much about the dude, other than the fact that he charges about twice as much as any store down in Rock Port. For all we know, he could be a mass murderer, hiding out here, waiting until the heat is off and he can move on."

"You know what bothers me?" asked Tracy.

He looked up. "I'm all ears. Tell me, Sunflower, love of my life, what bothers you?"

"My name is Tracy," she said, in a tone that should have alerted him to potential disaster, which he ignored.

"What's wrong with Sunflower? It's a perfectly beautiful name. It so describes you and your wonderful personality, like a flower on a hillside, with the sun beaming down on you."

"I don't want to be called that anymore. I've got a name. It's Tracy, and from now on, that is what I prefer to be called. You got a problem with that?"

He stood up and crossed the room. "Yeah, I do. You were Sunflower when we met and fell in love, and you've been my loving Sunflower for all these years, and I don't understand why you want to change all of the sudden. Why can't you be the little girl I promised to love for ever and ever?"

"Because I want more than this. Look around you. This isn't living, this is existing. We have holes in the roof, cracks in the siding, pipes that freeze in the winter and drip in the summer. I can't live like this anymore. No, let me be clear, I won't live like this anymore. I want more out of life, Harold."

"Don't call me that."

"You prefer Harry?"

"I prefer Star."

"You're hiding something awful, I can feel it. You lie to me and you lie to your son. Why? You talk about Young Tom hiding out, what about you? What did you do down in LA that you don't want people to know about? Not that you'd tell me, I'm only your wife and not even a real wife, a common law wife."

"We had a ceremony; you're my wife."

"With your friend the Reverend Thistle performing the gathering? Give me a break, Star, Harry, Or Harold, or whoever you are. We are living a lie and you don't care. Criminy, even the goats can tell you're full of crap and they don't have to live with you."

He reached his boiling point. "You don't want to live with me, you know where the door is."

She saw the anger in his eyes and wondered for a moment if he was going to hit her. "Violence, Star?"

He backed off. "I'm all about peace and harmony, Sunflower, excuse me, Tracy, and I won't dignify that with an answer. You do what you have to do."

She grabbed her coat off the hook by the back door.

"Where do you think you're going?"

She slid her arms into the coat, turned and gave him a sad smile. "Away from you."

She opened the door and walked straight out into the wind, and felt the tears rolling down her cheeks. She glanced at the door, knowing that she couldn't go back in there and face Star. She walked down the steps and headed across the yard toward the Seaver house.

#

Mary Seaver was washing up after the kids hurricane exit for school. It was like this every school day, with running around and problems with clothes and lunch boxes, and what Cindy could wear that wouldn't be too embarrassing, and little Billy complaining that Cindy was hogging the bathroom and why did girls need so long to get ready, then the rush through breakfast, hoping that the kids would eat anything on their plates, besides the lone strip of bacon and orange juice, then the complaint that they were starving just before it was time to bundle them up and send them off to the bus stop, then all was quiet. Every school morning was the same, and her husband was absolutely no help whatsoever. He slept in, then got up, grabbed a cup of coffee and a roll and headed out to his precious garage, leaving Mary with the lions share of child rearing. It truly wasn't fair, but arguing about it with her husband had proven to be a waste of time. So Mary did the work, fighting the tightrope of time that bound her to her tasks, then after the kids were off and gone, she started in on the clean up, and a few moments rest.

She rinsed the dishes and set them in the dishwasher and thought about her life. Was this what she was hoping for when she was growing up? Not likely. Sure, she wanted the home and the husband, family, and the comforts of a middle class life, but was there more that she was missing? She had the kids, and they were beautiful, wonderful, little people, whom she loved very much. They were kids, so they were messy and loud, and sometimes needed direction, but who didn't. Her home was perfect. It wasn't a mansion, but it had all the creature comforts that she wished for. Her husband was a good provider and was good to his children. So, why wasn't he more affectionate with her? This problem gnawed at her psyche to no end. It just wasn't natural. When they first got together, he couldn't keep his hands off of her, to the point where she was pushing him away, playfully, and they'd laugh, but sometime in the past year, he had lost all interest. Why? And when she asked him about it, he got angry and stormed out to his garage. Had she changed? Was she giving off some sort of sign that said don't touch? She didn't think so, but perhaps he did. Forget counseling. She suggested it and he told her he wouldn't go. Which left her where? Angry and resentful. She put the last of the dishes in the dishwasher, then wiped down the counter tops and the kitchen table.

A knock on her back door broke her musings. Mary looked though the pane glass windows at her next door neighbor, Sunflower waving at her. Mary walked over and opened the door.

"What's up?" asked Mary.

"I needed to talk to someone," said Tracy. "I hope I'm not interrupting anything."

"Come on in, I was just cleaning up after the kids." Mary turned and looked at her neighbor. "What's wrong?"

"How can you tell?"

"You look like you're ready to lose it, and I know that look. I've got it most of the time."

"You too?"

"Come on in and tell me about it. I'll put on some coffee."

They sat down at the kitchen table and Mary poured coffee into big white ceramic mugs, handing one to Sunflower, then added sugar to her own. Mary held onto the cup with both hands, feeling the heat coming through the ceramic. In the ten years that the two had been neighbors, they had built a trust, starting small, then growing with each encounter. Truth be told, back in high school, Mary and her friends would have laughed at Sunflower, labeling her a loser and a pot head, and the usual nasty things that high school kids said. But as she got to know the gentle redhead, she realized that there was a good listener with a good head underneath that hippie attire.

"So what's going on, Sunflower."

"I don't want to be called that anymore. Once upon a time, my name was Tracy Johnson. I never told you this, but I ran away from home when I was seventeen and decided that I needed a new identity. I became Sunflower. And for the past ten years, that's been just fine, but lately, well, it hasn't been as fine as it was."

"Problems with Star?"

"That's the thing. I don't know him anymore. And his name isn't Star, it's Harold. Or Harry. Either way, he's a liar and I don't want to be around him anymore."

"You can't mean that," said Mary. "You married for better or worse, right?"

"Even if he's a murderer?"

Mary gasped. "Star? I can't believe that."

"Nor can I, but I don't really know and it's driving me nuts. Ever since the murder, he's been evasive and when I call him on it, he clams up. For all I know, he killed that guy. The more I think about it, I realize that I don't really know that much about Star. We met at a concert in San Francisco and hooked up and I guess I was willing to let the past stay in the past, but what if he did something really bad in his past. I ran away at seventeen and changed my name, what about him? He told the police that he lived in LA, but he never told me that. Where's his family? Does he have one? Or is he some sort of mass murderer that killed his entire family and has been on the run ever since."

"Do you honestly see Star as a mass murderer?"

Tracy laughed, sipping her coffee. "Okay, probably not. But he's hiding something and husbands and wives aren't supposed to keep secrets from each other, right?"

"You wouldn't think so."

"Why, you're having problems too?"

"Other than the fact that Bill won't touch me? And when I ask him if he had anything to do with killing that guy he blows up? No, nothing much."

Tracy reached across the table and lay a hand on Mary's. "Do you think Bill killed him?"

"Probably not," said Mary, "but I'd like to know that's wrong with me that he avoids me. Maybe he doesn't like sex anymore."

"All men like sex."

"That's what I thought. So here we are, two married women with husbands that may or may not be murderers. Isn't that lovely?"

Tracy looked around the kitchen. "At least you've got a nice home. I live in a dump. And I look like a refugee from the Goodwill."

Mary eyed Tracy. "Maybe I can do something about that. You're about my size. You're a pretty girl, Tracy, but you can't tell with all your hippie clothes. Maybe what you need is a make over."

"That sounds like fun."

"Have you ever thought of cutting your hair? I used to be pretty good with a pair of scissors."

Tracy smiled. "I dream of it, but I can't afford going to a hairdresser."

"No need. You will be amazed at what I can do. This is going to be fun, something that I haven't had in a very long time. Don't go anywhere."

Mary ran into her bedroom and rummaged through her closet. She dug out some tops and old jeans that she didn't wear much that would look good on Tracy, grabbed a hand full of make up and scissors and headed back to the kitchen.

"You want change, I'll give you change. By the time we're done, you'll be a whole new girl."

#

Thomas Hoffman shuffled around his house, avoiding both the furniture and the half dozen cats lounging around the room. They were hungry, expressing themselves with a cacophony of noise. The problem was that Hoffman didn't know how to turn a feral cat away. It broke his heart seeing a little cat hunkered down by the side of the house during a torrential storm. Out of the goodness of his heart, he took the little creature inside, where it joined the chorus of underfed cats. Cat dander covered every surface, with hair and dust sharing air space in the small living room. All the rooms in the ramshackle house were like this. Cat hair covered the couch, the easy chairs, the bed, the dressers, the night stands, and the sideboards. Pictures of his life with his wife shared space with cat hair of all lengths and colors. Such was the life of a cat owner who couldn't say no to a stray cat.

It hadn't always been like this, but Hoffman was a lonely man. Ever since his wife passed five years earlier, he had nothing to do and no one to talk to, except for his cats. He named each and every one, though he secretly knew that he didn't get their names right and that in all honestly, none ever responded to the names he gave them. Still, it gave him a way of identifying one from the other.

Back when Estelle was alive, they had one cat. Her name was Basset, and she adored Estelle, following her around the house like a lapdog. Both Basset and Estelle were gone, replaced by Binky, Spot, Tiger, Blackie, Wooly, and Charlie, Hoffman's personal favorite, a tiger stripped fifteen pounder who was currently lounged across the top of the couch, his feet twitching in his sleep.

Hoffman had seen a lot of changes in West Harbor. He came to town a young man and worked the boats until a fishing accident in the forties left him with a bum leg. By that time he had already married Estelle Dupree, the prettiest girl in town, and had built a small house on Lilac Lane, the same house he currently lived in. After leaving the boats, he hitched on with the fish processing plant behind the school house. It was a large brick affair that ran twenty four hours a day during catch season, and lay idle during the off season. While the job didn't pay much, it gave the Hoffman's a living. Estelle stayed home and kept house, cooking and cleaning and preparing for a baby that never arrived. It was the one thing that Hoffman regretted, and this mostly for his wife; as a couple they were unable to have children. The doctors down in Rock Port said something about infertility, but Hoffman wasn't sure just who they were talking about, and was too embarrassed to ask, so the house was without the pitter-patter of little feet. Still, he and Estelle had a good life. They socialized, meeting with other young couples from the fishing industry. Hoffman had friends who came to port and drank too much and ended up on his couch, and even though Estelle shook her head at his choice of friends, was always polite and made sure that the young men in question got a fair nights sleep and a good breakfast before heading out to sea the next morning.

Life went on for the Hoffman's with the years passing by. The docks washed away for the third time in as many years and the boats moved their operations south to Rock Port, then the processing plant closed down. No fish to process, no need to stay open. The building fell silent, the windows broken by idle youth. There were no jobs to be had in West Harbor. Families moved away, and the houses fell into dust, eventually demolished by the county as safety hazards. All that remained of the processing plant was the cement slab of the general office that could be seen under the tall grasses that lined the north side of the village. The Hoffman's went on general assistance, bringing shame to Hoffman, a man who had worked all his life, then in a blink of an eye, he was old and alone, living with a half dozen cats.

He thought of the tricks that life had pulled on him, smiling at the goofy Tiger, still pawing air on the couch. When Estelle was still alive, he had a reason to get up in the morning, and now, maybe it was only the cats that kept him going. But he had a problem, a massive issue with money. It was hard enough to keep himself alive, but supplying cat food for his family, for that was how he viewed the feline presence, he needed more than he had. His social security check only went so far, and he couldn't very well kick his beloved cats out the door. So what to do? If he had an extra couple thousand, he could breath easier, and feed his cats in the process. But where was he going to come up with that kind of money. He sat and thought, then came up with an idea, one that was strictly out of desperation.

Hoffman reached for the phone and dialed a number, then waited. The other party picked up on the fourth ring.

"Hi, Old Tom here. I'll come to the point. I saw what you did. Don't care either way, but if you want me to keep my mouth shut, it'll cost you five grand. That's not my problem. Get the money and meet me at the old school house at six. That should give you enough time to get the money together. You're lucky I didn't tell no one. Silence is golden, right?"

He hung up the phone, sat back in his chair and smiled. Soon his troubles would be over.

8. More Bad News.

Tuesday morning came in with a fog and chill that was missing the last couple of days. Gone was the sun and Indian Summer, replaced by the usual cold mist that hung over the coast. The kids were bundled up tight as they boarded the school bus for another day of transport, and the village stayed indoors. Wood stoves were cranked up and rivulets of smoke escaped from brick chimneys, blending with the fog, disappearing into the mist. It was a day of quiet, with the newest residents hiding from the possible dangers that lurked out side their doors, while the older residents went about their business as usual. Bonnie Williams sorted mail, with Franklin for company, while Mary Seavers cleaned up the mess from her children, her husband already busy in his garage working on a cabinet, Jones stocked the shelves from boxes in the storeroom, and Star fed his goats, trying to avoid his wife.

All was quiet, until Bob Peterson noticed that there was a muted screeching coming from Old Tom's house next door. He knew that the old man liked to take care of the strays, and Peterson himself had complained bitterly to his wife about the health issue of having so many feral cats running loose on the property, but it did no good. His wife was a firm believer in keeping her nose out of other people's business, including that of their nearest neighbor, yet the howling was driving him crazy. He worked at home, trying to get an internet accounting service up and running and the cats were interrupting his train of thought.

Their's was not a fancy house, comprising of four rooms, with the living quarters on the left and the bedrooms on the side facing Hoffman's house. The back bedroom belonged to the two of them and he had taken the front bedroom, giving him a nice view of West Harbor, and enough light to make him not think he was living in a cave. There was a desk under the window and a couch along the side wall with the two windows overlooking their neighbor. From his vantage point, he could look out of the front window or the side, giving him nearly two hundred and seventy degree view of his surroundings. At the moment, he could see the half dozen cats perched on Hoffman's front porch. It wasn't as if Peterson didn't like Hoffman. He was a nice old man who said strange things, but Peterson was raised to respect his elders, so he cut the old man some slack, but the cats were driving him nuts. He tried putting classical music on the stereo to drown out the caterwauling, but it didn't work. Finally, he reached his breaking point. He would simply go over and tell the old man to feed his cats.

Peterson pushed away from the desk and walked out into the living room. His wife, Millie was wiping up the last of the dishes from breakfast and looked up at his arrival.

"I thought you were working."

"It's them damn cats. I'm going next door and talk to Old Tom and see if he can quiet them down."

"Don't be offensive, you know how he is about his cats. They are like children to him."

Peterson reached for his pea coat hanging on the hook, sliding his arms into the slots. "Don't you worry, honey, I'll be the soul of discretion. Me and Old Tom get along just fine."

"Be nice, He doesn't have any family."

"I'll be nice."

Peterson kissed his wife good-bye, then headed out into the fog. The chill was apparent as soon as he left the warmth of his house. The fog was thick enough to obscure all but the lane in front of their house, the Hoffman house to the east, and the old school house to the west. Peterson walked out to the lane, turned left and headed over to the Hoffman place. He sidestepped the cats, perched on posts and old tires, and sitting on the front steps, and knocked hard on the front door. He knew that the old man was hard of hearing, so he knocked again. Minutes passed with no response. He was ready to knock a third time, when he decided maybe just this once, it would be okay to see if the door was open. Perhaps Old Tom was sleeping and forgot about his cats, though that had never happened. Peterson turned the knob and was surprised when it opened in his hand. He stepped inside.

"Mr. Hoffman? Are you okay?"

There was no one in the front room, nor the kitchen in the back, though the howling cats could be heard through the thin walls. It was cold inside the Hoffman house, Peterson thought, clutching his coat tighter to keep what warmth he had inside his coat. It felt wrong being in the house, having never been inside more than the front room in the two years they had lived in West Harbor, but something didn't feel right. A quick inspection proved that, save for the cats, the house was empty.

He did find cans of cat food and a opener on the counter and decided that he would do the old man a favor. Perhaps he left town and forgot to feed his cats. Peterson opened a half dozen cans and brought them out to the front steps, setting them down quickly. The cats curled around his legs trying to get to the food. Peterson stepped off the front porch and headed back to his house, hoping that the affair was over. He was nearly to his gate when he noticed the front door of the school house was open.

"What the heck?" he thought, moving past his house and continuing onto the schoolhouse. For no reason other than curiosity, he walked up to the schoolhouse door and pushed it aside. It was dark inside, with some light coming in through the dusty windows. It was then he spotted the hand. He pushed the door all the way open and looked down. Now he saw the hand, attached to Old Tom's arm, and the angle the body lay on the wood floor.

"Mr. Hoffman? Are you okay?" Peterson ventured inside, and as he got near to the body, he noticed the blood pooled around Hoffman's head. Peterson knelt down and looked at the mass of blood on the back of the old man's head. He pulled a cell phone off his hip and dialed nine one one.

"Hello operator? I'd like to report a murder."

#

Ben Steele looked out the window at the fog and thought of how appropriate the weather was considering their case. There was a lot out there that he wasn't seeing, and if only the mist were to clear , he would he be able to see all that was going on. There was just too many people involved that might have killed Tony Chambers. No alibi's, no excuses, and worst of all, no remorse. If there were anyone on earth that more deserved to die, he couldn't see him. Chambers was a totally hated man and one that the entire community wished gone. For a fleeting moment, he wondered if the killing was done like in a Christie novel, with all the participants taking a wack at the deceased, thought he knew that there was only one killing blow that did the job, eliminating the need for multiple killers. Unless it was planned just that way, to make it look as if only one person had done the killing when in fact, it was a group effort. Perhaps Chambers was lured down to the beach by several individuals, and when he was being confronted by the group, one lone killer snuck up behind him and bashed him over the head. Steele knew that this was a stretch, but he was willing to acknowledge anything at this point.

He pulled out a piece of paper from the top desk drawer and wrote Chambers in the middle of the page, then his most likely candidates like spokes on a wheel around the deceased. Each had a motive, each had the opportunity, which was the killer? Louella Chambers had the most to lose, Star, real name Harold Gaithers, was suspicious, even if they couldn't find any history on the man, and Mr. Thomas Jones was definitely not telling them the truth. Then there was the hard-working, yet very angry, Bill Seavers. Which one did the deed?

Walker entered the room with a big smile on his face. "Tom Jones, not the singer, has been located."

Steele looked up. "Tell me something good."

Walker dropped a sheet of paper on Steele's desk and hooked a finger in his vest. "It took awhile to sort out all the Thomas Jones's that live in California, but it was worth it. Our boy did eighteen months in Chino for murder two, five years ago. It seems that Jones got in a bar fight down in San Bernardino, beat a guy to death and was sentenced to three to five, got out with good behavior. I told you he was our boy. History of violence, a murder on his record, it doesn't get much better than that, does it?"

"Bar fight, eh? So he has a quick temper and has the potential to kill when provoked. I'd say that gives us good reason to talk to him again."

Steele stood up and grabbed his coat of the back of his chair. Finally, things were coming together. Even with four good suspects, having one with a murder rap on his sheet made him the number one guy. He was halfway to the door when the phone rang. Steele walked back and picked up the phone.

"Steele. What's that? Another one? You're kidding. Right. We're on our way." He hung up the phone.

"Another what?" asked Walker.

"Murder, let's go."

Not much was said on the way back to West Harbor. The only information Steele got was that the victim was an elderly male, which narrowed it down some, but not much. They drove through the fog, carefully, for the road was slippery and wet, and managed to get to West Harbor unscathed. They crested the hill and Steele could see that the town was shrouded in fog, obscuring all but those structures nearest the south side of town. Louella Chambers house looked dark, the post office indistinct. The only other structure visible was the back side of Adam Franklin's house. As they rolled down the hill into the village, Steele could see a flashing red and yellow light of the deputy sheriff's car off to the north. The red neon open sign in the window of the Super Saver looked weak through the dense fog as they passed by, then they reached Lilac lane and the squad car, and behind that, Eddie Lawton's old chevy.

"How is it that he beats us every time?" asked Walker, staring out the window.

"Maybe they call him first," said Steele, "or he listens to the police band in his free time. Why don't you ask him?"

"He doesn't like me," said Walker. "If I ask, he'll just make fun of me."

They exited the car and walked up to the school house, the dim outline of the building firming up as they approached the building. The lights were on inside, casting a eerie glow through the fog that permeated the landscape. Wally, the deputy sheriff, stood at the door, with crossed arms and a stern look to keep the curious away.

"Hi, Wally," said Steel reaching the door. "Who found the body?"

Wally pointed to the house next door to the school house. "Neighbor of the deceased, name of Bob Peterson, found him this morning."

"Thanks, Wally," said Steele.

The detectives entered the schoolhouse and spotted Lawton bent over the stilled body of Thomas Hoffman. The crime scene photographer was snapping pictures from all angles, quickly documenting the scene, while the forensic team was dusting for prints and looking for clues that might aid the investigation.

Lawton looked up at Steele's arrival. "Got another one for you, Ben. Why are they doing this to me? I'm but a lowly public servant, trying to do as little as possible until I retire."

Steele knelt down to be at eye level with the medical examiner. "How did it happen?"

"Blunt trauma, just like the other one, with multiple blows. The victim resisted, judging by the defensive wounds on the arms. And there was considerably more force to the hits. From the looks of it, I'd say that somebody took a lot of shots to this poor guy's head. Just in case the first blow didn't kill him, the ones that followed did. From the amount of blood, I'd say he hit a main artery, possibly carotid, maybe the circle of Willis, hard to say until I get him to the lab."

"Time of death?" asked Steele.

"Sometime last night. If I were to guess, I'd say not more than twelve hours ago. Once I get him in, I can give you a better idea."

"Could it be the work of the same killer?" asked Steele.

"Maybe," said Lawton. "I'll need to clean up this blood to see what kind of wounds he suffered, but they were both blunt trauma deaths, and they lived in the same small town. I'd say that you probably only have one bad guy out there, but I could be wrong. As far as I'm concerned, I should be on a beach in Mexico, sipping a cool drink and checking out the senorita's, but nobody asks me."

"Give it a rest, Eddie," said Steele. "You want to retire, retire, put us out of your misery, but in the meantime, can the jokes and do your job."

Lawton stared at Steele. "What's got your panties in a bunch, Ben?"

Steele waved at the scene around them. "This. Another dead body in a place that hasn't seen murder in twenty years, now all of the sudden has two in less than a week. I'd bet your paycheck that they're related, but I can't for the life of me see how."

Lawton stood up, knocking the dust off his knees. "You'll figure it out, Ben, you always do."

"Thanks for the confidence," said Steele.

"Now," said Lawton, "can I finish up here?"

Steele and Walker left Lawton to do his job. They left the school house and entered the foggy outside where there was a scattering of locals standing and waiting to see what would happen next, the fog all but hiding their identities. Steele walked out to the middle of the half dozen and looked at the faces, all familiar up close.

"We've got another murder and will need to talk to each of you. Last time, we used the school house, obviously we can't do that this time. So go home and we'll be along to talk to you. Do not leave town until we've gotten your statements."

The locals melted away into the fog, turning their backs on Steele, and doing as they were told. Soon it was just Steele and Walker, standing in the middle of Lilac lane.

"So who's first?" asked Walker.

"The next door neighbor."

#

The detectives walked through the fog, and up the trim sidewalk to the Peterson's house, a smallish affair with no front porch and large pane windows facing the streets. There was an overhang to protect the visitor from rain above the door. Shingles were falling off the side and the paint was peeling, but the yard was clipped short and there was a new picket fence around the property that showed that someone was trying to improve the place.

Steele knocked on the door and was surprised on how quickly it opened, revealing a young man with hair over his ears and eyebrows, with a wary smile and a crisp handshake.

"Bob Peterson," said the young man. "We talked a couple of days ago."

"May we come in?" asked Steele.

"Sure, sure," said Peterson, standing aside to let the detectives in. "My wife has just made a fresh pot of coffee if you're interested."

"That would be nice," said Steele.

Peterson led them into the living room, a small space with furniture fresh from IKEA, the blond wood and bright blue fabrics looked inviting. Steele sat down on the couch, while Walker choose a nearby chair. There was a wood stove in the corner cranking out the heat. After the chill from outside, the air was practicably stifling inside. A young woman with a matching shag haircut and nice smile came from the kitchen with a tray with coffee cups on it.

"If you want milk or sugar," she said, "just let me know. Otherwise, I'll let you guys talk in peace."

Millie Peterson set the tray on the coffee table and did as she said, disappearing into the back bedroom.

"You'll have to excuse my wife," said Peterson. "This whole thing has upset her to no end. You see, we used to live down in San Francisco, where stuff like this happened all the time, and to be frank, we thought we left all that behind us. To find it in our little oasis is a bit disturbing."

"I can see that," said Steele, reaching for his cup. He tested the hot liquid, sipping slowly to avoid burning his tongue. "If you could just tell us what happened, we'll be on our way."

"That's easy," said Peterson, sitting on the opposite side of the couch. "I was in my office, that's the front bedroom over there, with a view of Old Tom's place. I have an on-line accounting service that's picking up and I work out of our home, which isn't to say that we're doing fabulous. Sorry, I'm babbling. Back to what happened. I was at my desk, trying to sort out a glitch in the software, when I heard the cats next door. Old Tom has, had, a lot of cats. They were hungry, making all sorts of noise. I tried to drown out their caterwauling, but it wasn't going to happen, so I went next door to see Old Tom. Maybe he was sleeping or something and couldn't hear them. Anyway, I went next door and knocked, then when he didn't answer, I found the door was open. I know I shouldn't have gone inside, but I was concerned for his welfare. I searched the place and couldn't find him, so I opened a half dozen cans and fed the cats."

Steele jotted down in shorthand what Peterson was saying. "So then what happened?"

"I was coming home, when I noticed the school was open. Now, that just doesn't happen. I thought maybe some kids were playing around in there, or maybe a bum decided to get out of the weather. Either way, I went to investigate and found him. Old Tom was a bit cranky at times, but was basically a pretty decent guy. Who could have done such a thing?"

"That's what we're trying to find out," said Steele. "Did you hear anything last night from the school house?"

Peterson shook his head. "Nothing. But we were watching a movie and went to bed kind of early."

"Any idea who might want to do this to your neighbor?"

"Not a clue. Like I said, Old Tom was a pretty decent fellow. He loved his cats more than anything. What's going to happen to them? I mean, we could probably take a couple, but he had like a dozen of them."

"We'll let animal control know about the situation," said Walker.

Millie came out of the bedroom. "They'll put them to sleep, won't they? Tom loved those cats. Surely, there's something we can do for them."

Steele didn't know what to say. While his boys had been at him for weeks about getting a dog, he had never had a cat, but he did have empathy for the animals. Perhaps the community could do something, but he wasn't sure what. In the meantime he had two murders to solve.

"Is there anything else you can add that might help solve these murders?" asked Steele.

The Peterson's shook their heads.

"I wish there was," said Peterson. "Old Tom was a good guy, and he certainly didn't deserve this."

"That poor man," said Millie. "And the worst of it is, the killer is still on the loose."

"He was for the first murder as well," said Steele.

"That was different," said Millie. "From everything I heard, Tony Chambers was a bully and a major jerk, one that the world would be well rid of, but Old Tom was a nice man who never hurt a soul. Maybe our little town isn't all that safe anymore. And to think that we left the big city to escape such things, and then here it is right in our face. I guess evil is just about everywhere."

Steele nodded. "Unfortunately so. Thank you both for your time."

They left the relative warmth of the Peterson house and walked back into the damp cold of the fog outside. They walked out to the lane, where they could see the body being taken out of the school in a black bag atop a stretcher. Steele watched the paramedics load the remains into the rear of the ambulance.

"You think she's right?" asked Walker. "About the evil, I mean."

"Naturally," said Steele. "Come on, Kevin, let's see what the rest of the residents have to say for themselves."

#

The detectives passed the ambulance on their way to the Super Saver. They walked up to the door and went inside, leaving the mist behind and coming face to face with Thomas Jones. The storekeeper looked up from his crossword puzzle at their arrival.

"Well look who's back," said Jones. "And before you accuse me of killing Old Tom, let me tell you right up front that he was one of the good ones around here. I had no reason to kill the old man. As far as I'm concerned, it's a tragedy and I hope you find the bastard that killed him."

"Admirable attitude," said Steele, "from a man who's served time for murder."

Jones stared at the two detectives. "So you found that out, big deal. I made a mistake and paid the price, and before you go all weepy-eyed on me, the son of a bitch pulled a knife on me and I was fighting for my life. If you look at the record of the sweetheart I put down, you'll see that he wasn't exactly a choir boy. I was out having a few and this asshole comes up to me and picks a fight. All I did was defend myself."

"That's not how the court ruled," said Steele. "According to the report I looked at, it was the other way around. You were the one who picked the fight and it was you that had the knife."

"Bullshit," said Jones. "What are you trying to pull here? I've seen the records and you know that it was the other way around."

Steele knew he was right, he just wanted to see what kind of reaction he would get from Jones. The explosive anger didn't surprise Steele, but did make him wonder if that enormous energy hadn't been applied in not one, but two murders. The first was easy to see. Jones had gotten into a confrontation with Chambers and was likely to have killed the man, but the killing of Old Tom made no sense, even from a hardened criminal like Jones.

"So what did he do to you that made you kill him?" asked Walker.

Jones leaned over the counter and stuck a finger in Walker's face. "Don't you try that crap with me, boy, I'll kick your ass, then throw you out the door."

Walker didn't flinch. "Try me."

Steele put a hand between the two. "Enough." He looked at Jones. "You got an alibi for last night?"

Jones shook his head. "I was here. I don't socialize, I work, I sleep. Maybe someday, I'll retire. What do you want from me?"

"The truth, Mr. Jones," said Steele.

Jones sat back on his seat behind the counter and picked up his crossword puzzle. "You guys wouldn't know the truth if it jumped up and bit you in the ass. So, do I need a lawyer, or what?"

"Not at this time," said Steele, "but don't leave town."

"Where am I going to go?"

They left the store and headed south on the lane.

"He's the one," said Walker. "I can feel it."

"Maybe," said Steele. "Maybe not, but he sure is an angry man. Time will tell."

#

The post office was lit up, casting a eerie glow through the fog, offering a beacon of hope for the passerby. Steele opened the door and let Walker enter first, then followed. Inside, they found Bonnie Williams behind the counter, with Adam Franklin sitting on a nearby stool, both staring at the detectives as they approached.

"Is it true about Old Tom?" asked Bonnie. "I heard through the grapevine, but I hoped the information wasn't true, but here you are, so it must be true."

"I'm sorry to say it is true," said Steele, walking up to the counter. He could see the shock on the woman's face, and worried for a moment that she might faint, her hands gripping the counter, white from effort, her face pale and her eyes unfocused. "Why don't you close up shop and go lay down."

"The post office never closes during business hours," said Bonnie, as if she was reciting the words. She looked up at Steele. "I'm sorry, I've known Old Tom my entire life. His wife used to make bead necklaces for the kids in the neighborhood when we were little, and they've always been here. I just can't imagine what's happening. I knew that the day would come when he passed, just as his wife did and my parents before her, but naturally, like in his sleep, not like this. I heard that someone bashed his head in, is that true?"

Franklin stepped off his stool. "Look officers, is this really necessary? Bonnie's not taking this very well."

Steele looked at the man. "We'll only ask a couple of questions, if that's okay with you?"

"Ask all you want," said Bonnie. "I will do everything within my power to help you catch the sicko who killed that gentle man, a man who just loved his cats and his community."

"Do you have any idea who might have wanted to kill him?" asked Walker.

She shook her head. "Not a one. He was a sweet old guy. Sure, he could be a grouch, who can blame him, but there was not one single evil bone in his body."

"Where were you from dinner time on last night?" asked Steele.

"I closed up shop just after five, like usual, then I went back to my place, made dinner and watched some TV, then went to bed."

"Did you see anyone out by the school house after dinner?"

"Not a soul," said Bonnie, "but I was in the back and honestly, the only thing I can really see from my place is the ocean and the beach. Sorry. I wish I could help you out, but I just can't."

"That's enough questions," said Franklin. "She didn't see anything, she doesn't know anything. Why can't you leave her alone? Can't you see that she's grieving?"

Steele turned his attention to Franklin. "Okay, how about you, Mr. Franklin? Where were you around dinner time on and do you have anybody that can verify that information?"

"I was making dinner. Chicken Curry with asparagus and hollandaise sauce, if you must know. There was a lovely program on PBS about immigrants that kept my attention right up to bed time. Anything else?"

"Do you know why someone would want to kill Mr. Hoffman?" asked Walker.

Franklin looked at Walker. "Obviously he did something stupid. Why else kill him? I mean really, he's been around town this long and nobody paid much attention to him, then along comes the first murder and days later Old Tom ends up dead. You want my opinion, I'd say that he knew something and was killed for it."

This actually was exactly what Steele was thinking, but what did Thomas Hoffman know that he died to protect? Steele was certain that they should have pushed Hoffman harder during their last visit, and if so, perhaps the man would still be alive today.

"You think he knew who killed Chambers?" asked Steele.

"I'd bet on it," said Franklin, "Or saw something that would lead him to believe he did. Either way, that's just how I see it. And I do feel bad for both Old Tom and for our community. Hopefully this will be the end of the killing, Lord knows we've seen enough to last us another twenty years."

"There's still the matter of apprehending the killer," said Steele.

Franklin smiled. "And I'm sure that you will do just so. Now, is there anything else? I think we should take your suggestion and have Bonnie lie down. She's experienced a terrible shock and a nice cup of tea might soothe her nerves."

Steele looked at the two residents. He knew that there wasn't much more he was going to get this day, but there was always tomorrow. He nodded.

"Thank you for your time. And if you think of anything that might help, just call the Rock Port Police and they'll let me know."

The detectives left the post office and stood out in the foggy morning. The sun was doing its best to break through, the orb setting like a golden ball surrounded by mist halfway up the eastern sky. There was no wind and the silence under the velvet blanket was like being inside a tomb. No noise, no sound, except for the crunch of their shoes on the pavement. There were more interviews to do before they could leave.

#

Next in line was Louella Chambers and her daughter, Margaret. There was a thin wisp of smoke coming from their chimney, and a weak light in the kitchen window to show that someone was home. They were almost to the door, when suddenly it was flung open, revealing Margaret Chambers blocking their entrance.

"What do you want? My mother doesn't want to talk to anyone right now."

"We just need a few minutes of your time," said Steele.

"We don't know nothing," said Margaret. "Go away."

"Can I talk to your mother?"

"She doesn't want any company, can't you understand that she's not feeling good?"

The door opened the rest of the way and Louella moved her daughter out of the way.

"I'm not feeling good right now," said Louella. "I feel just sick about Old Tom. He was so nice, and such a quiet man. Why someone would do that to him is beyond me. I just can't talk right now."

"Two questions and we'll leave you alone," said Steele. "Where were you and your daughter between dinner time last night and this morning."

"Here, she was with me. We ate some chicken pot pies for dinner, then looked at old scrapbooks until bed time. The fog was coming in, so I went out only for a moment to get some more wood, then stayed in the rest of the evening."

"Did you see anybody moving about when you went out to fetch the wood?" asked Steele.

She thought for a moment, then shook her head. "The fog was already too thick to see much past the road. Sorry I can't be of more help, can I go now?"

"What about your daughter?" asked Walker. "Did she see anything?"

Louella turned and whispered something to Margaret, then looked back to the detectives. "She don't know nothing. Good bye and good luck. I hope you find the killer soon, before there's nobody left in our little town."

She closed the door in their faces.

"If nothing else," said Walker. "she was quick and to the point. What do you think, boss?"

Steele didn't know what to think. This town was full of people who knew nothing, saw nothing, and apparently lived in blissful ignorance. "Somebody is lying, but I'm not sure just who. Come on, let's go ask some more questions."

#

The Seavers house appeared indistinctly as they walked up the lane, then grew more solid the closer they got. There was dew on the metal fence enclosing the front yard, and for once, the garage door was closed. The detectives opened the gate and headed to the front door. Seconds later, they were on the step.

Steele reached up and knocked, then stood back and waited.

The door opened, with Mary Seaver standing in the warmth of the entry. "Come in, we've been expecting you."

The detectives followed the Mary through the living room and on through to the kitchen where Bill Seavers sat at the table, his hands holding onto a coffee cup with steam coming off the top. He looked up at their arrival.

"I didn't do it," said Seaver. "That's what you wanted to hear, isn't it?"

"May we sit down?" asked Steele.

"Please," said Mary. "Coffee?"

"I would love some coffee," said Steele.

Walker nodded his head.

Soon, all were seated around the kitchen table, with the Seavers sitting adjacent on one half and the detectives on the other, all with steaming cups of coffee in front of them.

"Can we make this quick?" asked Seavers. "I've got work to do."

"Could you be a little more insensitive, Bill?" asked Mary. "Our neighbor had been brutally murdered and all you can say is that you didn't do it and could we be quick about this? How about a little respect for Old Tom?"

"Old Tom was a pain in the butt," said Seavers. "Everybody knew it. From the day we moved in here ten years ago, he's been nothing but an old jerk, always pissed off about something or other, and those cats of his are probably full of diseases, infecting our kids, and everyone around here. I'm sorry, but I can't say I feel sorry for the old guy getting bumped off. If that makes me insensitive, so be it." He looked at Steele. "So ask your questions so I can get back to work."

"Where were you last night from dinner time on through the morning?" asked Steele.

"Here. With my wife and children. We ate dinner, then watched some TV, then went to bed. Just like every other school night. Nothing special. I think I might have gone to the garage to check on something, but came right back."

Steele looked at Mary. "How about you?"

"Same. We stayed in. There isn't much reason to go out, really. The kids wanted to play outside, but the fog was just coming in and I thought they might catch a cold if they went out and played, so they were here with us. Not much happens around here."

"Can you think of anyone who might want to harm Mr. Hoffman?"

"Can't think of a one," said Mary. "It wasn't like that other horrible man who everybody hated. Old Tom was like a fixture around here, with his black suits, and all those cats, but every community had an odd duck or two. Ours was Old Tom. He used to yell at the kids when they ran down the lane past his house. I can't think of anybody who'd want to kill him. He was a little cranky at times, but that isn't a good reason to kill him."

"Did you see anyone lurking around the schoolhouse last night?" asked Steele.

"The fog was in and it was hard to see next door," said Mary.

Seavers pushed himself away from the table. "Is that it? I've got work to do. Bills to pay. You know how it is, right?"

And just like that, the interview was over. Seavers left the kitchen and walked out the garage door, and as the door clicked shut, there was a momentary silence in the room.

"You'll have to excuse my husband," said Mary. "He doesn't make time for others very well."

Steele stood up, with Walker following suit.

"Thank you for your time, Mrs. Seavers," said Steele.

#

Next in line was the home of Star and Sunflower, masked in the misty light, with just a few lights shining dimly through the fog. Steele thought of the interviews they had done following the untimely death of Thomas Hoffman. He was deeply dissatisfied with the answers to his questions, but more disturbed knowing that there was a murderer loose in this small community and no one seemed to care about it. What was wrong with these people? Didn't they worry about their own safety? Or was it more a case of the deceased died for reasons unrelated to them? Either way, Steele would keep at it, asking his questions, looking for guilt in the eye of the beholder, a off phrase, a shifty eye, or anything else that would help him break open this case.

"All this walking is making me sweat," said Walker. "Even with the damp air, I feel like I'm burning up inside."

"It's just exercise, Kevin. What would you do if you had to run down a suspect?'

"I could do it," said Walker. "I just wouldn't like it much. Are you sure this isn't your way of keeping my weight down?"

"Walking up and down the lanes of West Harbor isn't exactly like running a marathon."

"Feels like it to me," said Walker. "This is a waste of time, as far as I'm concerned. Jones is our killer, I know it. He went to prison for killing a guy and Chambers was going to expose him, so he killed Chambers, and the old guy saw it, so Jones killed him as well."

"There's only one problem with that theory," said Steele as they approached the house.

"And what's that?"

Steele stopped and looked at Walker. "If Jones did do the killing, and I'm not saying he didn't, why would he care if people found out that he did time down in Chino? It shouldn't affect the way he lives his life now."

"History of violence, boss. Jones wasn't afraid that people would find out about his past, he's simply a violent man and was pushed too far. So he killed Chambers, and doesn't want to go back to prison. I've got it all figured out. You'll see. Jones did the job. This is a total waste of time."

"Indulge me," said Steele. He knocked on the door and they stood back and waited.

The door opened and an angry Star faced them. "Now what? You come to accuse me of killing off Old Tom?"

"May we come in?"

Star stood off to one side. "Be my guest, but don't stay long. Me and my old lady are having a discussion and don't need your input."

They followed Star into the big room where they saw the new Sunflower, nee Tracy, dressed in a pair of form fitting blue jeans and a save the whales T-shirt, but that isn't what caught the detectives eye. The old hippie Sunflower, with her long flowing red hair and flowery dress was replaced by a stylish young woman sporting an a-line haircut that ended just below her ears, with make-up expertly applied. She looked absolutely stunning.

Steele was amused by how the transformation affected Star and Walker. While the former looked upset at the change, Walker was practically drooling over her new appearance.

"Welcome to the land of the Stepford wives," said Star, sweeping his hand over the room and ending on his wife.

"Ignore Harry," said Tracy, "Please come in and ask your questions."

"Like why you decided to become one of them?" asked Star, crossing the room. "You looked fine before, why change?"

"It wasn't fine before," said Tracy, stepping around Star.

"You look like a high school cheerleader," spat Star.

She twirled around and glared at Star, her hands on her hips. "What's wrong with that?"

"You always hated the cheerleader type. It's all her doing isn't it? I bet Mary Seavers put you up to this, right?"

"Wrong."

"I don't think so. Dude, you don't look normal. What happened to my sweet little Sunflower? I want her back."

"She's gone, dude. This is who I am. And the name is Tracy. You got that, Harold?"

"I don't go by that name."

Steele pushed himself between the two. "Enough. Let's sit down and talk. I've got a few questions for you both, then we'll leave you alone to work out your differences."

The two looked at Steele, then nodded. Since there was no couch, and only a futon and a bean bag chair in the living room, they moved to the kitchen, pulling up seats at the scarred wood table.

"I need to know where you two were between dinner time last night and this morning," said Steele.

Star shrugged. "Here. Where else, dude? I got, like, no other place to go. Me and the princess over there have been doing nothing but talking about her new look and how disgusting I am since yesterday afternoon."

"As much as I'd like to disagree with him," said Tracy, "what he says is true. We didn't go anywhere yesterday."

"How about last night?" asked Walker, finally finding his voice. He had eyes only for Tracy, seemingly mesmerized by her new look.

"I went to bed around eight," said Tracy. "He spent the night on the futon. I can't give him an alibi for the night."

"I was here!" exploded Star. "What are you trying to pull here, Tracy? You trying to get me arrested? Is that your plan? I was here all night, by myself, getting a crappy nights rest on the futon." He stared at Tracy, with a scowl. "A man is supposed to sleep with his wife, not on the couch. If you were a decent wife you wouldn't have made me do it, but you don't care about me, do you? It's all about Tracy, the little princess who only cares about herself."

"Look who's talking about selfish? All you care about is your precious music. Like it matters who played saxophone in some stupid quartet that nobody every heard of. You watch yourself, Harold, I might just have to do something about that music collection of yours."

Star popped out of the chair. "You touch my stuff and I'll take care of you."

"The way you took care of Old Tom?"

"Enough!" Steele put his hand out between the two. "One last question and we'll be on our way. Do you have any idea who might want to kill Mr. Hoffman?"

That stopped them. For a brief moment, silence filled the room.

"Not a clue, dude," said Star. "He was like a grandfather dude. The town elder."

Tracy shook her head, a tear forming in the corner of her eye. "He was a nice man who didn't deserve to die that way."

"Did either of you see anyone around the school house last night?" asked Steele.

They both shook their heads.

"We've been going at it pretty hard," said Star. "Genesis hid in his room, but I know the little dude heard what we said. I kinda of feel sorry about that, but sometimes the emotion just won't stay inside. Me and Tracy have some things we gotta work out. I can't speak for Tracy, but I wasn't paying much attention to stuff that was happening outside, it's been pretty intense in here."

Tracy nodded her agreement. "I wish we could tell you something that might help. I for one, hope you find the loser that did that to Old Tom."

Star seconded her sentiment. "We may not agree on some other stuff, but on that one we're together. Find the dude."

There wasn't much more to get from this interview, thought Steele. Perhaps there was more to their story, but that would come out later. If there was a later. They saw themselves out the front door and entered the mist.

"What did you make of that, Kevin?"

"Other than the fact that she's a total babe?"

"Yes, other than that."

"That Star doesn't have an alibi," said Walker. "With his wife and child in their respective rooms, he could have left the house, went to the old school house, killed Thomas Hoffman, and returned home without anyone being the wiser. How's that, boss?"

Steele nodded. "That is exactly correct. I'm glad you caught that part. That still leaves us where we were before. Lots of suspects and few alibis. There's a reason Hoffman was killed, and I believe Franklin hit it right. He saw the person responsible for the Chambers murder and died for it. If only he had told us what he knew earlier, he'd still be alive."

"So what's next?"

"We just keep at it," said Steele. "Sooner or later, our killer will make a mistake, and when he or she does, we'll be there to make the arrest."

9. Back to the Cop Shop.

The fog had lifted by early Tuesday afternoon, leaving a clear sky and unobstructed view of the apartments across the parking lot past the morgue, but giving Steele no clarity in his case. The first murder was simple. Tony Chambers was a man who irritated people and finally ran into someone who put a stop to it. Simple anger, simple murder. But the killing of Thomas Hoffman was something altogether different. Perhaps it was as Franklin said. Hoffman had seen the killer and died because of this knowledge. But the question remained, how did the killer know that Hoffman had seen him or her? Nearly impossible, unless Hoffman was in plain sight during the first killing, in that the killer had seen him, say on the bluff, or on the beach, and the killer knew that he had been seen. But that begged the question, if the killer had seen Hoffman, why did he wait three days to kill again? And why the schoolhouse? Then it hit Steele. Hoffman must have contacted the killer and arranged to meet at the schoolhouse. But why? To tell the killer that he had seen the act? Why would Hoffman do that? Steele stared out at the parking lot and thought of possible reasons.

The ringing phone disturbed his thoughts. Steele picked up the receiver. "Steele here."

"I've got some information for you," said Lawton, "If you and Sam Spade would like to come visit."

"We'll be right down," said Steele. He replaced the receiver on the hook, then looked at Walker, busy ready reports. "Ready for another trip to the morgue?"

Walker visibly paled. "Could you go without me? Lunch didn't agree with me and I don't want to throw up in front of Eddie. He'll just make fun of me."

Steele shook his head. "Come on, Kevin. This is what we do. Besides, Eddie will make more fun of you if you don't go."

"True, but that doesn't mean I'm happy about it."

"You sure you want to be a homicide detective? What happens when you get promoted to Lieutenant and have to do this stuff without me?"

"That'll be years from now," said Walker, pushing himself to his feet. "And by then, maybe I'll be used to the smell. It's not the dead body that bothers me, it's the way they smell laying on the table. Or maybe it's the chemicals down there. I'm not sure, but something about that place makes me want to run."

Steele grabbed his coat and headed for the door. "You're safer with the dead than with the living, don't you know that?"

"The living don't smell as bad."

"Obviously, you haven't spent much time on the wharf."

They left their cubicle and headed down the broad staircase, then out the back door and across the parking lot to the morgue. This time around, Shirley Withers was in place behind the desk, her gray shag haircut and half glasses were the only thing that could be seen above the partition. It wasn't until the detectives reached the desk that they saw the corpulent woman, with a paisley shawl busy working on a log book. She looked up at their arrival.

"Hiya, Ben. How's Arly and the kids?"

"Fine," said Steele. "How's Arnie?"

"My stupid husband is still working on that stupid model railroad of his. Lord knows how much money he's put into it so far." Shirley noticed Walker rolling in behind Steele. "Hiya, Kevin. Did you take some Dramamine before coming down here? I know how sensitive your stomach is."

"I'm fine," Walker muttered.

"That's nice," said Shirley. "You boys can go on back, Eddie's waiting for you."

They crossed behind the desk and headed down the long hallway, their shoes clacking on the old tile floor as they reached the entrance to the anatomy room. The same gray walls met them, along with the chemical smells, and in the center of the room, stood Eddie Lawton, wearing his not so white lab coat over his pale green scrubs. Lawton looked up at this arrival.

"Thanks for coming down so quickly," said Lawton. "I found out something pretty interesting. Come here, let me show you."

Steele walked over and joined Lawton standing over the body of Thomas Hoffman, laying face up on the Gurney, a sheet covering him from the neck down. In death, Hoffman's gray face looked serene and quiet. Lawton pulled the sheet down to the waist, revealing a thin, hollow chested Hoffman.

"See these marks on the arms? From the look of the welts, I'd say he was hit with something thin and strong. A piece of rebar, maybe an iron pipe. Now, look at the wounds on the back of the head?"

The two leaned over to better see the deep gashes on the back and side of Hoffman's head.

"Long and thin marks. Very similar to that on the back of the arms, but this time there were many more indentations. The single blow on Chamber's head was sufficient to kill him, but this time, there were a least a half dozen blows, with several ones that grazed the skull, before the final two did the job, and judging from the blood flow, post mortem, I'd say that the killer applied several additional blows for good measure. This man was dead before the beating stopped."

"Kevin, you want to see this?" asked Steele.

"I'm good," said Walker from his place against the back wall.

Lawton looked over at the chubby sergeant. "You sure you're a homicide detective, Walker? This is part of the job, son."

"I can see fine from here," said Walker.

"No you can't," said Lawton. "Man up and come over here and see what I'm talking about."

Walker pushed himself away from the wall, and cautiously crossed to the center stage, holding onto his stomach as he neared the body. When he reached the body, he glanced down a the gray face and the thin chest, and started to waver. Instinctively, he grabbed the side of the gurney to keep from falling over.

"Good boy, Spade," said Lawton. "Now, look at the blows. See the ones on the arms? Defensive action. And the ones on the back of the head? See them, Spade?"

Walker's eyes danced along the areas of interest, before settling in on the blows on the back of the head, cleaned up and hair removed to better show the damage.

"What do you see?" asked Lawton.

"Besides the dead guy?" asked Walker. He leaned in closer, holding one hand over his nose and breathing through his mouth. "The blows aren't symmetrical, indicating that the assailant was flailing away at this poor guy, hitting what he could. I'd say the fellow that did this kind of damage was in a rage at the time of the killing."

Lawton stood back and smiled. "Good work, son, that's exactly what I wanted you to see. Give you some time and you might end up a homicide man after all."

Steele watched the interaction with amusement. He knew what Lawton was doing, in fact approved of the act, and was gratified to see Walker step up to the plate.

"Anything else, Eddie?"

"I haven't had a chance to do much with the rest of him, but I thought you might want to know about the state of mind of the killer. I'll let you know if I find out anything else of interest."

"Thanks, Eddie," said Steele.

Lawton looked over at Walker. "Good work, Spade."

The detectives left the morgue, waving goodbye to Shirley along the way, then re-entered the sunlight of the now warm afternoon. Walker looked pleased with himself.

"You okay?" asked Steele.

Walker smiled. "Never better."

#

By the end of the work day, Steele and Walker were no closer to solving the mystery than they were at the beginning, with one more unsolved on the books.

They reviewed notes and interviews and all the forensic evidence that had been accumulated for the two murders, and in the end, they were stumped. Steele spent the afternoon thinking of the possible suspects, amazed and unhappy with the number of people who might have had something to do with the murders, all without alibi's, all with a reason to kill. The evidence in the death of Thomas Hoffman proved to be even more dissatisfying for he was a well liked resident of the community, and his death seemed to hit several people hard. So what did Hoffman know? Who did he see? And did this knowledge cause his death?

At five o'clock the two detectives went their separate ways. Walker had plans to get together with a few friends, and Steele went home to his family.

Though it was early evening on this semi-warm October evening, Steele still made the time to do a little home maintenance before dinner. The gutters needed to be cleaned out, something that he had been putting off for a month, but with the upcoming winter rains, he needed to get the job done, and this was as good a day as any. He changed into his jeans and a denim work shirt, set the ladder alongside the house and scooped out the dead leaves and gunk that filled the narrow cavity, dropping the mess onto the ground. He made quick work of the back, going up and down the ladder, moving it from one side of the house to the other, then raked the debris into a black plastic bag, tied the top and dropped the whole thing into the garbage can alongside the garage. It was nice manual labor that kept his hands busy while he mulled over the case.

Steele wasn't sure what to make of the lies and half truths he was sure the residents of West Harbor told him. Was Louella innocent in the death of her husband when she had the most to gain by his demise? Was Thomas Jones truly reformed from his past life of danger? Was Star anybody of consequence that might wish either of the deceased dead? Too many suspects. And too many possibilities.

Steele took the ladder around to the front of the house and repeated the process, climbing up and down, moving the ladder, scooping out the matted leaves, then finally raking up the mess into a large black plastic garbage bag, a twist tie, and joining the other one in the can. He was just putting the ladder away when Arly stuck her head out the door.

"You almost finished, Ben? Dinner's ready."

"As much as I can do today."

Steele smiled at his pretty wife, and followed her into the kitchen. "Smells good in here, what are you cooking?"

"Chicken Divan, with mushrooms and au gratin potatoes." she leaned in and gave him a quick kiss. "You better clean up, you smell like rotten leaves."

Steele left her in the kitchen, passed the boys sprawled out on the living room floor watching TV, then down the hall and into the master bedroom. He stripped off the work clothes and hopped into the shower, did a quick wash, then got dressed in his brown suit, dress shirt and tie, and headed back to join the rest of his family.

Ten minutes later, they were seated at the table, with Steele and his wife at the two ends and the boys on opposite sides in the middle. The surface was covered with steaming chicken and potatoes and green beans and rolls. After a quick prayer of thanks, Arly filled the plates for the boys, then herself, while Steele filled his own plate. Soon, they got down to the business of eating.

"Did anything happen at school today?" Steele asked the boys.

"You bet," said Devin. "Genesis got into a fight with Jimmy Conlin that the teacher had to break up. It was awesome. Oh, sorry, he don't like being called Genesis no more."

"Doesn't like being called Genesis anymore," corrected Arly.

"Whatever," said Devin. "He told everybody that his name is Mike and he traded his tie dyed shirt for Trevor's old forty-nine shirt, which is old and has a hole under the armpits, but Mike didn't care. He said he didn't want to wear tie dyed stuff anymore."

"So what was the fight about?" asked Steele.

"Jimmy called him a hippie loser, like usual, only this time, Genesis, or Mike, or whatever, decided to fight. He can't fight, swings like a girl, and some of the other boys were ready to join in, but Cindy Seavers gave them the eye and they backed off. She sure is a hottie. She was right there for him, telling him to punch Jimmy in the eye. It was so cool."

"Fighting isn't the answer to everything," said Steele. "Is this Jimmy boy a bully?"

"Nah," said Devin. "He likes Cindy and thinks he can impress her is he beats someone up, which is kinda stupid when she likes Genesis, Mike, not that the kid knows. He's pretty dense sometimes."

"How well do you get along with him?" asked Steele.

"He's a weirdo, dad. I don't hang out with him. I told you, he can't play sports, doesn't know cars, or super heros, or any cool video games. It's like he lives in some kind of time warp. Basically, I feel sorry for the kid, having nothing good to play with and from what I hear, no television, no games, nothing but some smelly goats."

"That's the way his parents want to raise him, that's their business," said Arly. "How would you like it if someone criticized the way we were raising you?"

"I'd smack him upside his head," said Devin. He thought for moment, then grinned. "Okay, maybe I wouldn't, but I get your point. I should be nice to the kid, right?"

"That's right," said Steele. He looked at his younger son. "How about you, Aaron. Did anything exciting happen today for you?"

Aaron talked for the rest of dinner, telling one story after the next about his class project, the "mysteries of the far east", and his classmates, and the funny way that his friend can blow milk out his nose, and how the teacher farted in class and everybody laughed, and about the movie they saw on butterflies, and on as the food on the plates disappeared.

Arly had baked apple pie for desert that all enjoyed. Then it was time to clean up after dinner, with the boys chattering the entire time as they helped bus the dishes, and carry the remains of the dinner to the kitchen. Then Arly rinsed the dishes, putting the leftover in Tupperware, and Steele loaded the dishwasher.

Afterwards, the family settled into the living room, with Steele and Arly on the couch, and the boys on the floor, and they put on a family movie about a gentle bear. It looked to be a nice ending to a busy day, when the phone rang.

Steele looked at his wife. "I better get it."

"Why not just let the machine pick it up."

Too late. Steele was already off the couch and over to the phone by the kitchen. He caught the phone on the fourth ring.

"Steele residence, Ben speaking. What? Okay, I'll be right there." He hung up and walked over to his wife. "I've got to go to West Harbor."

"At this hour? Why?"

"There's a domestic disturbance in progress that needs my attention."

"Why can't they just send out a deputy?"

"Because it involves one of my suspects. Sorry, honey, I've got to go." He leaned over and kissed his wife. "Don't wait up, this might take awhile."

#

There was a lot of noise coming from the barn sitting on the far eastern edge of West Harbor by the time Ben Steele rolled up. He had made one quick stop to pick up Walker on the way, they rolled north on the trunk highway as fast as they could go. Already sitting in front of the driveway was a deputy sheriff's car, and a half dozen locals, standing in the near darkness, watching the scene unfold.

Steele pushed past the Seavers, the Groves, and the Peterson's on his way to the front door. The door was wide open, with light spilling out onto the broken sidewalk, with loud voices flying out of the structure, indistinct, yet heated.

"Come on, Kevin, let's see what's going on."

They entered the home and saw Star and Tracy standing feet apart with Wally, the deputy Sheriff, standing between them.

"I can't believe you'd do that to me, after all I've done for you," shouted Star.

"You hit me," shouted Tracy.

"You broke my records!"

"You're lucky I didn't break them over your head."

Star spun around the deputy and swatted Tracy, knocking her head back. "You know how much those albums cost? Those were collector's items."

Tracy stepped back, a little blood dripping from the side of her mouth. "I don't care. You lied to me."

Steele took it all in, the two combatants, the knocked over furniture, and most importantly, the small child hovering in the doorway leading to the bedroom with abject fear on his face. It was clear that the boy had never seen such a spectacle in his life, and for that brief moment, Steele felt sorry for the little boy. Steele did what he had to do. He walked between the two and held out his arms, keeping the two fighters apart.

"Listen up," said Steele. "This is over as of right now. Do you hear me?"

Star tried to get by Steele. "She started it. Like dude, out of nowhere she comes in accusing me of killing off Old Tom and how I was a killer and a liar, then she started breaking my records, like was that necessary? I mean, dude, what was I supposed to do?"

"Stop being a liar for one," spat Tracy from across the room. "And a husband isn't supposed to hit his wife."

"I barely touched you, dude," said Star, pushing his long hair out of his face. "If I wanted to hit you, I would have smacked you from here to sundown. You don't know what a hit is."

"That's enough," said Steele. "Kevin, take Star over to the corner and get his statement."

Walker took Star by the elbow and led him away, with Star complaining the whole way.

"Just look what she done to my collection. Dude, there were some valuable albums that she destroyed."

Steele nodded at Wally, who had taken up a position in front of Tracy to protect her from further attacks. "I'll take it from here, Wally. Can you make sure the boy is okay?"

"Sure thing, Lieutenant."

Steele watched the deputy walk over and kneel down so that he was face to face with Genesis, their voices low and unheard from ten feet away. Steele directed his attention to Tracy.

"Are you okay?"

"I'm alright," said Tracy. "I don't know what came over me. We haven't been getting along very well since I've decided to stop being Sunflower. I guess he needed to keep me pigeon holed as his little hippie wife, then Tony Chambers comes to town and he got all secretive and nothing's been the same ever since."

"How many times did he hit you?"

"A couple of times. To tell you the truth, I'm a little afraid of him right now. For all I know, he could be the one who killed both of them, and living right here with me. I just don't know him like I thought I did. Not that he ever talked much of his past, and that didn't bother me much before, but when Tony Chambers came along, it suddenly become something bad. I'm not sure what happened to Star, but something did and he's not been the same easy going guy he's been the last ten years. All of the sudden, he's all secretive and sullen. He's definitely hiding something, and I'm afraid of what it might be."

"You said you're afraid of him. Would you like to press charges? We can take him with us and maybe find out what he's not telling you."

She looked over Steele's shoulder at her husband being interviewed by Walker. Star was waving his hands, pushing his hair out of his face, then looked over at Genesis, deep in conversation with the deputy.

"I would like to press charges," she said.

"Fine," said Steele. "We'll take him with us. In the meantime, will you be okay alone out here?"

"You mean with a murderer out on the loose? Maybe Star is the killer and I don't have to worry anymore."

"Do you think he did the killings?"

She shook her head. "Honestly? I don't know what to think anymore other than the fact that he's not the man I married. I don't know what's going on with him, but I would feel better knowing. Even if it's bad, at least I could deal with it, this uncertainty is eating me up. You take him in and see what you can get out of him. I haven't been too successful."

"We'll do that," said Steele. "And you can decide tomorrow if you want to file assault charges, okay?"

She smiled at him. "That would be okay, I guess. It's a terrible thing, suspecting your spouse of murder, isn't it?"

"Not ideal, no." Steele took a card out of his pocket and handed it to her. "If you need police protection, give me a call and I'll see to it, okay?"

The detectives left with a subdued Star in tow. The neighbors were still there, but no one said a word as Walker helped Star into the back seat, then slid in next to him. Steele looked at the faces watching them and wondered if he had the killer, or if he or she was still out there. He started the car and took off.

#

Star was booked and fingerprinted in the Rock Port police station, then taken across the parking lot to the jail, housed in the same building as the morgue, with the morgue on the south side of the building and the jail on the north. The front room of the jail was small, with a desk, manned by the sergeant of the watch, behind this office, were the two interrogation rooms, followed by the cells, all ten of them, with a short hallway between the line of five. At this moment, only two were occupied when Star was brought in, a drunk and disorderly man named Flowers who was currently sleeping off his battle with the bottle in the first cell to the left, and a transient in the opposite cell who had made the mistake of trying to shop lift four bottles of wine from a local store. The rest of the cells were empty. Two uniformed officers put Star in the second cell on the right, closed the door with a resounding clank that echoed off the walls.

"How long am I going to be here?" asked Star, his forearms resting on the cross bars of his cell.

"That depends," said one of the uniforms.

"On what?"

"On whether your old lady presses charges."

The two officers left the cell area, closing the steel door behind them, leaving Star with a passed out gentlemen across the short hall and a transient in the cell adjacent to his own.

Star sat down on the cot in his cell and worried. Just how much trouble was he in? And more importantly, were his fingerprints on file? Rock Port was a long way from Los Angeles, he reasoned, and they probably didn't have a state of the art computer system for tracking criminals. At least that's what he told himself. In the meantime, there was nothing more he could do but wait it out. He felt anger toward Sunflower. How could she do this to him? Would she really press charges against him? Wasn't it bad enough that she destroyed half of his albums? Fear gripped him hard. He rolled onto the bed and stared up at the ceiling and thought about what might happen to him.

"You got a cigarette?"

Star turned his head and saw the transient, with his full white beard and missing teeth, and three layers of clothes. "I don't smoke."

"How about something to drink? Got any wine on you?"

"I don't drink."

"You're kidding, right? Everybody drinks. I drink. All my friends drink. What's the matter with you that you don't drink? You think you're better than me?"

"Leave me alone," said Star turning away from the transient, his face to the empty cell on the other side.

"You can't ignore me," said the transient. "I've got the right to free speech. I can say whatever I want to. It's a free country. You can't make me shut up. Just try and see where it gets you. I can talk all I want."

Star put the pillow over his ears to drown out the transient's raving, which helped muffle the voice, but didn't silence the speaker, nor stifle the stench of body odor, old whiskey and bad oral hygiene that floated into his cell like a cloud of stink.

"So now you don't to talk to me? You suck, mister. I thought hippies were supposed to be full of love and all that crap. You ain't no hippie. You're a hippie in disguise. I'll bet you vote Republican. I bet you drive one of them fancy cars. Look at me, you piece of crap. Quit ignoring me. I hate it when people ignore me. I've got constitutional rights you know. You talk to me, mister."

Star pulled the pillow tighter against his ears, trying to stop the flow of verbal abuse coming from the transient. What seemed like an eternity only last ten minutes, with the volume rising with each invective.

The door flew open and the desk sergeant stood next to the transient's cell. "Shut up, Willie."

The transient shifted his gaze to the man in uniform. "Or what? You going to beat me? Tie me up and give me the water torture? Maybe punch me in the face? Wouldn't be the first time."

The sergeant walked over to the transient's cell. "Put a lid on it, Willie, or we'll up the charges and send you down to prison. They love hobo's in prison."

That shut him up. Star looked over at the conversation, wondering just what happened to hobo's in prison, but he didn't really care. All he wanted was some peace and quiet where he could think of a way to get out of situation.

The sergeant left and the transient sat down on his cot, staring at Star. In a quiet voice, the bum said: "I still see you, hippie boy. I'm not done with you yet. You just wait, I can talk all night if I have to and there ain't a damn thing you can do about it."

Star lay back on his cot and worried about his predicament, and the likelihood of listening to the ranting of a transient all night. He closed his eyes and tried to picture a meadow, with a warm breeze and fluffy clouds. Peace and harmony. Love and tranquility. He could hear the muttering of the transient, but it was in the background. The events of the day had mentally and physically worn him out and he fell into that state between sleep and awake, trying desperately to reach a place of quiet salvation.

"Time to talk, Harold."

Star sat up and tried to get his bearings, then it came back to him in a hurry. Detective Steele stood on the opposite side of the bars, nodding at him.

"The name is Star."

Steele nodded at the sergeant. "Let him out, Bill."

The sergeant took a large key off his chain and opened the cell door. Steele entered and took Star by the arm and led him out the door.

"Come on, Harold," said Steele.

"I told you, my name is Star."

Steele looked at him and smiled. "Not according to your police record."

At that moment, Star knew that the game was up. They knew who he was. It was now just a matter of time before his entire criminal record would be thrown in his face. This was the moment he had been dreading for the past ten years. What would happen now? Would he face jail time? Would they send him back to Los Angeles to serve his time? Would he have to shame his family again? He let himself be guided through the steel door and into the interrogation room on the right.

Detective Sergeant Kevin Walker was already inside the drab walled room, sitting at the scarred table. The room looked like a tomb, with faded yellow tiled floor, institutional green walls, no windows, and one old table. Steele sat Star down on the lone chair on one side of the table, then turned and closed the door before joining Walker on the opposite side. There was a small stack of papers on the table in front of Walker.

"So, Harold," said Steele. "We ran your prints through the computer and came up with a lot of interesting things. You lied to us, Harold. Your last name is not Gaithers, it's Caithers. Close, but no cigar. And according to your records, you did three runs in Juvie down in Los Angeles, and were a known accomplice with a couple of fellows who did home invasion robberies in the Hollywood hills." Steele picked up the top sheet and glanced at it. "One Frank Andrews and a fellow named Terry Mills who was killed by a retired deputy sheriff. Sound familiar? Says here that there is an outstanding

warrant with your name on it. It seems like you left some
unfinished business down south."

"That was a long time ago," said Star. "I'm not the
guy I was back then."

"Still," said Walker, "It shows a life of crime."

Star raised one hand. "Whoa. Dude, that was a
long time ago. That isn't who I am now."

Steele leaned in and eyed Star. "Really. How
about this for a scenario, Harold. You were part of that
home robbery where your buddy got himself shot, you run
and hide and then along come Tony Chambers who says
he's going to blow the lid off your secret life, so you kill
him, and then along comes Tom Hoffman saying he saw
you do the killing, so you kill him as well. How am I
doing so far?"

Star sat back in his seat and began to sweat. "This
is so wrong. Dudes, I couldn't have done any of that."

"You saying my story isn't true?" asked Steele.

Star licked his lips. "Look, maybe some of what
you said is true. Not that I'm saying I had anything to do
with that home robbery thing. I knew Frankie and Terry,
and I heard that he got shot, but that doesn't mean I was
with them. You can't prove otherwise. And sure, I got
into some trouble when I was a kid, who doesn't? But that
don't make me a killer."

"Maybe it does and maybe it doesn't," said Steele.
"But I bet if we sweat you long enough, you'll cop to the
killings."

"I thought I was here because I hit my old lady a
couple of times."

"That's what brought you in, yes," said Steele.
"But that isn't the only crime we're looking at. Right

now, you're number one on a very short list of possible guilty parties. You want to make a confession now and plea bargain for a better deal, let me know."

Star clammed up. This was a nightmare that had no end. He crossed his arms and stared at the two detectives.

"Why did you do it, Harold?" asked Walker. "Tell us and get it off your chest. I know you want to tell someone."

Star looked from one to the other. He only had one last thing to say. "I want a lawyer."

10. What happened to our little town?

It was a bright sunny Wednesday morning with a light wind coming off the ocean, bringing in the scent of salt and a freshness that seemed to wash over West Harbor, bringing a new beginning. Bonnie looked out the window of the post office and watched the big yellow school bus pick up the children and head up north, over the hill and on to pick up more children, and then all was quiet in their little village. Changes were coming to her little town that she had no control over and it made her feel decidedly uneasy. She turned and faced her morning tasks with trepidation, uncomfortable for the first time in years with her routine. It just didn't seem right, she thought, filing the letters and circulars into the correct boxes, that she should be doing such mundane things when there was murder afoot. Still, what else could she do? The mail had to go out.

Bonnie finished her tasks, then turned and walked over to the front door, staring out the window. Why wasn't Adam Franklin on his way with her steaming cup of coffee like every other morning? He'd been coming over so long that he was a part of the routine, so where was he? She looked over at Franklin's neat little bungalow across the street. The house was closed up. Where was he? She flipped the closed sign to open, then made sure that all the shipping labels were stocked as well as the change of address forms and the bin holding the mailing boxes was full, then turned and walked behind the counter and sat on her stool and thought of her existence.

Was this what she expected from life? Waiting on customers, watching life from the comfort of her stool? Waiting for something to happen to her? Life had happened to her all too much for her to do much other than sit and watch. Her mother died, then her father, and somewhere along the line, she became post mistress and her life was settled, but what about all the things she missed in life? Where were the husband, children, and all that went with that? Where were her big holiday celebrations? Graduations? Homecoming dances? All seemed to bypass her and now it was too late. Suddenly, she felt very sad about her life.

Bonnie stared out the window and thought these things, wishing that she had done things differently. Somehow, the two murders didn't affect her all that much. Tony Chambers was a bully who deserved to die, and Old Tom really missed his wife, so his murder, while brutal, seemed okay for he was now with her. But what about Bonnie Williams? What about her life? Should she chuck it all, move to San Diego, and maybe marry a nice retiree? Was it truly too late for her? Or was she stuck with inertia, living out the remainder of her life in her home town? She looked up at the sight of Louella approaching the front door.

Louella opened the door and entered the post office. She looked like an old Russian woman, bundled up in a heavy overcoat, her neck and face covered with a tan scarf, with only her thatch of curly gray hair and thick glasses visible.

"Good morning," said Louella, unwrapping her scarf. "It's gotten so cold lately. I had to throw on extra wood."

"It's not that bad out there, is it?"

"Cold," said Louella. "But it may just be me. It seems like I've been cold every day since Tony died, and lord knows that was a blessing. You heard about the house and all that? Of course you did, the whole town knows, I'm sure. Anyway, he's gone and it seems like he took the warmth with him. At least the fog is gone. Wasn't that awful?"

Bonnie pushed off the stool. "Terrible." She grabbed Louella's mail from the slot and returned to the counter. She handed it to Louella. "So how is it with Margaret back in town. Are you having a nice visit?"

Louella shook her head. "You want the honest truth? She's driving me crazy. She has this insane notion that Young Tom is interested in her, which is the silliest thing I've ever heard. He's at least twice her age, and I don't mean to be mean, but my daughter isn't exactly a beauty queen."

"He likes her like that, does he?"

Louella nodded. "I find it hard to believe, don't you?"

"Well you never know with men," said Bonnie. "Did you hear about Star and Sunflower? I mean Tracy, she doesn't want to be called Sunflower anymore."

"I heard the police come, but I didn't want to talk to them anymore. Honestly, I didn't care about Tony, but it wasn't right about Old Tom. You, me and Old Tom were the oldest residents in town, and now he's gone. I just feel like a hole's been cut in my heart. I can't believe that someone would want to harm that nice old man."

"He wasn't always nice," said Bonnie, "not that I want to speak ill of the dead, but Old Tom could be a mean drunk in his day. You weren't around here, like I was, when he worked the boats. Lordy, those men could drink. That was back in the day when the Anchor Steam Bar was still around, but I agree with you. Something's happened to our little town and I don't know if it will ever be the same again."

"Personally, I just want to be left alone. I hate to say this, but I wish Peggy would just go home and leave me be. All she does is complain about this and that, like I can help her out, but that doesn't stop her, and I'm sick and tired of talking to the police about these awful murders. You want my opinion, I'm glad they took Star away. Maybe that will be the end of this and we can go back to the way we were."

"You think he did the killings?"

"I have no idea, but the police are pretty smart fellows, so if they think he did it, then he probably did."

"They took him away for hitting Tracy, not murder."

"That was just an excuse to take him down to Rock Port where they could put the screws to him. You mark my words, Bonnie, he did it. You saw him argue with Tony, and from what I heard, he had a violent streak. You can never tell about some people, and even though he looked harmless to us, inside, he was stone cold killer. But the police have him now, and everything will be fine. Now, all I've got to do is get Peggy to go home." She wrapped her scarf around her face and nodded to Bonnie. "Stay warm."

Bonnie watched her leave. Was it that simple? Star did the murders? And what about Young Tom being interested in Margaret? Nobody was interested in

Margaret, at least not in that way. With Star caught, would things go back to normal? And more importantly, was this what she wanted? She sighed and stared out the window.

#

Tracy sipped her coffee and looked across the kitchen table at Mary Seavers. She could hear Bill Seavers pounding on something through the door leading to the garage. Her mind was in turmoil, wondering just what she should do. She told Mary all of what had transpired the night before and Mary had listened quietly, not commenting until Tracy finished her telling, then the two sat and drank their coffee. The sun shone bright and cheerful through the window, casting long shadows across the table and tiled floor.

"So what are you going to do now?" asked Mary.

"I'm not sure," said Tracy. "I can't very well leave Star down in jail, even if he deserves it, but the thing is, I'm not sure that I should let him out. I mean, as long as I'm waiting to press charges, the police can do their thing and see if Star is guilty of more than just slapping me around."

"Do you honestly see Star as a double murderer?"

"I have no idea. I can't say that I really know my husband, even after all these years." Tracy sipped her coffee. "His real names is Harold Caithers, he has a juvenile record of stealing cars and was suspected of being part of a home invasion robbery deal in the houses above Hollywood, and ran off when one of his partners got killed in the middle of a robbery. He ran and changed his name, grew his hair long and became Star."

"So he has a past," said Mary. "That doesn't make him a murderer."

"No, it makes him a liar. He never told me any of that, and probably wouldn't have if Tony Chambers hadn't come to town and got himself killed. I could have gone blindly through life as the wife of a murderer and wouldn't know it."

"Star a killer? Is that what's bothering you? If so, I don't think you have to worry about that. So he has a past, big deal. Hasn't he been the model of peace and harmony since you've known him?"

Tracy thought about that for a moment. "True. He hasn't hurt a fly, but you're right, that isn't the only issue. Aside from his lies, and maybe I can get past those, but there is still the big issue. The pink elephant in the room, so to speak. I don't want to live like a hippie anymore. I just can't do it. I want what you have. I'm not asking to live in a mansion, just a nice home, with central heat for the winter and central air for those summer days when it gets above ninety. I want a house that doesn't have holes in the ceiling, a place where you can't hear the mice in the walls, a television set–star says that TV is evil and won't have one–and a microwave oven, and nice furniture."

"How is Star supposed to give those to you on what you make as goat herders, no offense."

"That's another thing. I'm sick and tired of the goats. They smell, they make a lot of noise, and to be truthful, they bite when they're angry and they're angry a lot. So I say, get rid of the goats."

"Does Star have any skills to sell? A job he could do? Would you need him to cut his hair and conform to something he doesn't want?"

Tracy shook her head. "I don't know what I want. I don't know if Star has any skills, if you want the truth, and I doubt seriously that he would cut his hair, not that it's a deal breaker if he doesn't, but it's worse than that." she paused before speaking, then said: "the reality is, even if he changed, cut his hair, got a job and fixed the house, I'm not sure I want to be with him anymore."

"Divorce?"

"Maybe, I don't know what I'm doing. Genesis informed me this morning that he wants to be called Mike from now on, and doesn't want to be a hippie boy anymore. And I can't say I blame him. All the other little boys look and act the same and he doesn't want to stick out. Maybe he's going through the same things I am. I just don't know what to do. If I stay with Star, he's going to have to make some major changes, which I have doubts that he can do, and I still might resent the fact that he lied to me. Trust is a hard thing to get back. And if I divorce him, then what am I to do? Move back to my parents in Southern California? Get a job down in Rock Port? Go back to school? Tell me what I should do. And what about Genesis? Do I take him with me or leave him with Star? It's too much for me right now."

Mary drank more coffee, then carefully set the mug back on the table. "So what are you going to do in the immediate future, about Star being in jail and all?"

This was the issue that kept Tracy up most of the night. Was Star a murderer? Did he belong in jail? And if not a murderer, was she in danger if she didn't press charges. The last thing she needed to worry about was whether Star, once released, would turn violent against her again. He looked plenty angry when the cops took him away. Did a night in jail make him worse? He slapped her, an act of violence. Would it escalate? And say she didn't press charges and he came home, did she want him there?

"What do you think I should do?" asked Tracy.

"My advice? We take Bill's truck and go get him, and bring him home and you can tell him how you feel and what you want. If you're worried about how he'll react, you can talk to him here. If it doesn't go well, you can sleep on our couch until you figure it out. How's that?"

Tracy felt gratitude for her neighbor. She stood up and gave Mary a hug. "I couldn't do this without your help."

Mary patted Tracy on the arm. "Come on, let's go get your jailbird."

#

Adam Franklin sat in his living room and looked out the window at the post office. He could see Bonnie moving about inside, setting up for the day. He watched the school bus come and pick up the children, then head north to Monroe to pick up more of the county kids before heading back to Rock Port for the school day. Franklin was in a quandary. He had finally broached the subject of love with Bonnie and was unsure of how to proceed next. He couldn't just blurt out that he loved her, though he did, for that might scare her away. It had been a long time since he needed to woo a girl and he was out of practice. How would she react to such a pronouncement? Would she smile and say she loved him back? Or shake her head and tell him to go away? It was too much for him. He just couldn't face the rejection, but he needed to know.

The morning passed and he made himself busy, cleaning and dusting, and generally doing everything he could but go over to the post office and tell Bonnie that he loved her. He spotted Louella head to the post office and was jealous of her conversation with Bonnie. She didn't stay long, bundled up like a babushka, Louella shuffled home, leaving him with a clear view of Bonnie sitting on her stool, looking out the window. It was as if she could see right into his house, and for a moment, he worried that she might be doing just that. He shifted his chair and put some distance between he and the front window, but still giving him a view.

He glanced over his shoulder at the kitchen, where the pot of coffee sat. He had brewed a full pot of French Roast, the aroma of the dark beans floating into the living room and tickling his nose. He knew he should go pour a couple of cups and walk over to the post office. She would be waiting for him. She would be excited to see him. He smiled. More likely, she would be excited to see the coffee. He had been bringing her coffee for the past year, building a trust and an expectation, and today was the first that he had skipped the routine. Surely she would wonder what happened to him, he reasoned. Maybe she would come over and see him to see if everything was alright. He liked that idea. Bonnie concerned about his welfare. Then he worried. Maybe she didn't care if he brought coffee and it was only in his imagination that she

liked the effort. Who was he fooling? She was bright and
beautiful and he was an old widower who lived with the
memories of his dead wife. Why would she be interested
in him? He tried to push these thoughts out of his head.
He was selling himself short. He was a nice fellow who
could offer her companionship in their latter years.
Someone to share the last portion of their lives. There
weren't many others vying for the job. Why wouldn't she
want him?

Franklin sipped his coffee and noticed that he had
let it go cold. He crossed the room to the kitchen and
poured another cup, then walked back to his seat and
looked out the window. The morning passed as he sipped
his coffee, refilling the cup when it got empty, then back
to the window. As the morning hours passed, he realized
that Bonnie wasn't coming over to see him. It was
disappointing, but he came up with possible reasons for
her not doing so. She had a job to do, and couldn't leave
the post office unattended. She was respecting his
privacy, and was waiting for him to act like he always
did, bringing the coffee to her. She was busy with phone
calls. She was busy with sorting mail. He sighed. Or
maybe, she just didn't care. His emotions ran the gamut
from love to despair like a yo-yo, rebounding with each
up tick, then crashing down once again.

He spotted a moving vehicle coming from up the
lane, shifted in his seat and watched the truck pass, with
Mary Seavers and a prettied up Sunflower, now Tracy,
riding shotgun. He had heard the disturbance the night
before and watched the police haul Star away. Domestic
violence was the rumor passing through the village, but
Franklin wondered. Perhaps they were taking Star in for

questioning and wouldn't that be just fine. A murder solved and peace would come back to the village. But what if the police didn't have enough to convict? Was there still cause for worry? Franklin didn't approve of hitting a woman, under any circumstance, and felt that Star should be punished for the deed, but what about Tracy? Would they stay married after the fact? A man who hits his wife once would do it again, thought Franklin. But that wasn't his problem. His was centered on the post office.

Franklin shifted back and stared at the closed door of the post office. If only he had the nerve to walk over and profess his love. How difficult could it be? He had practiced a dozen different variations in his speech, discarding each in turn as too sappy, or too stilted, trying to come up with the exact words that would win the affections of the girl he loved. He imagined her moving in with him, and how that would change his life. He would have to pack up all his pictures of his wife and their life together, but she would have understood that he didn't want to be alone the rest of his days. She wouldn't have begrudged him some happiness. So he thought of what he would say to Bonnie, hoping for the exact right words that would get her to not only acknowledge his love, but would return the same to him.

He sipped his coffee and found that it had gone cold once more. He had enough coffee in him to float a boat. He set the cup on a nearby table and settled in, watching and waiting for Bonnie to come outside. Perhaps if he could talk to her outside the post office it would be easier. While he waited, he practiced his lines.

\#

Bill Seavers handed over his keys to his wife and Tracy. He stared at the transformation of his next door neighbor and was amazed on how good looking Tracy was. Underneath all that hippie garb was a knock out, hidden in billowing dresses, long hair and no make-up. He waved good-bye, then went back to his work, still thinking about how lucky Star was to have such a beauty married to him. Seavers then thought of his own wife, just as beautiful as Tracy, and felt a tinge of sorrow for the way he had been treating her. He knew that she wanted more intimacy, and he was being a jerk about it, but money was tight right now, and he knew what would happen if he let himself enjoy his wife in that way again. The last thing they needed was another child, something that Mary had been hinting at for some time, and even if she promised that she would use protection, a part of him didn't believe it. And the clothes she wore were driving him insane. She looked so good it hurt, and his will power was weakening.

He stared at the beginning of his next project, a cabinet, and tried to get excited about it, but was still thinking of his wife and how good she looked. Seavers took a piece of paper and some pencils and mapped out the dimensions for the cabinet, planning out the materials needed, and the sizes to be measured and cut, and thought of the murders. Anything to keep his mind off sex.

Two murders in less than a week, with several guilty parties. Seavers thought of each in turn. While he couldn't see Louella killing her husband and Old Tom, she was the one with the most to gain from Tony

Chambers untimely demise, but was she a murderer? Then there was Star, sitting in the local jail. Could he have done the killings? It didn't seem possible that the hippie had enough anger in him to do the job, or the guts to do it. Star definitely had his troubles, Seavers had heard all about the big fight from the night before, but was he capable of killing another human being? Seavers wasn't sure. That left him with Thomas Jones. What did the community really know about Jones? That he came to town a couple of years ago and opened the Super Saver, that he gouged the locals for the privilege of shopping nearby, and that he lived in the back of the store. So, where was his family? And more importantly, why did he come to West Harbor in the first place. It's not like this little village was on the way to anything. Here on the coast, all was quiet, was that what attracted Jones to West Harbor? Or was there a more sinister reason for Jones coming to town. Perhaps he was hiding out, trying to keep his past a secret, and as far as Seavers was concerned, Jones had done a pretty good job of that. Seavers didn't know a thing about the man. And he heard all about the altercation Jones had with Chambers on the day the latter died, conveniently behind the Super Saver. The more Seavers thought about it, the more likely it seemed to him that Thomas Jones was the killer. As far as Old Tom was concerned, it was probable that the Hoffman witnessed the murder and was killed to keep his silence. It all made sense. Hoffman was a man with a past, was confronted by Tony Chambers, killed Chambers, and then to cover up his crime, killed Old Tom to keep him quiet.

Seavers put down his pencil and looked out that garage door, across the field that separated his street from the Super Saver. All was quiet in the sunny landscape outside, but he knew that evil lurked just around the corner. In this case, in the form of Thomas Jones. Seavers knew that he was facing a potential killer, but he didn't care. Nobody else was willing to step up to the plate to protect this town. The new comers stayed inside, old man Franklin would probably faint dead away, leaving what? The post mistress? Seaver knew what he needed to do. He headed out the garage and started down the lane. He would solve this thing once and for all.

#

Thomas Jones sat behind the counter of his store, working his ever present crossword puzzle and thought about the recent disturbances to his peaceful existence. It was bad enough when Tony Chambers got himself killed on the beach below the Super Saver, but Old Tom's passing had created a problem that required some drastic action. He tried to not listen as the Peterson's muttered in the aisles as they picked at the can selection, and saw the look of suspicion in their eyes when they came to the counter to pay for the food. Jones watched them walk out the door, whispering to each other as they made their way up the lane past the school and wondered just what it was that they were talking about. Were they accusing him of the killings? And then there was the police, with their less than subtle approach to his situation. Certainly, Jones had a past, who didn't? But that didn't mean that he was the one doing the killings in this little town. He had come here to escape all that, but it seemed to follow him like a bad stink. It was just a matter of time before the police hauled him in for questioning, then what? Would they arrest him? Throw him in jail? Even with no proof, sometimes the police took the most likely candidate and ran him up the flag pole and Jones had to admit, he looked the guiltiest of the lot. It was just a matter of time before it got worse.

Jones drummed his fingers on the counter, unable to concentrate on his puzzle. Maybe it was time to be moving on. He didn't want to, having tied up most of his savings in the store, but he had some put aside that would carry him through in his next location, but the truth of the matter was, he didn't want to leave. He liked West Harbor, he liked being an independent business man, and he even liked the not so pretty girl up the road, even if she was half his age. She would have been good for him, he thought with sorrow, knowing that he had mostly made up his mind to leave. The pretty girls had no time for him, but he did okay with the less than pretty ones, and this one had potential, not that he would ever find out if it was to be or not.

The bell above the door rang as a customer came in. Jones looked up to see Bill Seavers standing in the door way.

"Something I can help you with?" asked Jones.

Seavers walked over to the counter and stared at Jones. "As a matter of fact, there is."

Jones waited. He could see that Seavers was worked up about something and was curious what it was.

"You don't talk about yourself much, do you?" asked Seavers. "Why is that? What are you hiding that you don't want the rest of us to know?"

Jones sat back on his chair and eyed Seavers. "I run a store, I'm not an information desk."

"So you say, but why is it that there isn't a murder in this town for over twenty years and yet we have two within a week, both within a stones throw of your store."

"You accusing me of murder?"

"Maybe I am. So what of it? We don't know you. And two people suddenly die and you're right in the middle of it. You're hiding from something and I'll bet it was something terrible. Did you kill someone somewhere and come here to hide?"

Jones put his hands on the counter and stared at Seavers. "Get out of my store. In fact, stay out of my store. You're business in not welcome here anymore."

Seavers shook his head. "That's not going to cut it, Jones. You're a murderer."

Jones came from behind the counter and grabbed Seavers by the shirt and pushed him toward the door. While Seavers might have been a pretty good high school athlete, he was no match for the powerful Jones. One second they were at the threshold, the next, they were outside. Seavers tried to punch Jones, was blocked and Jones popped the smaller man on the nose, knocking him to the ground. Jones ran over and kicked Seavers as he tried to stand up, then reached down and pulled Seavers up and pushed him away.

"Go home to your wife," said Jones. "And stay away from my store. I don't want your business."

Seavers wiped blood off his nose. "You won't get away with this, Jones. I'm going to call the police and tell them all about you."

Jones shook his head and walked back inside, the taunts of Seavers filling his ears as he walked away.

"This isn't over, Jones. I'm not done with you."

Jones let the door close, shutting out all but the dull muted sounds of Seavers still outside, pointing his fingers and shouting at the building. Jones flipped the close sign to face the street and locked the door, then headed back to his living quarters. Maybe it was time to leave. Suddenly, his peaceful existence was threatened. He pulled a suitcase off one of the nearby shelf, opened it up and lay it on the bed, then began to pack. Perhaps he had stayed longer than he should have, but there wasn't much to be done about that. It was time to move on.

11. New Evidence

Star spent the night in jail, trying to ignore the hobo at the end of the line of cells--the jailer took pity on Star and separated the two men--but it was a fitful sleep at best. The detectives brought him back to the interrogation room in the morning and hammered him with questions. What had he done in Los Angeles that sent him packing? What had he and Tony Chambers talked about that caused him distress? Were was he during the two murders? Was he a killer in disguise? Star took the questions, asked in a dozen different ways, all giving him a headache, but in the end, he was still holding his own, though he was tired and worn from the sleepless night and barrage of questions. Finally, they put him back in his cell and left him there to think about it. He lay on the bunk, staring at the ceiling. Even without a confession, Star had enough distrust of the police to believe that they could hold him indefinitely. It was the police state, he decided, that allowed them to keep him in jail, without legal recourse. He had talked to a public defender after the first go round, but the kid, being fresh out of law school, wasn't sure if the police could keep him or not. The only advice the lawyer gave Star was to keep his mouth shut, which he was already doing to the best of his ability. In the meantime, he lay on the bunk and wondered when the next session would begin.

It was all a nightmare, and as hard as it was for him to admit, it was all his fault. He should have never kept a secret from Sunflower, his beloved wife, who now hated him. Would it have mattered if he had done things differently? Say he told her about his past, would that have kept her from changing into a stepford wife? Doubtful. She would have been understanding, at least that's what he told himself, but would it have made a difference? She had changed, without giving him any warning, or had she? Was there a middle class housewife hiding inside her that he failed to see? And even if he saw the signs, what could he do about it? He was a goat herder, not exactly a lucrative profession. How was it possible to give her what she wanted? What seemed so ideal no more than a week ago was now crashing down around his feet. He liked being a hippie goat herder. The money wasn't much, but it was enough to put food on the table, but not much more. He knew that she admired the Seavers house, but so what? For a brief moment, he got angry at her, as if this whole mess what her doing. If she hadn't changed, then he wouldn't be sitting in jail, wondering if he would ever get out. But deep inside, he knew that this wasn't true. He hit her, his beautiful wife, because she broke his precious albums, all because he was afraid to tell her the truth. So here he was, ready to face possible prison time, all because he was scared of what the truth might do to his marriage. It's a sad life, he told himself. But what was the alternative? Could he change? Cut his hair, become Harold Caithers once more and make something of himself? Go back to school? Get a real job? Live in a house that looked exactly like everybody else's? He just wasn't sure it was worth the effort, but one thing he knew for certain. If he didn't change, he would lose his wife and child for they would move on without him. Suddenly, he was very depressed.

"This sucks," he said aloud.

"You talking to me, hippie?"

Star turned his head and spotted Willie the Hobo from four cells away, leering at him.

"That's right, hippie boy, I'm talking to you. Don't think I forgot how rude you were last night, but I'm willing to let bygones be bygones. You and me, we could be pals, you know, once we get out of here. I know things."

"What things?"

"You was talking in your sleep, boy, and what a mouthful you had to say. So who's this sunflower you talked about? Your sweetheart? Well you can forget about her. She's the one that put you in here, didn't she? That's right, I told you I knew things. So what are you going to do now? She don't want you back, so you got nowhere to go, am I right? Don't answer, I know it's true. So you can come with me. I've got friends. They don't mind if I bring along another lost soul. We get by, and there's plenty of good food out there that's hardly been spoiled, just a little brown around the edges, but you can scrape that off if you're hungry enough."

"I didn't say I was going to join you."

"Don't go all high and mighty on me, boy. You're in deep trouble. The police don't care about me, I'm just a pest to them, but you might go down hard. You mark my words, boy, you ain't going home to your woman. She's rid of you, you hear? Nobody wants you no more. You might as well get used to the idea."

Star put the pillow over his ears, trying to drown out the old man's words, but it wasn't working. He slammed the pillow on the bed. "Shut up! Don't talk to me."

"What's the matter, hippie boy? Truth hurts, don't it? You should be nice to me, I'm all you've got on the outside. We'll get a nice place, you and me, and then we'll be pals, right? I ain't had a pal for a long time, it'll be good to have someone to talk to again. You'll see, you and me, we're going to be best pals."

Star sprung from the cot and raced to the bars separating him from the hobo. He wanted to slap the silly grin off the hobo's face, maybe knock out the remaining teeth, but he was too far away. "Will you please shut up! I'm not going to be your pal."

"So you say," said Willie. "But in the end, you'll see that I'm right. I ain't smart, but I know things."

The sound of the opening door stopped conversation. Both jailed men stopped to look at the two uniformed men entering the cell. They passed by Willie and headed toward Star.

"You ain't gonna let him go are you?" asked Willie.

One of the uniformed officers, a young man with a clipped moustache stopped in front of Star's cell, reached into his pocket and pulled out a set of keys. Moments later, he opened the door and nodded at Star.

"Your wife dropped the charges," said the officer. "You're free to go."

#

Detective Ben Steele watched the three West Harbor residents walk across the parking lot from the jail to a large pick up truck parked in the lot. Star walked with his head down, near but not touching his wife, while Mary

Seavers walked a good ten feet away, giving them space
to talk. Even from his distance on the second floor, Steele
could see that the conversation wasn't going well. Tracy
held her arms crossed tight across her chest, looking
everywhere but at Star, while her husband moved around
like a monkey on a stick, jumping in front of her,
gesturing, waving his arms, trying to get her attention.

"He's not doing very well, is he?"

Steele turned and saw Walker staring out the other
window. "Not for lack of trying."

"She's hot," said Walker. "I don't see them
together. Maybe before, but not now. She could have
whoever she wanted, looking that good."

"Maybe she wants to stay with her husband."

"Not much chance of that," said Walker. "Look at
them. She's all closed up and he can't even get her
attention."

"It's none of our business," said Steele, "other
than whether or not Star is our killer."

Walker shook his head, standing up. "I don't see
it. Even with his juvie history, I don't see him as our
killer. First of all, can you see him taking down a man of
Tony Chamber's size? I can't, and second, he doesn't
look like he'd have the guts. I mean, look at him, he can't
even face up to his wife, how is he supposed to face down
a guy like Chambers and kill him? I just don't see it. How
about you, boss? What do you think?"

That was the question. Steele truly wanted Star to
be the killer, for it would solve the mystery, clean up the
cases, and allow him to go on a romantic weekend with
his wife, but was that the correct thing to do? Walker's
assessment seemed correct, and Steele was satisfied that

they had gotten as much as they could from Star during their two interrogations. The man simply was a weak, pathetic guy who messed up as young man and had been living in fear of discovery ever since. The goat herder thing was just the easy way out, giving him an income without bringing much attention to himself.

"You're probably right," said Steele. "As much as I would have liked him for the job, he probably didn't kill those two men."

"So what now?"

The double ring tone of the phone interrupted his next comment. Two rings meant an outside line. Steele picked up the phone. "Rock Port Police, Steele speaking."

"I know where the murder weapon is," said a high pitched voice.

Steele covered the mouthpiece and tapped Walker. "Get a trace going on this."

Walker picked up a phone on his desk and spoke quickly into the receiver.

"For which murder?" asked Steele.

"West Harbor, don't waste my time. You're probably trying to trace this call so I'll make it simple. The murder weapon is in the tall grass behind the Super Saver in West Harbor. You should be able to figure out the rest."

The caller hung up, leaving Steele with a dial tone. He looked over at Walker. "You get anything on that?"

"They weren't on the line long enough," said Walker. "What did they say?"

"He or she, hard to tell which, said we'd find the murder weapon behind the Super Saver."

Walker grinned. "What did I say from the beginning? Jones is our killer. Isn't that what I said?" He took his hat off the rack and slapped it on his head. "Well? Aren't you coming?"

The two left the station, walking out into the crisp air, and Steele's car. Minutes later, they exited the parking lot and headed north on the trunk highway. There wasn't much to say along the way, with each man left to his own thoughts. Steele wondered about the caller, man or woman he told Walker, but in truth, he was sure it was a man, faking a high pitched voice to keep him from recognizing the speaker, for Steele was certain that the caller lived in West Harbor. So why not identify himself to the police? Usually there was a reward for such information, why did this person not wish to take the reward? And then there was the nature of the call. Knowing where the murder weapon was meant any number of things. Did it belong to Jones? Was he the killer? Was he stupid enough to throw the weapon in the tall grass behind his store? Wouldn't he know that finding a murder weapon so close to his store would implicate him? Then again, maybe he wasn't thinking at the time. Which led to the possibility that Jones was the killer, but how did the caller know about the location of the weapon? Had he seen it thrown there? Or was the caller the killer, trying to implicate Jones? Too many what ifs, thought Steele, as they crested the hill and drove on down to West Harbor.

They passed Louella's house and the post office, and stopped in front of the Super Saver. All was quiet in the village when the detectives exited the car. As they rounded the store, they spotted Jones loading up his already full car. Even from twenty feet away, Steele could see that the back seat was full, the trunk open, and Jones carrying a closed box to the open trunk.

"Where you going, Mr. Jones?" asked Steele as they approached the store keeper.

Jones set the box in the trunk and looked at the detectives. "I've had enough of this little town. It's time to move on."

Steele moved in closer, shortening the distance between he and Jones. "Really? This wouldn't have anything to do with the murders would it?"

Jones shrugged. "Time to move on, what can I say. I've had it with these local yokels."

While Steele talked, Walker, wearing latex gloves, moved around the back of the building, pushing the tall grass left and right.

Jones looked over at Walker. "What does he think he's doing?"

"Don't worry about him," said Steele. "We're talking about you. You've lived here a couple years and suddenly it's time to move on? Come on, Mr. Jones, you can do better than that. What's the real reason you're leaving?"

"That ain't none of your business. I can move if I want to. I'm tired of this place, is that a crime?"

"No, but this is."

Jones and Steele looked over to where Walker stood, holding up a tire iron in a large plastic evidence bag.

Jones dropped the box he was carrying and took off toward the beach, with Steele right behind him. The two men dropped to the sand below the dune, with Jones in the lead, and Steele at this heels. Jones' slight lead disappeared quickly with Steele digging in, then with a flying leap, Steele tackled Jones, knocking the two to the ground. Jones struggled to get free, but Steele was fast, pulling a pair of handcuffs from a side pocket. Second later, he had the Jones cuffed, with his hands behind his back. Steele helped Jones to his feet.

"Thomas Jones, you're are under arrest for the murders of Tony Chambers and Thomas Hoffman."

Steele recited the Miranda rights as he hauled Jones across the sand to a waiting Kevin Walker.

"You've got the wrong man," said Jones. "I didn't kill anybody."

"Except for that guy down in San Bernardino," said Walker as they pushed Jones into the back of their car. They secured Jones, then got in the front seat, putting the evidence bag on the front floor board, then headed south, with their suspect in tow.

"Why did you do it, Jones?" asked Walker over the seat.

"I'm done talking," said Jones.

Walker turned to Steele, a big smile plastered on his face. "I told you he was our guy."

#

Star sat on the outside passenger window, looking out at the passing landscape. He had tried to talk to Tracy, to no avail, and was now sullen and angry. It just wasn't right, all that had happened to him during the last twenty-four hours. They rode in silence, each to his or her own thoughts. He glanced over at Mary and Tracy and wondered just how it was possible that he was riding with the kind of women he always yearned for, back in the day, but had dismissed as vacuous shells since his transformation some ten years back. If his friends could only see him now, he thought, for the two women were truly beautiful. A redhead and a blonde. Who could ask for more? Reality crashed in his subconscious, bringing him back to face facts. The blonde was only in the vehicle to help Tracy, and Tracy didn't look like she was all that fond of him anymore. It was a bittersweet ride, traveling with these two beautiful women who wanted nothing to do with him. Still, he was grateful to be out of the cell and away from his next best friend, the hobo, Willie, and his smelly breath and missing teeth.

Such was the luck that he escaped one reality for the cold air he rode in, wedged between his wife and the door, a woman that he had known intimately for the past ten years, sharing his bed and his life, yet now seemed distant and cold. What had happened to their marriage? Was it all Tracy? Or did he have something to do with the change. It was easy to blame the recent lies on Tracy's change of heart, but there was more to it than that. Why hadn't he seen that she was unhappy as a hippie goat header's wife? What was wrong with that picture? All these years, they shared moments, and for what? Was it all just a waste of time? A lesson in futility? Waiting for the day when Tracy awoke and decided to move on? Then he thought of life without her. Would he survive? What would become of him with no one to look out for him? And what about their son? Would they be one of those too modern families with split custody, moving their son back and forth between residences? Or worse, would she try for full custody, leaving him out in the cold?

They rounded the curve and passed a car coming from the other direction. Star noticed the detectives right way, then saw who was sitting in the back seat.

"The cops are taking Young Tom," said Star.

Mary looked in the rear view mirror at the retreating automobile. "You sure?"

"They have him in the back seat," said Star. "I knew he was the one."

Tracy turned her head and stared at Star. "Just because they're taking him in for questioning doesn't mean he's the killer. For all we know, you're the one and we're taking you back so you can kill again."

Star pushed his hair back and shook his head. "I told you, dude, I'm not the guy. Okay, so I lied a bit about my past, I'm not proud of it, okay? But that doesn't make me a killer. I was a dumb kid and did dumb things, and that's all. Three stints in juvenile hall doesn't make me a bad guy."

"So why didn't you tell me all this when we met?" asked Tracy.

He looked down. "Because you wouldn't have gone out with me if I told you the truth and as far as I was concerned, you were the most beautiful woman I'd ever seen and I didn't want to lose my chance."

That got her quiet. She stared at him, with just the slightest hint of a smile, though she seemed to be fighting herself to keep it just slight. "Is that so?"

"Dude, you were a total babe, and I knew that if I didn't make my move, you'd be with some other dude faster than I could say what happened."

"So how about now?" asked Tracy. "Am I still a total babe?"

"You are," said Star. "And I hate to say it, but you look like somebody who wouldn't give me the time of day. It's just like high school all over again. You and Mary over there look like a pair of cheerleaders and you know that there wasn't a chance that the A list kids would have anything to do with the stoners. Not then, not now."

"But you quit that stuff years ago," said Tracy. "And you don't have to stay the way you are. The police know all about you now, there's nothing to hide. Not that I'm happy about your lies, but I can sort of see why you might have wanted to keep your past a secret, but that's over now. You are free to do as you wish. No longer must you hide behind the persona of Star, the hippie goat herder. You can be anything you want now."

"Dude, you made me spend the night in jail," said Star.

"Dude, you hit me," said Tracy. "I am sorry about your records. I just got so mad that I lashed out at the one thing I knew you loved more than me."

"It wasn't right," said Star. "They put me in a cell with a crazy man yelling at me all night long. But I guess I can see your point. I was wrong to lie, and I guess one night in jail won't kill me. At least I finally faced up to all that fear. Dude, you have no idea how long I've worried about this coming out, and then there it was and there was nothing I could do about it. I was seriously thinking that I'd be sent down to Los Angeles to face charges. Fortunately, the statue of limitations saved me. But at least that's over. Thanks to you, I am now free of my burden."

Mary laughed. "That's pretty deep. Are you two going to kiss and make up or what?"

Tracy turned and faced Star. "What do you think? Are you ready for some changes."

Star felt a stone in his stomach. "I'm feeling a lot of fear here, dude."

Tracy leaned over and kissed her husband, then pulled back and smiled. "Face the fear, Harry."

"I hate that name, can you call me Star, please?"

"Fine, but I still want to be called Tracy, and no more stepford wife crap. You got a problem with that?"

"I can live with that." He smiled. "I don't have to cut my hair, do I?"

#

The detectives brought Thomas Jones into the police station, where he was officially booked and fingerprinted and taken to the same cell to sit and wait to be interviewed. The drunk in cell number one had been released on his own recognizance and told to keep his nose clean, Willie the Hobo, in the cell opposite was still on board, happy to have a new prisoner to torture. Jones lay on his bunk and stared at the ceiling, his hands laced behind his head. This day was turning out to be a major bummer. He shouldn't have let Bill Seavers get to him. Why run when the murders were still unsolved? It made him look bad. And having the potential murder weapon show up behind his place was unreal. How did it get there? And more importantly, how did the police know where to look? There was definitely something bad going on in West Harbor. Someone was setting him up to take the rap, but who? Who didn't like him enough to sic the police on him? Jones was busy running down the names of the West Harbor residents and came up with Bill Seavers. He was the one. He must be. Seavers had confronted Jones in the Super Saver and forced the store keeper to make a rash decision. The more he thought about it, the surer he was that Seavers was behind this whole thing. Did that make Seavers the killer? It seemed likely, how else would he have the weapon nearby, ready to place behind the store? As loathe as he was to admit it, Jones knew that he was in deep trouble. Having a murder weapon show up behind his store at the exact time he was packing to leave town made him look like the number one suspect. So what could he do? A lawyer would tell him to keep his mouth shut, and he would, to a degree, but he needed to get it across to the police that this wasn't his doing. He was being set up because of what? Availability? Hatred? Or even convenience? He was baffled by the intrigue.

"Hey, Baldy? You alive down there?"

Jones turned his head and spotted the hobo at the far end of the cells. "You talking to me?"

"You see any other baldy's here?"

"Watch your mouth, old man. Show a little respect."

"For you? Why should I? What're you going to do? Come down here and beat me up?"

Jones stood and crossed to the bar separating him from Willie. "Keep it up, wise guy. You know why I'm here?"

"Jaywalking?"

"Two murders," said Jones. "You think it's wise to piss me off?"

That shut the hobo up. The old man sat back on his cot and stared at Jones, working himself up to say something, but nothing came out.

"That's what I thought," said Jones, returning to his cot and his musings.

He had no more than laid back down when the door at the end of the jail opened and the two detectives walked in, accompanied by the sergeant of the watch. A quick turn of a key and the cell door was open.

"Come with us, Mr. Jones," said Steele, standing on one side of the open door.

Jones walked out of the cell, with a detective on either side, and they headed for the interrogation rooms. Jones paused as they reached Willie's cell and pointed a finger at the hobo.

"Watch your mouth," said Jones.

The hobo remained silent, watching as the four men left the jail.

Steele ushered Jones into the interrogation room on the right and sat him down on the lone chair. The detectives took up the chairs on the opposite side and the sergeant of the watch exited the room and shut the door behind him.

Steele pulled out a notebook and pen and looked at Jones. "You're in a world of hurt, Mr. Jones. A history of violence. Time in prison for second degree murder. Two murders within a hundred yards of your store. A murder weapon found behind your residence. And to top it off, you were running away from the scene. What do you have to say for yourself?"

"I'm being set up," said Jones.

"Really?" asked Walker. "Is that all you can say?"

Jones stared at Walker. "Do I look stupid enough to stash a murder weapon behind my store? If, in fact, I did kill either of those two guys, wouldn't I have been smart enough to fling the tire iron into the sea? Why would I leave it out in the open like that?"

"Maybe you're not as smart as you think you are," said Walker.

"You're an idiot," said Jones. "Both of you are. Can't you see how much of a set up this is? Sure, I have a past, but I've paid my debt to society. Someone is banking on that information to keep themselves safe from being caught. I'll admit that it wasn't all that smart to pack up and try to leave town, but I figured my time was up there. I know when I'm not welcome and when it's time to move on. In my estimation, it was time to move on."

"What about the tire iron behind your store?" asked Steele.

"What about it? It was planted there, obviously, by someone who wanted me arrested. Well, here I am, but you've got the wrong guy. I know, I don't have a decent alibi for either of the killings, but neither do many others in town. Any of my neighbors could have done the killings, or for that matter, someone from out of town could have done the job."

"Why would someone from out of town kill two in West Harbor?" asked Steele.

"I have no idea," said Jones. "I just know that I didn't do it. It's your job to figure out the real killers, not me, but I do have an idea who might have done it."

"This should be good," said Walker. "The some other dude did it defense."

"I'm serious," said Jones. "You want the truth why I was leaving town? Bill Seavers came into my store and made a big stink, accusing me of doing the killings, yelling at me that I was the guy. I was thinking about it and maybe he's your guy, forcing my hand, leaving the tire iron for you to find. Say, how did you know it was there in the first place?"

"An anonymous phone call," said Steele.

Jones sat back in his seat and crossed his arms over his chest. "Well, there you go. Someone out there is setting me up, and if you want my opinion, I'd say it was Bill Seavers."

"Why would Seavers kill Chambers and Hoffman?" asked Steele.

"I've got no idea," said Jones. "You're the big detectives, it's your job to find out. Now, I've said enough. You want any more, I'd like a lawyer."

"We're not done with you, Mr. Jones," said Steele.

"For the moment you are," said Jones.

The detectives spent another fruitless ten minutes, grilling Jones about his whereabout during the two murders, looking for chinks in his story, but got stonewalled for the efforts. Each question was met with silence and a shake of the head. Steele knocked on the steel door. When the sergeant of the watch opened the door, Steele nodded at Jones.

"Take him back to his cell."

#

Steele sat back in his chair and sighed. He had a man in jail who looked good for the murders and nothing to prove that he did the job. After their initial interrogation, Jones lawyered up and refused to say another word, sitting with his arms crossed over his chest, staring at a spot on the wall behind the detectives. While the circumstantial evidence pointed to Jones as the killer, Steele had doubts. Like the man said, why would he leave a murder weapon in plain sight when it would have been easy to chuck it in the ocean, buried forever beneath sea and sand? And why would he attempt to leave town if he knew that the police would come for him? A sign of guilt or a indication of his worn out welcome in West Harbor?

And then there was the phone call, the untraced, unidentified caller, who sent the police to West Harbor? Who was this mysterious caller and why didn't he or she identify themself? Was it as Jones said? Could this mystery man be Bill Seavers trying to pin the murders on Jones when in fact he was the killer? And if he was the killer, what was his motive? Steele had reviewed the transcribed notes of the Seavers interviews and nothing in them indicated a motive for the killings. Certainly, Chambers may have flirted with Mary Seavers, but was that motive enough to kill the man? Steele wasn't sure, but did believe that regardless of who killed Tony Chambers, Thomas Hoffman died because he knew the killer and said something, but to whom? Jones? Seavers? Or any of the other colorful characters of West Harbor? It was a quandary.

"We should put him on a polygraph," said Walker from the adjacent desk. "I know he was the guy. Just because he turns into a clam doesn't make him innocent."

"What about the phone call turning him in? Doesn't that look like a set up to you?"

Walker shook his head. "A concerned citizen, that's all. Jones is our boy."

"He left a murder weapon behind his store? How did this concerned citizen know it was there?"

"How should I know? Maybe he saw Jones throw it there and was just waiting to tell someone."

"They waited four days to call. Hoffman would still be alive if we had this information on say, Sunday. I'm thinking Mr. Jones was right about being set up."

"It's a trick, boss. Honestly. He killed Chambers and Hoffman saw it and probably tried to blackmail Jones and got killed for his effort."

"And some other concerned citizen just called in to let us know about it? Something isn't right about this whole deal."

The phone rang, disturbing their discussion. A single ring tone. A inside phone call. Steele picked up the receiver. "Detective Steele. What's that, Eddie? I'll take the good news first. Well, that's something. Okay, give me the bad news. Gotcha. Thanks, Eddie." He hung up the phone and looked at Walker. "The blood stains on the tire iron matched both victims."

"So we got the murder weapon, we knew that. What was the bad news?"

"There was a smudged fingerprint on the handle of the tire iron."

"How can that be bad news?'

"It doesn't match the prints we took from Star or Jones. There goes your number one suspects."

"Maybe Jones stole the tire iron from somebody and wiped his prints off."

"Before he set the tire iron in the grass behind his store? I doubt it. Unfortunately, it looks like Mr. Jones was telling the truth about being set up. Which means, the killer is still on the loose."

12. Back to the Drawing Board

Bonnie Williams got on the phone and made the calls that needed to be done, making sure that the grave hole diggers were brought in to prepare the site up on Cemetery Road for Thomas Hoffman's burial. It was a gloomy day, gone was the sun from the day before, replaced with a misty morning under a dark cloudy sky. The kids were bundled up, running down the lane to catch the big yellow school bus, then the bus was gone, heading north to complete its run, leaving the town quiet and still outside her window. She made a flyer and posted in the front window, asking for help putting together a pot luck for Old Tom's wake, then sat on her stool and looked out the window.

She was sure she was missing something, some act that was necessary, but couldn't think of what it might be, so instead, she sat and stared out the window and thought about her little home town and all that had happened in the last week. Two weeks ago, she would have said that West Harbor was a boring little town, where nothing happened, then there were two murders and the police were in and out of town, taking first Star in for questioning, then he returned, only to have Young Tom taken in. Was this the end? Was her next door neighbor guilty of these horrendous crimes? Would life ever return to normal?

Bonnie spotted Adam Franklin crossing the street with two cups of coffee in his hands and smiled. As much as she hated to admit it, she had gotten used to Franklin and his morning coffee, and their usual gossip session that started her morning. Having him gone the previous day was disconcerting. Why hadn't he come at his usual time bearing her hot caffeine? Was he ill? Or avoiding her for some reason?

Franklin juggled the two cups in one hand and arm, and used his left hand to open the door. Seconds later, he was inside, handing her a steamy cup of coffee.

"Going to rain out there," said Franklin. "I felt a few drops coming over."

Bonnie took the offered cup. "Looks like it might be wet for Old Tom's funeral."

"That it might," said Franklin, hopping onto the stool on the customer side of the counter. "Does that bother you?"

"Oh no. I like the rain, and it seems appropriate, don't you think? A hard rain for a funeral? It just wouldn't seem right having a bright sunny day on such a sad occasion. I liked Old Tom and feel pretty bad about the whole thing."

"It's pretty sad, that's for sure. So what can I do to help?"

Just as she was about to speak, she noticed a deputy sheriff's car pass by the post office with Young Tom riding in the front seat.

"Will you look at that," said Bonnie.

Franklin twisted his head around in time to see the car and occupant riding past. "What's going on? I heard that police took him in."

"I guess they didn't have enough to hold him," said Bonnie. "First Star, and now Young Tom making trips to the police, and now both are back. Does that mean neither of them killed Old Tom?"

"I'm not sure what it means. Maybe they're still gathering evidence or something. I thought for sure it was Young Tom, didn't you? He seemed so likely, being close to both killings and all, but what do I know? I'm just an old man with too much time on my hands."

"You are not an old man," said Bonnie. "Older maybe, but definitely not old. So you want to know what you can do to help out? Simple. I need to run down to Rock Port to talk to the people at the mortuary, and see what I can do about getting a preacher out here for the service and my car has a flat tire. If you're not too old, do you think you could change the flat for me? I've got a pretty good spare tire, but no tire iron. It's been so long since I've had to change a tire, the darn thing has gone missing on me. You've got a tire iron, don't you?"

"I certainly do," said Franklin, "but I have a better idea. Rather than get all wet changing your tire, why don't I simply drive you to town? I would enjoy it immensely and if you were agreeable, maybe we could do lunch down there as well. I know of a couple restaurants down there that would be perfect. What do you say?"

"What about my duties here? I can't just close up the post office for hours on a work day?"

"Sure you can," said Franklin. "Look, how much mail came in for pickup today? Not a whole lot I'd say. So what if you close up for a couple of hours. The people around here would understand. You're already committed to going to Rock Port to set up the funeral, what's another forty-five minute lunch with me at a nice restaurant?"

She thought about it for a moment, wondering what the people in town would think if they saw her drive off with Franklin. West Harbor was a small town and people liked to gossip, but she wasn't sure if she wanted the gossip to be about her. Would they laugh at her for being a silly old maid, chasing after the only available bachelor in town? Did she care? It had been so long since she had been out on a date that she wasn't sure exactly what the etiquette was for paying. Was this to be Dutch treat? Or was he paying? In the old days, the person asking did the paying, but had times changed? Regardless, did it really matter? She had the money, even if he didn't and truth be told, the offer was appealing. She looked over at the waiting Franklin.

"I would love to go to lunch with you."

#

Star sat across the kitchen table from Tracy and gave her his best smile, the one that won her over in the first place. He knew that he had passed one hurdle, talking to Tracy in the truck on the way home, but now he was alone with her and he needed all his charm to keep her with him. In the final analysis, he knew that he wanted to keep his wife, even with the name change and as little as he wanted to admit it, he dug the new look. Back in high school, a girl that looked as good as Tracy did now wouldn't have given him the time of day, and yet, the once shy and painfully plain girl and blossomed into a stunning beauty. It was hard for him to see why she would want to stay with him, being all hippie and long hair, but still, here she was, waiting for his response. And he knew that the next words to come out of mouth better be the ones she wanted to hear. This was no longer a matter of few records being broken, this was marriage survival, something he never saw coming. All these years, he talked of the universe and their place in it, never worrying that his precious wife would consider living her life without him. He had been selfish, taking for granted that his wife would want to stay with him. Such arrogance, he thought, and now, like a cloud shifting and the sun coming through, he saw clearly that he was wrong, but how could he fix the problem? That he wasn't sure.

He glanced outside at the falling rain, so appropriate, he decided for his mood, and for the importance of this moment. The now, the future, depended on him in a way that he was never prepared for. All his life, he had been a follower, taking the easy path, not making any difficult decisions. Even his choice to run had been the easy route. Better to run than to face the consequences. Star didn't have that luxury now. He needed to make the right decision this time around.

"So I was thinking," said Star.

"And?"

"We don't have a car, so it will be difficult to find a job down in Rock Port, but if you want, I can try to get a car loan."

"What kind of work can you do?"

"Well that's the thing," said Star. "Sadly, I don't have a lot of skills, so that would mean an entry level job, doing whatever I could. It won't pay much, but it would be a start, but I do have a better idea." He paused. This was the moment of truth. "I was thinking about expanding our operations here. Take out a small business loan, build a small family business right here. We've got the property for it, and if the Seavers don't like the noise and smell, we could option some property north of the schoolhouse, where the old fish plant used to be. It would be far enough away from town that the noise and smell shouldn't bother anyone, and it would bring industry back to West Harbor."

"You can't even keep the goat shed in good repair."

He smiled. "That was the old me, the slacker, the one that went with the flow. I've seen the light, and that would be you. I don't have a lot of marketable skills right now, other than being a goat herder. Why not make the most of that? The goats like me, I like the goats. We get more goats, open our business big time and market the milk and cheese to the grocery stores here on the coast. Right now, we're selling ourselves short, sending off the milk to some producer who makes money off of us, when in reality, we should cut out the middle man and make the money ourselves."

"What do you know about the business? You know how to open a dairy?"

"I can learn. I was pretty good in school, when I wasn't getting into trouble. Why not give me the chance to prove I can do more?"

"And what about our son? He doesn't want to be called Genesis anymore. Can you deal with that? He want's to live a normal life. Watch TV, eat normal food, hang out with his friends, be called Mike. And look at this wreck we call a home. This isn't what I want for my life, and as good as your plan sounds on paper, what is the reality of it actually happening?"

He knew that what she said was true. He had been a slacker for so long, absorbed in his hippie existence, it would be difficult to change. Was he up for the challenge? He looked across the table at his beautiful wife.

"I want to try, that is if you're willing to stick by me long enough to see if I can do the job. I know that's asking a lot, but I truly believe I can give you all that you want. I'll research how to run a dairy, find out what we need, apply for the business loan, pick out the site for the dairy, and I'll fix the goats shed, and the fence, and everything else I can do to make this work. What do you say, Tracy? Will you give me another chance?"

She stared at him for so long that he got nervous, then slowly nodded. "Another chance, but you better be telling me the truth, Star, or I'm gone. Me and Mike will leave you and your goat herder dreams and find a better life for ourselves. And if I hear you refer to me one more time as a stepford wife, then the deal if off. Do I make myself clear?"

"I believe I get your point, Tracy. So where do we go from here?"

"Old tom's funeral tomorrow. You can be a slacker for one more day., then it's nose to the grindstone time."

"I can't do the funeral thing," said Star. "Really, I can't. I know you might believe that I didn't kill Old Tom, but I bet there's some here in town that still think I did. I can't possibly attend when people are talking about me behind my back. Sorry, no funeral."

She stared at him. "It's disrespectful, Star. We go as a couple or I go alone. Is that what you want? To start off our new beginnings with a mark against you?"

He knew when he was beat. This new forceful Tracy was something he wasn't used to. In the past, he simply did as he pleased, no problems, no arguments, now suddenly, he had lost control of the situation and the roles were reversed. Suddenly, Tracy called the shots, and he knew that he would do what he could to keep her, so he would do as she said. Even if it meant having to endure the looks and stares of his fellow citizens. He would stand tall and look them in the eye and dare them to accuse him. He was many things, but a murderer, he wasn't.

Star nodded his head. "I'll go to the funeral."

#

The whine of the electric saw split the air, with wood particles flying off the board as Bill Seavers rolled it through the rotating steel blade. He was working on the inner drawers of the cabinets, with measured pieces of wood to his right and cut ones to his left. The project was coming along nicely, and with good time put in, should be completed in less than a month, giving them a little extra money for the Christmas holidays. He placed the cut wood pieces on the pile and picked up another piece. Seconds later, the screech of the saw filled the air as the blade bit into the wood.

"Bill!"

Seavers continued pushing the piece through to the back side, carefully rolling the piece straight on through, keeping his eye on the pencil line he had etched on the wood.

"Hello?"

He finished the cut and placed the two pieces on the stack to the right, then turned and spotted his wife in the doorway. Seavers pushed the safety goggles to the top of his head and walked over to Mary.

"Is it lunchtime already?"

"No it isn't," said Mary coming down the steps into the garage. "I just got off the phone with Bonnie. She called the funeral parlor and found out how much a casket would cost for burying Old Tom. He didn't have insurance to cover the cost and Bonnie wanted to know if you would be willing to make a casket. Nothing fancy, she said."

"That's still going to cost us some money."

"He was our neighbor, Bill. Think of it as good will. And if you'd like, I'll pass the hat and see if anybody will chip in to help pay. Really, you have the skill and the cost would be a lot less than if we bought one from the funeral home."

He thought for a moment, he had never built a coffin before and the challenge was enticing. Should he make it out of pine, like the old west, or cedar? He still had some velvet from a foot stool he made and the batting needed for the filling. It could be done fairly cheaply, with his labor being the biggest cost.

"I'll build the coffin. When's the funeral?"

"Tomorrow."

"Then I better get started."

She stood her ground. "That's not all I came out here for. We need to talk."

Seavers groaned. He hated it when she said those words, for they were always bad. What would it be this time? A leak in the bathroom? More money for the kids? A new play set for the back yard?

"What did I do now?"

She walked over and stared at him. "It's not what you did, it's what you're not doing."

He was confused. This wasn't a normal way to start a conversation. "What are you talking about?"

"The question is what did I do to make you not want me anymore?"

Seavers stared at his pretty wife. He could see the anxiety in her face and in the way she held her body. She was tense, there was no doubt about it. "Why would you ask such a question? You're my wife, of course I want you."

She shook her head. "Not in that way. Bill, are you serious? Do I have to spell it out for you?"

"Please do. If this has to do with making more money, then I'm working as hard as I can. I try to make enough to cover our expenses and still have enough for your shopping sprees."

She put her hands on her hips and stared at him. "You are the most obstinate man I've ever met, Bill Seavers. I ask you if you still want me in that way and you talk about clothes. Look, I've been dressing as flattering as I can, hoping that you'd get the hint, and even talked about having some lunch sex to get you in the mood, and all you can say is that you provide money for clothes? Are you kidding me? Is my looks? I know I'm older than when we were in high school, so are you, but back then, you couldn't keep your hands off of me, and now I feel like I'm living like a nun. So I ask you again, and this time, buster, you had better come up with a better answer. Are you not attracted to me sexually anymore?"

It was Seavers turn to feel flustered. This was the issue he was avoiding, hoping that it would go away, but now he had no choice but to speak his mind and face the consequences.

"I'm still very attracted to you."

"You don't show it."

"Okay, fine, you brought it up. You want to know what I'm thinking? You dress too sexy for this little town. I see the way you look and I'm thinking that every man in town would like to have sex with you."

"So why not you? You're the one I'm married to."

"Because I don't want any more children." There, he said it and now waited for her response.

She stared at him for a moment, then laughed. She was laughing at him. And not just a giggle, but a full out barking laugh.

"Is that what's bothering you? You should have said something sooner. Here I was thinking that you didn't like me anymore, and actually was worried that you might like Tracy better, don't give me that look, I saw the way you stared at her this morning, and all along you've been avoiding having sex because you didn't want children? Why on earth didn't you say something? We can talk about this you know."

"I thought you wanted to get pregnant again?"

"Who told you that? It wasn't me. I'm good with the two we've got. You don't want a third it's fine by me. Being pregnant and going through childbirth is no picnic. Make an appointment down in Rock Port, take care of it, and there will be no more babies in this house. Is that all that's been bugging you? The thought that I wanted to get pregnant?"

He felt stupid, and a little turned on. "Yep."

"Well we've got some condoms left over from the last time you were in the mood, if you're still attracted to me."

"I am."

"Then why don't you come in for a little early lunch and you can show me how much you're attracted to me."

Seavers was grinning as he placed the goggled on the nearby work bench, then followed his wife to the kitchen door, hitting the automatic door closer as they entered the house. It looked like making a coffin would have to wait for just a bit.

#

Louella sat in her chair and stared out the window at the falling rain. She was mad for the way the town had rallied around the death of Old Tom, but completely ignoring the death of her husband. Not that she wasn't grateful for Tony's untimely demise, but it just rubbed her wrong that her neighbors were doing do much for one but not the other. Wasn't she suffering just as much, more so? Old Tom left only his cats, who Louella was certain only cared about the keeper of the food cans? Didn't she have to face the expense of a funeral and all that went with it? Then why was she being left out of the town generosity? She saw the note in the post office, asking for help with Old Tom's wake, but nothing was said about her husband's funeral arrangement. It was as if the town only saw one death as important, and it sure as hell wasn't Tony Chambers.

Then there was the police, coming and going, asking questions, disrupting the quiet nature of the town, sticking their noses where they didn't belong, and with all that, she figured they should have caught the killer by now, but as far as Louella knew, only Star and Young Tom had been brought in and released, which left them where? With unsolved deaths, which could only mean more intrusive action by the police. She was sure that the killer was Young Tom, shifty eyes and secretive, but Star certainly looked good for the killings, yet both had been questioned and released. Having a killer loose didn't bother her much, for losing Tony meant that she didn't have to leave her house, and the death of Old Tom was probably the result of his sticking his nose in where it didn't belonged. That was something that Louella was good at avoiding. She keep her business to herself and wished that others would do the same.

She didn't see the conflict in wanting people to keep out of her business and helping her with the burial of her husband. Her brain didn't work that way. So she sat and stewed, staring at the rain. According to the radio weather report, this latest storm was just beginning, with more coming in from the west, with guaranteed rain for Old Tom's funeral the next day. She was so caught up in her musings, that she didn't notice Margaret coming in from the bedroom.

"Mom? You okay?" Margaret crossed the room and leaned against the window, with the falling rain providing a backdrop for her. "You're so quiet, I thought you might be asleep."

That was another thing that was bothering Louella, having Margaret underfoot. It wasn't so bad when her daughter was little, she was used to the company, but all her time of living alone had made her protective of her privacy. The problems were many, starting from

Margaret's mere presence. The girl was loud, and argumentative, and worst of all, secretive. Whenever Louella asked a question, Margaret had told her to mind her own business, or that she didn't want to talk about it, or just ignored the question and changed the subject. It was like living with a large disagreeable pet, one that Louella wished would just go home.

"I'm okay, just thinking about your daddy's funeral. The whole town's looking at burying Old Tom right, but don't see that we've got one to plan too. It ain't right what they're doing. No respect. Your daddy lived here too, and nobody seems to care that he was murdered and needs to be buried too."

"Don't be like that, Mom. Daddy wasn't exactly nice to these people. From what I heard, he treated folks around here pretty bad."

"Don't you disrespect your daddy. He may not have been the best father, but he was your daddy."

"Who treated me bad too, Mom. Look, I'm sorry Daddy's dead, I am, but there isn't much I can do about it."

"You could feel bad."

Margaret stared at her mother, pushing her bangs out of her eyes. "Like you? He was going to kick you out of here and put you on the street. Face it, Mom, Daddy wasn't a nice person. He told me he wished I'd never been born. What kind of dad says that to his only daughter? It hurt a lot, Mom. You remember the police asking where I was on Friday and I told them that I was with a married man? I made it up. I didn't want to tell the police the truth. You want to know where I really was? I was down at the free clinic talking to one of them social workers, crying my eyes out. How would you like to be told you weren't wanted? I cried and cried, then went home, making sure my roommate wasn't around. As far as I'm concerned, I'm glad he's gone. And these people around here probably feel the same way."

"What about the funeral cost? I don't got no extra money for that sort of thing?"

"I'll talk to the police about it, okay. Look, Mom, I can't stay here no longer. I've got a job and a life down in Rock Port. You should come and visit me. You've never even seen my place or where I work. You want, I'll take you right now. How would you like that?"

Louella shook her head. "Gotta be here for Old Tom's funeral."

"After all you just said about how the town's treating you so badly?"

"Gotta do it. Just because they're disrespecting me don't me that I should do the same back. I knew Old Tom. Need to pay my respects. When exactly is it that you're leaving?"

Margaret looked at the floor, then looked up at Louella. "Right now. I was just packing. I know you like having your space and figured you wanted me gone. I know you wouldn't say nothing, but I could tell." she smiled. "So, I guess this is it for awhile. It's been nice seeing you, Mom."

Louella pushed herself out of the chair and hugged her daughter. "You take care of your self down there. I hear there's a lot of crime in Rock Port."

Margaret sniffled. "Almost as bad as here."

The two separated and Margaret went into the bedroom, quickly returning with her two bags. She smiled and waved one last time, then headed out into the rain, leaving Louella alone with her thoughts. One minute after she was gone, Louella began to cry.

#

Thomas Jones sat behind the counter of the Super Saver and looked around at his domain, wondering just what he was going to do. He had his morning crossword puzzle opened, and not started, the blank spaces on the page challenging him to do something. Pick up the pen, start with the top left clue and begin his morning routine, but this was no ordinary day. His brief encounter with the police left him confused. They had processed him, just like they did in southern California, then put him in a cell, then interrogated him, and then put back in the cell. He had asked for a lawyer and refused to answer questions, but that usually meant more time in the cell and several more questions, with the police trying to trip him up in some way, to get him to confess his crimes, but none of that happened. The first part, fingerprints, cell, initial interrogation was as expected, it was being released without a word of explanation that left him concerned. Was he off the hook? Why did they release him? Was he no longer a suspect? These questions gnawed at him. His car was half packed and his certainty at running was no longer a given. For the first time in his life, Jones felt paralyzed with inaction. He just didn't know what to do.

The bell over the door rang as Margaret Chambers entered the store.

Jones looked over at Margaret, her homely face giving away nothing. "Can I help you, miss?"

She walked up to the counter with a ten dollar bill in her hand. "I need some gas to get out of here."

"Leaving so soon?" In spite of his troubles, Jones was still in interested in this less than pretty woman. Another time, perhaps he would have pursued her harder. "Don't you like our little town?"

"I was born here, what's to like?"

He shrugged. "So where are you going from here?"

"Home. I live in Rock Port just down the road." She paused, then smiled. "I know I'm being silly, but when we first met, I got the impression that you were interested in me, but that couldn't be, right? I'm half your age and well, I'm not exactly the kind of girl that most men are interested in."

"I think you're selling yourself short," said Jones. "You are as pretty as you need to be, and if you want my frank opinion, age doesn't matter all that much if the two parties get along. And for your information, I am interested in you. In spite of the age difference."

"I noticed that your car was full, you leaving West Harbor?"

That was the issue. Jones looked at the girl. "Four hours ago, I would have said yes, but a lot has happened in the past four hours."

"What happened, and where would you go?"

"Two questions? Fine. The first one is easy, I was taken in for questioning for the double murders, I'm sure you know all about them, and the second one is harder, I had no idea where I was going."

"You know that Tony Chambers was my daddy, didn't you?"

That surprised Jones. "No, I didn't. I'm sorry for your loss."

She stared at him. "You didn't kill my daddy, did you? I know there's a lot of rumors going on around here and one that I heard was that you and my daddy got into a fight on the day he died."

Jones held up one hand. "I swear, I did not kill your daddy. But I will tell you that I didn't like him much. He was a real pain in the ass, pardon my French, and I figured someone would take him out someday, I just didn't expect it to be that day."

"And the police took you in for questioning?"

"And released me hours later. I honestly don't know what to do. I can't believe I'm saying this to you, but I don't have a lot of people I can confide in. You want the truth, I was getting ready to leave this place when the police showed up. Somehow, I got fingered for the killings, and miraculously, a murder weapon appeared behind my store."

"How did it get there, if you didn't put it there?"

"Another mystery," said Jones. "And the thing is, someone called the police and told them about it."

"The real killer?"

"Most likely, but listen to me, all I'm talking about is me. You're probably feeling pretty low right now, having your daddy taken away like that."

She leaned against the counter. "Well, that's the thing, really, I don't feel that I've had that great of a loss. I mean, I should feel bad, right? He was my daddy, and all I can think of is the last time we talked. I don't know why I'm telling you this, you being a complete stranger and all, but the last time we talked, my daddy told me that he wished I was never born, that if he had his way, he would have made my mom take care of it. How do you like that for a daddy to say something like that about his only daughter?"

"That's a terrible thing to say about such a pretty girl."

She gave him a look. "I know I'm not a pretty girl. You don't think I see myself in the mirror every morning?"

"Being pretty is more than just looks," said Jones, warming to the subject. In spite of himself, he was flirting. "From what I can see, you strike me as a honest girl and judging from the fact that you came to town to help your mother through a difficult time, you have a good heart as well. Those are good traits to have."

"You're pulling my leg, mister."

"Call me Tom."

She smiled. "How old are you, Tom?"

"Forty-one, how old are you, miss?"

"Twenty. So you're twice my age."

He shrugged again. "It's just age. Do you have a name? Or do I keep calling you miss?"

She stuck out her hand. "I'm Margaret Chambers."

"I apologize in advance, but you don't really look like a Margaret to me, I'd say you're more of a Maggie. Has anybody ever called you Maggie?"

She made the pretense of thinking, then shook her head. "But I like it." Her face clouded over. "I don't know if I should change my name after all these years."

"Your name, you can call yourself what you like. Say Maggie, I know I'm a lot older than you and you probably got boys camped on your door step to take you out to lunch, but if you have the time, and want to do something fun, could I give you a call sometime?"

"You got a piece of paper?"

Jones ripped a sheet off a nearby notepad, and handed her pen and paper.

Margaret jotted down her name and number and handed it back. "I'm usually home in the evening. I can't believe I'm doing this. I've never given my number out."

He took the paper. "Then I feel honored." he turned and hit the gas pump switch, then turned back to Margaret. "Put as much in as you want, on me."

"Thanks, Tom. You'll call me?"

"I'll call you."

She turned and walked out of the store without so much as a backward glance.

Jones watched her leave, then looked down at the paper she had given him, with the name Maggie scrawled in a big loopy letters and the phone number underneath. Maybe he'd stick around a little longer.

#

Adam Franklin drove Bonnie to the police station where they were informed that the body of Thomas Hoffman had been released to the Morrison Mortuary on Front Street. A quick five blocks later, they were in the mortuary, where they were told that the Seavers called to say that they would provide a coffin, cutting the costs of the funeral immensely. Then they drove to the church to hire a pastor to do the service. Then it was lunch time.

Franklin was having a good time driving around with Bonnie. Even if it was a sad situation, for Franklin, it was like going out on a date. It was just a little before noon by the time that all the errands had been run, all within one hour of the time they left West Harbor, leaving them enough time for a leisurely lunch. Franklin picked out a cozy sea side restaurant, called Poseidon's Palace.

The Palace was a small affair, built on the south side of town, with a covered sun room overlooking the ocean crashing onto the rocks a mere thirty feet away. There was a small cove to the north with a stretch of sand, normally full of sun bathers, but with the cold rain outside, the beach was deserted. Not so the restaurant. With little to do, the tourists were flooding the available eateries. There was but one table available when Franklin ushered Bonnie inside the dark wood interior.

"You're in luck, sir," said the woman behind the counter. "A table just opened up with a view of the sea."

Franklin couldn't believe his good fortune. First he was able to spend some quality alone time with Bonnie, during which they chatted about little, but enjoyed the silences that filled the time between sentences, and now, here he was, taking her out for a romantic lunch. What could be more perfect that this? As he followed the woman with the purple dress to his table he wondered if he would have enough nerve to say what he needed to say. There would be no more perfect time than this to propose marriage, though he wasn't sure he could just blurt that out. Perhaps start with a declaration of love, he decided as he held out Bonnie's chair for her.

"Thank you," said Franklin to the greeter. He sat down adjacent to Bonnie and smiled at her. "Alone at last."

"Except for the fifty people around us," said Bonnie, nodding at the full house, each table full of diners, some families, some couples. All animatedly talking as they ate their lunches. "This is such a nice place. Are you sure you can afford this?"

He dismissed the comment with the wave of a hand. "Nothing but the best for you, my dear."

They opened their menu's and Franklin's heart stopped for just a moment. The prices were a little on the steep side, at least for Franklin, with entrees hovering in the thirty dollar range. Still, he was with the woman he had been in love with for the past several years, and he figured that the price was worth it, just to have her with him. They would enjoy a wonderful meal and he would be able to say what he needed to say. He hoped.

"What are you going to have?" asked Bonnie.

Suddenly, Franklin felt his stomach flip flop with anxiety. How was he going to eat when he was this nervous? Don't show nerves, he told himself. He forced himself to look at the menu, trying to find something that would be easy on his system. He quickly discounted the high end lobster tail and pricy steaks, then rolled his finger down the line, looking for something that he could stomach.

"Well, it all looks so good, I'm not really all that hungry. I was thinking about this Shrimp Louis salad, but I might have the halibut. What about you? Are you hungry?"

"Starved," said Bonnie, glancing at the entries with a smile. "It's been a long time since I've been out to dinner. And it all looks so good. You won't think poorly of me if I get a steak would you? I haven't had a good one in a long time."

"Eat whatever you like," said Franklin, mentally adding up the cost for the meal. The expense would make a dent in his monthly budget, but this was a special occasion. "Have a drink if you wish."

"May I?"

"You may."

The waiter came along and they placed their orders, Bonnie had the petite sirloin with caramelized asparagus tips, and a mai tai, while Franklin opted for the halibut with rice pilaf and steamed broccoli, with a tall beer. The waiter disappeared and the two chatted about the town, and the magnificent restaurant and just about everything except the two murders back in West harbor. The drinks arrived first, followed quickly by the food. All conversation stopped as the two ate the delicious food. Finally, the meal was over and they sat back in their chairs.

Franklin stared at Bonnie, enjoying the view. She was so beautiful, and for this brief moment, she was all his. The knot in his stomach tightened as he worked up the nerve to broach the subject that he had been wanting to discuss ever since he got her in his car. She was wiping her mouth with the linen napkin. It was now or never.

"Bonnie, do you remember our discussion the other day about love and how you said that it had passed you by?"

"I remember. What about it?"

"And you said that you doubted if you'd ever get married, because it wasn't in the cards? Well, what if it were?"

She leaned in closer. "What are you not saying, Adam?"

This was it. The moment he both dreaded and wished for. "I think you know that I hold you in the highest regard, Bonnie, and except for my wife, I've never felt this way about another person. Ever since my wife died, I've been a lonely man, except for when I'm with you. Somewhere along the line, I fell in love with you."

Silence met his statement like a lead balloon, dropping his spirits steady as Bonnie stared at him. Then she smiled and he felt better.

"I know. I've known for a long time" She reached out for his hands. "Adam, you are a warm, kind man, and I'd like to say that the feeling is mutual, but it isn't. I like you, a lot, but I'm not sure what love is. I'm not familiar with the feelings."

"But you like me, that's a start," said Franklin, trying to recover from the bombshell. He had professed his love and got the equivalent of a kiss on the cheek in response. But at least she said she liked him, that was positive, maybe love would come later.

"Of course I like you, you're my friend, but I'm not sure if I can be more than that. Can you live with that?"

Time to go for broke. "Do you think you could ever fall in love with me?"

She shrugged. "I can't say. Maybe. We do get along pretty well. It's just," she shook her head.

"Just what?"

She looked up. "Just that I never considered the possibility before, that's all, and obviously, you have."

Franklin changed the subject, and tried to keep the look of dismay off his face during the paying of the check and the drive home. He was depressed by Bonnie's reaction, but, looking at the bright side of things, at least she didn't say that she would never fall in love with him, which meant that it could still happen. He took this small ray of hope in his heart and drove the two of them back home.

13. Funeral Day.

Friday morning came in with a blustering wind, dark clouds overhead, and pouring rain as the sky lightened for the day. The children were put on the bus, leaving the town in mourning, covered by a shroud of darkness, with the rain picking up as the morning light filled the village. The locals braved the elements, huddled in their overcoats and hats, hiding beneath the yellow, and blue, and black umbrella's as they made their way out of their cars, or walked up Cemetery Road, and the site of Thomas Hoffman's burial plot. There was a hole dug, with a casket suspended over the hole on a electronic stand, ready to lower the casket at the end of the service, the entire affair covered with a large blue tarp that kept most of the rain off the casket. The grave site next to the open hole was that of Hoffman's late wife. The rest of the stones on the hillside overlooking the town represented a half century of West Harbor life, including Bonnie Williams' parents, and the old mayor, back when such a post existed, plus dozens of locals who had lived and died in this small hamlet. It was a forlorn cemetery, with a broken down fence to keep animals out and supposedly the memory of the deceased inside.

Pastor Richard Lewiston had come up from Rock Port to perform the ceremony, a man who knew nothing of Thomas Hoffman, but there wasn't much the town could do about that. Hoffman wasn't a church going man.

Ben Steele and Kevin Walker stood behind the crowd, watching the backs of the residents huddled as close to the protective tarp as possible without falling into the hole. The rain came down at a slant, obscuring most details of the town below, with a dimly lit sign in the Super saver bravely winking through the mist, and the top of the school house showing itself.

Walker turned up the collar of his coat and pulled his fedora a little lower on his head. "Miserable weather, boss. Remind me why we're here again."

"To show our respects," said Steele, "and to attend the memorial following the service. It wouldn't look right for us to barge in on the wake. Much better to follow the crowd."

"And you think we can get fingerprints from everybody in town?"

"Best chance. Everybody will be there, I hope, and this is easier than trying to get them all down to Rock Port. Trust me, Kevin, this will work out just fine."

Walker shuddered. "I think I'm coming down with a cold."

"Hush," said Steele, "the pastor is ready to begin."

"Friends and neighbors," said Pastor Lewiston. "Please, let us celebrate the life and death of Thomas Hoffman."

The residents moved in even tighter. Standing in the front row were Bonnie Williams, with her hand resting in the crook of Adam Franklin's arm, next were Star and Tracy, with the Seavers next to them. Louella Chambers stood off by herself, staring at the ground. The Peterson's, Graves', and Duncan's stood off to one side, an alliance of newcomers who wished to show their respects, but weren't too close to the deceased. Thomas Jones was conspicuous by his absence.

"We are here today to show respect to Thomas Hoffman, a good man, husband, friend, neighbor and keeper of cats, who was taken from this life too soon. Who knows the ways of the almighty, that would cut a man's life short. In his infinite wisdom, all things are done for a reason, one that we mortals are unable to understand. We need to be grateful for the moments, the minutes, the hours and days of our lives, living as good Christian men and women, exalting the lord our savior, living for the day when we are reunited with the lord, our god, our maker. In this Thomas is blessed, for he is now standing on the right hand of the lord.

"Thomas was preceded in death by his wife of many years, and he is now back with his loving spouse after so many years apart. Life is a short moment in space, death an eternity, making the choices man makes here on earth so important. Every lasting life, that's what Thomas now has, after the transitory existence he experienced while living on earth. Blessed it be that he is now in the Kingdom of the Lord. While death is viewed as a farewell, it is also a celebration, for the moment Thomas left this earth, he walked the streets of gold in heaven. No more aches and pains of mortal life, for eternal life is what awaits us. Thomas now has that. Let us bow our heads in prayer."

"Oh lord," said Pastor Lewiston, "Please watch over the soul of Thomas Hoffman and all these good men and women who are here today. Watch and care for them as lost sheep, looking for safe haven in times of trouble. Watch and keep them, warm their hearts and souls, and keep a place for them in the majesty of your house. For all this, we are grateful servants to the one, the lord of all lords, and the right hand of God almighty. Amen."

A scattering of amen's were muttered by the few, then the pastor closed his bible and looked out at the faces. "I suggest we go inside before the real rain starts."

The mourners split off in two, the umbrellas dancing across the wet grass to the cars for those who drove, and down the road for those who walked. Soon it was just the casket, the pastor and the two detectives.

Steele walked over and shook Pastor Lewiston's hand. "A real nice send off, Pastor."

"Thank you. It's hard when you don't really know the deceased."

"Are you going to stay for the wake?"

"Absolutely," said Lewiston. "I'm starved and I expect the food to be good. It usually is for these country affairs." he glanced back at the casket. "Sad to think that the man was murdered."

"Don't worry, pastor," said Steele. "We'll get the killer."

Lewiston smiled. "If it is in the lord's plan to do so, I'm sure you will."

The pastor turned up his collar and headed toward the few cars remaining in the parking lot, leaving Steele and Walker in the rain.

"Boss? Getting wet here. Can we go?"

Steele took one last look at the casket, then nodded. "Let' s go find our killer."

#

The residents of West Harbor made their way to the home of Bonnie Williams. They entered the side door, walked up the short steps to the living room, and were embraced by the warmth of the wood stove. Bonnie welcomed each guest as they entered. Being a private person, following in the footsteps of her very private parents, Bonnie had never had more than a couple people in her home at one time, mostly staying to herself. But this was a special occasion, one that she was happy to host. There was food scatted across the kitchen counter top that separated kitchen from living room, with tuna casseroles, and fruit jell-O's, and quiche, and rolls, and bean casseroles, and lots of desert bars, along with a punch bowl filled with pink lemonade and a stack of plastic glasses next to the bowl.

The noise level was high as people came in from the rain, talking about the funeral, and the rain, and the cold. Bonnie was on hand to take their coats and put them in the spare bedroom, then back to the door to welcome the newest arrivals. They all came, Pastor Lewiston, the Duncan's, followed by the Graves', and the Peterson's, all chatting together, then Louella, and the Seavers, all bounding up the stairs into the living space. Star and Tracy arrived on the heels of the Seavers, and the younger men and women stared at Tracy as she took off her coat. The hippie girl was gone, replaced by a striking redhead that turned the men's faces and the women's scowls. Not everybody was pleased with the transformation. The last to arrive were Steele and Walker, brushing the rain off their coats as they hit the doorway.

"Let me take your coats," said Bonnie as she relieved them of their outer garments. "Have something to eat."

Steele glanced at the room full of people, some on the couch, others in the chairs, the rest standing around talking. The muted sound of rain could not be heard above the din inside. He could see the rain slamming against the window and the churned up sea beyond, but not much more than the first hundred feet or so.

"What are we going to do, boss?"

"Did you bring the evidence bags and a marking pen?"

"In my pocket. How do you want to work this?'

"We need each and every one of these people to give us a sample of their fingerprints and the most logical way is with the punch glasses. The whole thing would have been a wash if not for the plastic glasses. Your job is to play host, get them punch and when they need a refill, take their glass, put it in a evidence bag, mark the bag and get them a new glass."

Walker looked around the room. "There's a lot of people here. How am I going to do that without getting them mixed up?"

"I'll help you. Look, the Duncan's are ready for a refill. Go get their glasses and I'll get the refills."

It looked to be a tricky operation, but it went fairly smooth. Walker moved in and asked if the Duncan's wanted more punch. They seemed grateful not to have to get up, and Walker took the glasses by the bottoms, and moved into the crowd, then waited until he got to the kitchen before placing them in evidence bags and tagging them. From there, it was easy. He brought new glasses to the Duncan's and moved on to the next couple. Steele helped out, waiting for people to set their glasses down, then offered to get them refills. He took the glasses to Walker in the kitchen and they were bagged and tagged. Meanwhile, the party rolled on.

"Attention everybody," said Bonnie, standing in the middle of the room. "This is a wake to honor our dear neighbor and friend, Old Tom, so I think it would be appropriate if we shared memories of him. He was the oldest member of the community and lived a long life here. If you have something you want to share, just raise you hand and talk. No need to stand, unless you want to. So, who wants to go first?"

Silence met her request.

"Okay," said Bonnie, "I'll start. I first met Old Tom when I was a little girl. I couldn't have been more than around five or so and my parents let me play after school with my friends, this being back when West Harbor was a lot bigger than it is right now. There was a bunch of us, playing in the sunny backyard of the school and our ball ended up in his back yard. I was elected to get the ball and you know how Old Tom was with kids, so I was scared, walking up to the door, and when I knocked, Mrs. Hoffman was there with a plate of cookies and the ball and I thought it was a miracle, then Old Tom stuck his head out from the kitchen and told me that I'd better watch were I kicked my ball. Next time, he'd squash it like a bug. I grabbed the ball and ran, completely forgetting the cookies."

"Did you ever kick the ball back into his yard?" asked Peterson.

"As a matter of fact, we did," said Bonnie. "No more than a week later, the same thing happened, and there was Old Tom, holding the ball, and staring at me as I rounded the corner. He tossed it to me and said, in the deep voice of his. "You almost hit one of my cats." it was then I realized that he was only trying to protect his cats."

"I've got a cat story for you," said Peterson, standing up to address the crowd. "I know we've only been here for a year or so, but we live next to him and those cats can make a noise. When they're hungry, they could wake the dead." He stopped talking when he realized what he said, then continued. "Sorry, anyway, there I was, trying to work and all those cats were doing their thing, and I look out the window, and there's old Tom, opening up cans of food for the cats and singing to them, and doing a little jig, and the cats, I swear, sat on the porch and watched him like he was an entertainer. It was the funniest thing, seeing Old Tom, in his black overcoat and white hair, dancing and prancing in front of the cats."

"He loved those cats," said Tracy, standing up. "I brought him cheese and milk, knowing that he didn't have much money, and every time I brought the cheese, he would thank me, then take the cheese and divide it into small portions, then kneel down and make sure each and every one of his cats got some, leaving nothing for himself. That was the kind of man, Old Tom was."

"Not in the old days," said Louella, from the chair in the corner. "He was a fighter and a brawler. He worked the boats, then worked at the warehouse and boy howdy that man could drink. And then there was hell to pay. Old Tom might have turned into some kind of pussy cat, but in his day, he was a man who got riled easy and fought often."

"But he loved his wife," said Bonnie. "That man doted on her like she was the queen of England. He gave her everything he could, and was heartbroken when they couldn't have any kids."

A silence fell over the room.

"He didn't like me," said Star. "And he said that my goats smelled."

"They do smell," said Seavers.

"Be nice, Bill," said Mary Seavers. She looked at the faces around her. "Old Tom was always a gentleman with me. He had the nicest manners. He always tipped his hat and wished me a good day."

"How about a toast to Old Tom," said Bonnie. "Everybody get a glass." she waited until all complied, then raised her own. "To Thomas Hoffman, our dear friend and neighbor, may you rest in peace."

"Here, here," said several in unison.

"What a load of crap," said Louella, putting her glass down on the nearest table. "Here you all are, celebrating the life of one who died, and ignoring my husband's death. He died too, you know." She stood up and faced the crowd. "You're all a bunch of hypocrites. Honor one without the other? Hogwash. I lost my husband and I don't see no fancy funeral for him. What about me? What about my grief? I ain't going to sit here and take any more of this."

Louella moved through the crowd and was half way to the door before Bonnie stopped her.

"Don't leave, Lou. I'm sorry for your loss, but most of these people didn't know Tony, not the way you did, and Old Tom was part of the community."

Louella shook off Bonnie's arm. "So was Tony. One time he was, maybe not anymore. Sorry to have ruined your party."

Stunned silence followed her departure, then everybody began talking at once.

"People, could I have your attention for just a moment." Bonnie stood in the middle of the room. "While I do understand that Lou was hurt, this is not about her or Tony, this is for Old Tom. Please, stay and help honor the memory of our departed friend. Thanks to the generosity of you folks, we have plenty to eat. Stay, eat and continue to share the life and times of Old Tom. Please. Pastor Lewiston, perhaps you could bless the food and start the line."

The pastor did as he was told. A quick prayer, thanking the good lord for the food, fellowship and good memories were followed by the pastor taking the first paper plate and filling it full of the casseroles and salads and cookies spread before him. Soon all were eating and chatting as if Louella's outburst hadn't occurred.

Walker picked up Louella's glass and slid it into an evidence bag, then rejoined Steele by the kitchen.

"Got them all, boss. What next?"

"Put them in the car, then come back. We should show our respects, have something to eat, then head back to Rock Port and see if he can get the glasses analyzed."

And so they did. Walker took the evidence bags to the car, then returned and took his place in line. The party was in full swing by the time the two detectives made their way to the door. They left the warmth of the party, and walked back out to the cold, biting, rain.

Once they were in the car, with the heater going full blast, Walker nodded at the bags in the back seat. "There was one that we didn't get, but that's only because she wasn't there."

Steele nodded. "Margaret Chambers, I know. But if we need, I'm sure we can find her in Rock Port. And if none of these pan out, then we'll know who did it."

Steele put the car in gear, and they pulled onto the blacktop and the short drive back to the city.

#

It was early afternoon by the time Steele and Walker returned to the Public Safety building in Rock Port. The rains continued, coming down in sheets, limiting visibility to a hundred feet. They grabbed the dozen plastic bags and headed from the car to the back of the building, getting soaked in the short walk, then brushed the extra moisture off when the reached the comfort of the back entry. The police lab was located in the basement of the building, with a metal door blocking the doorway off the back entry, all but hidden from the general public. Most people entering the building, came in from the front, with its open and inviting wide stairwell, but here in the back, it was small and cramped, with one door leading to the front lobby, one to the outdoor, and the last, to the lab below.

"What happens if none of these match the one found on the tire iron?"

"We cross that bridge when we get to it, Kevin. Think positive. We may have our killer's prints right here in our hands."

"I don't know, boss, that seems pretty simple. I mean, wouldn't the killer know that they left prints on the murder weapon?'

"I don't think so," said Steele. "I believe whoever did the job was going to pin this one on Mr. Jones. Without the found print, we'd have kept Jones here, and pounded on him until he confessed, but unfortunately for our killer, he or she left a print. Trust me, Kevin, we're close on this."

Steele grabbed hold of the door knob and pulled open the heavy door, keeping his other hand clutching the evidence bags. He headed down the steps, the noise of his footfalls echoing off the yellow walls. There was no frills to this hallway, like the morgue across the street, expense had been spared, with faded yellow walls, bare cement stairs, and industrial lights hanging every fifteen feet from the short ceiling. At the bottom of the stairs was another metal door.

Here was the depository for the public works, the file rooms, evidence rooms, storage, lost and found, and at the end of the short hallway, the forensic lab.

Steele opened the lab door, glass above and wood below, and the detectives entered the realm of Dominic Rodriguez, a thin reedy man with a pencil moustache and thinning hair. He always seemed to be looking down his nose at people, but that was only because of his six foot six frame. He had dark eyes that gave away nothing, but only Steele knew that he sent money to children's charities around the world. Rodriguez didn't want his fellow workers to know of this, fearing that they might take that for him being nice, and the last thing he wanted was friends. He controlled the lab and those around him like a captain of his ship. This was his lab. Period.

The forensic lab consisted of a large room, with tall counters with shelves above and the obligatory sinks at the end of each row. Beakers and Bunsen burners took space along with vials of chemicals for testing, work books for each station, and along the outside walls, rows of green file cabinets to store results of each test run. The lab was both a repository of all previous work, and a working station for work to come.

There were three lab technicians, busy at the stations, who didn't as much as look up when Steele and Walker entered their domain.

Rodriguez noticed them and walked over to the counter top that separated the lab from the general public.

"Detective Steele," said Rodriguez.

"Mr. Rodriguez. How are you on this wet afternoon?"

Rodriguez sniffed. "I can smell the rain, but down here, we're not given the luxury of windows, as you know, but I'm sure you didn't come down here to discuss the weather."

Steele nodded at Walker and they placed the plastic glasses within evidence bags on the counter. "You found a print on my murder weapon."

"Smudged one, but yes. So?"

"I'm trying to match that print with one that you can pull of these glasses." Steele explained how they acquired the glasses and whose prints would be found on each. "We wrote the name on the bags to identify the owner of the prints, all we need you to do is pull the prints of each glass and create a file for each individual, then compare those prints with the one you found on the tire iron."

Rodriguez sniffed again. "Is that all?"

"That's it, how soon do you think you can do the job?"

Rodriguez looked at the dozen bags, as if mentally adding up the time for each glass, then looked at the clock over the door, then back to Steele. "Taking prints off a plastic glass is a fairly easy procedure, but time consuming. Baring unforseen circumstances, we should have these done by mid-morning tomorrow, give or take an hour."

"Work your magic, Dom," said Steele. "There's a killer out there waiting to be caught."

"And you think it's one of these people?"

"We're hoping. How soon can you get started?"

"I'll put a couple of my best people on it immediately."

The detectives left the lab and headed upstairs to their desks to wait for the results. Even though it had been nearly a week since the killing of Tony Chambers, now that they had the killer in their sights, the anticipation of ending this investigation was excruciating.

#

Steele sat at his desk and looked out the window at the falling rain, the morgue and jail obscured in the dimmed light, the apartment building across the street a mere blurry square. There was little traffic on the streets and for all purposes, there world outside was empty of life, leaving Steele with his thoughts. The one that bothered him the most was that the murderer of Thomas Hoffman had been one of those attending the service. The question was, which one?

"You know what gets me?" asked Walker hanging up his coat and adjusting his wide tie. "We let Jones get away when we had him safe in jail. He's the killer, plain and simple."

"How do you suppose Jones could have done the killing? His finger print didn't match the one on the iron."

"That's the beauty of it, boss. Jones puts the murder weapon in the grass behind his place just to divert attention from him being the killer. A set up? I don't think so. So what that the fingerprint that doesn't match. Don't you see? He's setting himself up for the job alright, knowing that we'd eliminate him. He puts the weapon behind the house and makes the call. He gets somebody else to touch the tire iron before this all happens, then after he kills Chambers and Hoffman, he simply wipes off his prints, hides the weapon in plain site, calls it in, and lo and behold, we come along and he looks like he's leaving. You ask me, it's all a set up to make him look innocent, but I'm not buying it."

"That seems a little far fetched," said Steele. "Why not look at the obvious. Somebody else is trying to frame our Mr. Jones, and he had the misfortune of trying to run at the exact time that this other someone made the call and sent us running. It could be Mr. Jones is innocent."

Walker sat down, shaking his head. "I see him as the bad guy, boss. He's a proven killer and has a history of violence. So even if you find that mysterious print matches someone else in the village, that doesn't necessarily mean that they did the killings. It could be just as I said, Jones got somebody else to touch the iron, and put it aside for the moment he could magically bring it out and frame himself."

Steele tried to see Walker's logic, following it through its natural path. Everything Walker said was possible, but was it probable? And was it also true that having a fingerprint match wouldn't necessarily identify the killer?

"Okay, I see you point," said Steele. "So what would you suggest as our next step?"

"First thing would be to bring Thomas Jones back here and sweat him for how ever long it takes to get him to confess."

"And if he doesn't?"

"Then I'd bring back Star. There's a lot we don't know about that guy. He could be the guy that set up Jones for the fall. I can see him making the call, hiding the tire iron, and getting away with murder."

"But why kill Tony Chambers?"

"From what everybody says, the guy was a major league jerk. Sooner or later someone was going to punch his ticket, and the time came last week. Bring Star back in, bring them all in one at a time. Sweat them. Drill them with questions until somebody cracks."

"The women as well?"

"Why not? Just because they're the fairer sex doesn't mean that they don't get mad enough to kill. I know what you're going to say. Chambers was a big guy and it'd take a lot of force to kill the guy, but a lot depends on the level of anger in the killer. You hit the guy at the right spot, with enough force and, yes, even the women could have killed him. And if we're looking at the women, I'd say our number one suspect would be the ex-wife. You thought I forgot about her, didn't you? She had the most reason for wanting Chambers dead."

"What about the killing of Thomas Hoffman?"

"Collateral damage. I think Franklin had it right. Hoffman saw something and the killer took him out."

Steele leaned back in his chair and thought about that for a moment. "Let's talk about that. Hoffman was killed in the schoolhouse. The question is, did Hoffman arrange to meet there or was it a chance deal? The school house is not exactly the place to meet. Why not in Hoffman's home? Or that of the killer? Did the killer follow Hoffman to the school house? Or did they chase him there? And another thing, why wait until several days go by before killing Hoffman. Something must have happened to trigger that event."

Walker shrugged. "Maybe Hoffman ran across the killer somewhere in town, mentioned that he had seen the deed and wanted to talk about it."

"But why? If you saw a killing and knew that the killer hadn't seen you, why advertise that information?"

"Maybe the killer knew that he was seen, approached Hoffman, set up the meeting, then came and killed him."

"Or maybe Hoffman approached the killer. Why would he do that?" Steele snapped his fingers. "Maybe he wanted to blackmail the killer. That would make sense. The secrecy. A meeting in the middle of the night when no one was around. I'd bet he wanted money from the killer to keep quiet."

"Makes sense, but that still doesn't give us how they met up, or who did the killing."

It was true. Steele nodded his head. "Back to square one. While we wait for the lab, we can go over the notes again, maybe something will come up."

The rest of the afternoon was spent in review, the detectives re-reading the interview notes, and the forensic reports, until it was quitting time.

Walker took his coat off the hook and slid his arms in. "I'll tell you one thing, boss. This case has given me a powerful appetite. I feel like making something huge tonight. Or maybe I'll just pick something up. That would be better. As hungry as I am right now, I can't wait to shop and cook. Then I'm going to watch an old movie and go to bed. How about you?"

"Home," said Steele. "Arly will be waiting."

Walker waved one hand. "See you tomorrow, boss."

Steele watched him go, then straightened up his desk, putting files away, still thinking of the case. There was something he was missing. If he could only put his finger on it, he knew that he'd have it done, but was it? The dark shadow of an idea kept him company as he finished up his routine, making sure his desk was clear and ready for the next day. He was reaching for his coat when it came to him. The thing that they had over looked. It was certain that Hoffman talked to his killer, and while it was possible that he had confronted the killer at the market or out on the lane, there was a more plausible explanation. Steele picked up the phone.

"Betty? I need a favor. I know, quitting time. Just make one call for me, will you? Thanks. I need the phone records of Thomas Hoffman, yes, that's the one. As soon as possible. Thanks, Betty."

Steele hung up the phone and headed for the door. There was nothing more he could do but wait.

14. The Wrap Up.

Saturday morning came in with high clouds and sunny skies, leaving the air crisp and cool, with the upcoming winter rains still ahead. It was the middle of October and the wind coming in from the Pacific ocean stung the flesh, the last days of summer well behind for those that lived on the coast. Ben Steele slumbered in his bed, hidden under the layers of comforters and blankets, warding off the cold morning air. He woke slowly, thinking of nothing more than how nice it felt to stay huddled under the mass of cloth. Steele could hear the muffled sound of his two boys in the front room, watching the usual Saturday morning cartoons, and something else. He stuck his nose out from under the blankets. He could smell bacon cooking, and coffee brewing.

Steele pushed back the sheets and blankets, braving the cold chill of the room, and quickly dressed, heading out to the meet the aromas that tickled his nose. As he headed up the hall, he could now hear, distinctly, the sounds of the cartoons, and his wife in the background.

"Boys, breakfast is ready," said Arly.

Steele entered the kitchen, walked over and gave his wife a kiss. "It sure smells good in here."

She smiled at him. "Are you talking about me, or the bacon?"

"Both." He poured himself a cup of coffee and sat at the table. "How long have you been up?"

"Since the boys woke me a hour ago," said Arly. "You were sleeping and I didn't have the heart to wake you up, but since you are, can you get the boys to the table? Breakfast is ready."

Steele spotted the two boys sprawled out on the living room floor, faces glued to the television set. "Aaron, Dev, if you're not here in the next two minutes, I'm turning the TV off."

Like little robots, the two boys stood up and crossed into the kitchen and sat down.

"We're missing a good show," said Devin.

"Yeah," echoed Aaron. "Space Rangers are the coolest."

"Eat your breakfast," said Steele, "then you can go back to the Space Rangers."

The four sat down and ate, with Arly loading up the boys plates with scrambled eggs, crisp bacon, and buttered toast, then poured orange juice for each boy, before loading her own plate. Steele ate his food and listened to the boys talk about what they planned for the day, starting with Space Rangers, and then moving on to a ball game down at the school yard, with Aaron complaining the whole time about not being included in Devin's plans, and Devin complaining about what a pain in the rump Aaron was about most everything in life. Just a typical Saturday morning at the Steele household.

The boys bused their dirty dishes to the sink, then ran back and resumed their position in front of the television set, expressing their displeasure at missing the show, then it was just Steele and Arly left to clean up the rest of the mess. Steele cleaned up the table, then dried dishes while Arly washed, the two working as a team.

"So what are your plans for today?" asked Arly. "Going to work?"

"Just for a little bit," said Steele. "I've got some leads that hopefully will pan out. With a little luck, we can wrap this case up today."

"That would be nice. I could call my sister, she'd come up and watch the boys so we could get away, if you'd like."

He reached over and hugged his wife. "That'd be great, but one step at a time. Let me see what I can do about solving this first, okay?"

She kissed him. "You can do it."

Steele left his wife and family and drove down to the station. All was quiet on the second floor of the Public Safety Building, being a Saturday, but the police department was still humming along, even on a skeleton crew. Steele spotted the two folders on his desk before he sat down. He hung up his coat and made himself comfortable in the seat before opening the first of the two, the results of the phone records. It didn't take long to see that Thomas Hoffman had made but one phone call on the day of his death, and the phone company was kind enough to give him the corresponding name with the number. He set this folder aside and picked up the other one. There was note attached to the front of the folder.

"We stayed late to finish this. You're welcome."

Steele recognized the handwriting of Dominic Rodriguez and smiled. He could already hear the captain complain about the overtime paid out for the service. Steele opened the file and scanned the results. Rodriguez and his crew had taken the prints off the glasses and transferred them to a standard fingerprint chart, each identified with the name of the print owner. The last sheet of paper was a typed analysis of the prints, in comparison with the one found on the tire iron. Steele read the results with some surprise, but was happy that the owner of the print and phone number called matched. Steele picked up the phone and called Kevin Walker.

Walker answered on the third ring. "Your dime."

"We've got our killer," said Steele. "I'll pick you up in fifteen minutes."

#

Bonnie Williams sorted through the mail, doing what she had done six days a week for the past thirty years, without thinking too much about it, but today, she was distracted. So much had happened with the last week, that was difficult for her to concentrate. So little happened in West Harbor that without looking at a calender, the seasons came and went but the years were all the same, except for everybody getting older, then along comes Tony Chambers and the balance is upset. First one murder, then another. Nothing was going to be the same again. Then there was her constant morning companion, Adam Franklin, with his usual cup of coffee and banter. Had he been in love with her the whole time he was pretending to be just her friend? Was this something that she wanted? It was all too much. Now here he was, professing his love for her. What was next? A marriage proposal? Was that something she wanted?

She shook her head, trying to sort out her feelings. She liked Franklin, but did she love him the way he seemed to love her? Did she want to get married after all these years of being single? Could she change? Could she move out of her house? Or worse, could she allow another person to live with her. Hosting the wake was the first time in many years that she had entertained, and it had drained her, not to mention stressed her out worrying about the mess and what the others might do to her home. Bonnie knew that she was being silly, but the thought of having another person around scared her. She was used to living alone. Period. But what of Franklin? Now that he had opened the door, would he continue to knock until she let him in? She remembered the look on his face at the restaurant, having blurted out his love for her, and the expectation that she would return the sentiment. Could she?

Bonnie slid the mail into the appropriate slots without looking at the items, something she normally did, wanting to know who was getting what from whom, liking knowing the business of her fellow citizens, yet today, she filed the mail without a second glance. She was certain that there was something wrong with her, but couldn't put her finger on the reason for his discontent. Perhaps she needed a vacation. It had been awhile since her last escape.

She was out front, straightening out the postal forms when she spotted Adam Franklin coming from his house, with two cups of coffee, one for each hand. She watched him approach, the butterflies in her stomach building to a crescendo as he neared. She turned the lock on the door and flipped the open sign over, then grabbed hold of the handle and pushed the door open.

"I thought you might be missing your coffee," said Franklin as he took the steps into the post office. "We didn't get to talk much yesterday."

Bonnie worried about that remark as she walked around the counter and sat on her stool. "No we didn't."

Franklin sat on his familiar perch and looked at Bonnie. "You look beautiful. Has anybody ever told you that?"

Bonnie sipped her coffee. "Not since I was about twelve. My dad used to say that, but he seemed to be alone in that attitude."

"Well you are," said Franklin. He looked like he wanted to say something, but wasn't sure how to begin. "Well, here we are."

"Like we always are. What is it that you want to say, Adam? I can see it on your face that you've got something in mind."

"Well, yes, as a matter of fact I do," said Franklin. "Have you thought any more about what we discussed at lunch the other day? I know that I told you that I would wait for an answer, but I truly can't wait much longer. It took every bit of nerve I had just to tell you that I was in love with you, and to have you not say anything has got me worried, like maybe I should have just kept my big mouth shut."

She reached across and lay a hand on his. "Adam, you know I'm fond of you. Over the past couple of years we've become good friends, and I do love you in part, but I'm not sure that my love for you is the same as yours is for me. Do you understand what I'm saying?"

"That you love me," said Franklin, beaming. "That's what I wanted to hear. I know, maybe it's not same kind of love, but what is love anyway? Just two people who care about each other right? I know you care about me, and I have to tell you, it's been a lonely five years for me since my wife died, and I truly didn't think the day would come when I'd be able to replace the joy and companionship that she gave me, until I started talking to you."

"You're getting ahead of yourself, Adam."

"I know, but I've got to do this before I lose my nerve completely. I know that you might not feel the same about me as I do about you, but I think that love grows over time, and even if you only feel a friendship love at this time, that doesn't mean it won't grow into something much more, and I'm betting that this love will turn out to be a deep, life affirming love, the kind that last through the ages and beyond. I know that I don't have much to offer you, other than a nice house and a decent pension, but between us, I believe we'd do nicely together."

"Are you asking me to marry you?"

Franklin smiled. "See, even when I babble, you understand what I'm saying. Yes, I want you to marry me. Please say you will and make me the happiest man on earth."

Bonnie's brain processed the information quickly, seeing all the young men of her past, the loves that came and went, and the moments when marriage seemed imminent only to be pulled away at the last minute, all leading to this moment, what might turn out to be the one and only marriage proposal she would ever get in her life. It was true that she wasn't in love with Franklin, but she did like him and maybe it was as he said, that over time the love would grow. All her life, love was just out of her reach, bad timing, and bad luck, and yet in spite of it all, here she was, facing the biggest decision of her life. She looked at Franklin's hopeful face.

"I don't see a ring. You propose marriage, you should have a ring to back it up."

He slid off the stool. "Hold that thought. I've got a ring. Don't go anywhere."

Franklin headed out the door, half jogging to his house, leaving Bonnie alone with her thoughts. Was this what she wanted? She watched Franklin disappear into his house. She hadn't committed yet, there was still time, but not much longer. She smiled. Being married did have a nice ring to it.

#

Thomas Jones opened the Super Saver, flipping on the neon open sign, then walked outside and dropped a quarter in the newspaper box, lifted the lid and pulled out the morning paper. He looked around at the village, gauging his feelings for the place that he had called home these past two years. The cool wind tickled his bald pate, reminding him of the upcoming winter. It seemed like yesterday that he rolled into town and took over a failed business, cleaning the shelves, stocking the can foods, and ordering the delivery of gas for the empty tanks below the parking lot. A lot of water under the bridge, he decided, walking back inside.

Jones flipped on the over head lights, then settled in his spot at the counter, with his view of the store in front and the town outside his little window. He opened the paper and began to read, working his way though the front sections of the paper, before turning to the crossword puzzle on the back page. He had just folded the paper when he noticed his first customer for the day. Even from a distance, Jones could make out Bob Peterson approaching, clutching his coat and keeping his head down, the shag haircut giving him away. Minutes later, the door opened and Peterson entered.

"Kind of chilly out there today," said Peterson.

Jones put the puzzle aside. "Winters coming. Nothing can be done about that."

Peterson nodded. "Millie hates the cold. Says she wants to move south, but I tell her that we can't afford to move, and besides, no matter where you are, the weather isn't perfect, right?"

"You're right. Make the best of where you are."

"That's what I've been telling her. It doesn't matter anyhow. We're not going anywhere. Millie didn't want anything bad to happen to Old Tom's cats, so guess who now has a bunch of cats to feed? That's right. We split the lot up, we and the Duncan's, each taking six, and now I've got the screaming meanies right outside our door. I'm holding to keeping them outdoors, like Old Tom did, but Millie wants to make indoor cats out of them. Can you imagine the noise that six cats can make? It about drives me crazy. I suggested making a little cat house out in the back yard, but Millie says that it's inhuman to treat them like that. They're out door cats, I told her, but she's fighting hard to turn that around."

"Old Tom spent a lot of money on those cats," said Jones.

"I hear that, but will Millie take no for an answer? No way. She says we have to take them or the county will put them all to sleep. You want my opinion, some of them cats aren't all that healthy anyway, but you didn't hear that from me. Millie would have a cow if I so much as suggest that the cats aren't going to live long. I believe they miss Old Tom, but I could be wrong. You ever had cats, Mr. Jones?"

"I never had time for pets."

"Me either. Anyway, Millie sent me over for cat food. Which aisle?"

"Back wall, with the pet supplies."

Peterson followed directions, disappearing from view for a moment, then returned with a dozen cans of cat food. He set them on the counter. "Maybe I should be buying this stuff in the case. Any chance of a discount if I buy bulk or should I shop down in Rock Port for that?"

Jones thought about it for a moment. He had been nothing more than a mercenary in the price wars, holding to his thirty percent profit margin for so long that it was difficult for him to consider anything else, but he was a member of this community. Shouldn't he help out where he could? That is, if he was going to stay. With all that had happened during the past week, he wasn't sure he wanted to stick around, but if he did, would it hurt to help out where he lived?

"I'm sure we could come up with something that would be fair to both of us," said Jones, not sure exactly what kind of deal he was offering.

Peterson reached into his pocket and pulled out a twenty. "That'd be real nice, Mr. Jones. I don't want to give my business to Rock Port, nothing personal, but those businesses aren't in West Harbor. Shop locally, right, Mr. Jones?"

Jones rang up the purchases, bagged the cans and gave Peterson his change. "That would work for me."

Peterson took his bag, then paused. "I heard a rumor that you were leaving town. Is that true? We need you here, Mr. Jones."

And just like that, Jones make his decision. Leaving town was no longer an option. He was needed and that was something he had never been in his life. Living a marginal existence meant that coming and going were of little concern to those around him, but for the first time, he had become a member of a community. It was a strange feeling for Jones, having never experienced it before. He looked up at Peterson.

"I'm not going anywhere."

"That's good." Peterson waved with his free hand and headed for the door. "See you around, Mr. Jones."

Jones watched Peterson walk away, clutching his coat with one hand and holding onto the bag of cat food with the other. The early morning sunlight cast long shadows off his body as he moved away from the Super Saver. Jones turned and looked at the store he had created out of thin air. During the two years of his thirty percent markup, he had put away a little money, for there wasn't that much money to make off the two dozen people who lived in West Harbor, but maybe it was time for a price reduction. He could still make a profit if he cut his thirty percent to fifteen, and be doing a service to the community. The reality was, some of his fellow citizens shopped in Rock Port anyway, because of the exorbitant prices he charged. Perhaps they would shop more at his store if he didn't charge so much. It was a novel idea for Jones, not being naturally altruistic, but what could it hurt? And maybe it was time to do a little remodeling in his living quarters. He had never intended on staying long, but had that changed as well? It would be nice to have a storage shed for the can goods and such, leaving his living space larger. Not having shelves of product facing him every waking moment was a pleasant thought. Maybe he could get a couch. Changes were coming.

Jones picked up his crossword puzzle and started the grid, working the top left corner, then his gaze shifted to the bulletin board on the wall under the window to the outside world. Here were his price lists, and delivery dates, and tucked away in one corner, a piece of paper with the name Maggie on it, complete with phone number under it. He set the paper down, and picked up the phone, took a deep breath, then began to dial.

#

Star braided his hair into one long pony tail, and trimmed up his scruffy beard, then left the bedroom and walked out and joined his wife and son at the breakfast table. Tracy was dressed in jeans and a sweatshirt. Genesis wore his San Francisco forty-nine shirt and jeans. Star smiled at his family and thought about the future. He had made some big promises the day before, and wondered if he would be able to fulfill his goals. Was it possible to make a decent living out of goats? Was he able to start up a dairy and give Tracy the life she wanted? Or would he fail miserably, and watch his wife and child walk away from him. This was a turning point for Star, and the not knowing was causing him a lot of anxiety. Still, Tracy and Genesis were still with him, and he hoped, would stay with him. He sat down at the head of the table and smiled at his family.

"So here we are," said Star.

Tracy returned his smile, but he was sure it wasn't as sincere as he hoped. Was there some sadness behind it? He and Tracy had talked late into the night about their future together and the steps he would need to insure that it was a happy union, and by the time Star went to sleep, nightmares invaded his quiet rest, leaving him tired and achy the next day. Still, she was smiling. That had to account for something, he decided.

"So what are you plans for today?" asked Tracy.

Here it was, he thought, right up front. What was he going to do?

"Well, I know very little about starting up a dairy, so I thought I'd take things slowly." Star saw the look on Tracy's face. Disbelief or sadness? He wasn't sure. "So I thought I'd see if I could borrow Bill Seavers truck and run into Rock Port and do a little research in the library on the subject. There must be dozens of books that could help us get started. I've never applied for a business loan, but I think we'd better off if we knew what we were talking about before filing papers. What do you think, Tracy?"

She nodded. "That makes a lot of sense. What about the rest of the day?"

"That's easy," said Star, feeling like he was making good progress. "The goat shed needs a lot of work, as does the fence in the back yard. We've got plenty of nails and wood. And it looks pretty sunny out there. I could do some repairs and maybe talk to some people about getting some more goats. We're going to need a lot more goats if this is going to work."

Genesis sat and watched his parents talk, waiting for his moment to speak. When Star stopped talking, Genesis jumped in. "Could we get a TV set, dad?"

Star looked at his son. For years, he had been calling television the vast wasteland, culturally depraved, and morally reprehensible, yet he knew that his boy went over to the Seaver household and watched cartoons and movies and all that he hated. Was getting a television set selling out to a society that craved instant gratification? What would happen if his son was exposed to more and more television? Then he thought of his own upbringing. They had a television set, and he grew up watching sit-coms and movies and sports, and the only reason he went off the rails was because of boredom. For a while there, he craved the excitement, and the danger of being a thief, and of course the money was good and he had that little problem with drugs. Still, was it TV that caused him all his woes, or was it his own choices that led to his running away and changing his name? He made a decision.

"Sure. I'll look into it while I'm in town." he looked over at Tracy. "I know what you want, and I'll try to get it for you, but this is all very new to me."

"I know, but we'll work it out."

"And you think that having all the nice things that the Seavers have will make our marriage work?"

"I'm not sure," said Tracy, "but Mike and I need a normal life. That means a lot of changes. I'll come with you to town and see what I can do about helping out the family. Either a job, or start taking classes at the community college. If this dairy project is going to happen, we'll need to know something about small business administration and accounting. I can do that. Or look for a job. There's no reason for me to be sitting around her all day if you're working with the goats and Mike is at school."

"What kind of job?" asked Star.

"The kind that pays money. I'm pretty good with money, need to be better, but I've saved a small sum, enough to buy a used a car, and a television set, which is a good start toward our future."

Star smiled. Our future, she said. Maybe he could pull it off. Maybe living like the rest of the world wasn't such a bad thing. And he had to admit, he didn't much care for the leaky roof, or the lack of central heat, and there had been days when he wouldn't have minded sitting around the television set with his family, watching a good movie and eating popcorn. He was still a young man, not yet thirty, and he had a whole life ahead of him, why not make something of it.

"It's not going to be easy," said Star.

"Nobody said it was," said Tracy. "And there's one more thing I think you should do, but this one is on you."

He waited for it.

"I should think that you would be proud of Mike and me and would want to boast a little. You're a family man, don't you think you should call your family and tell them about us? It's been ten years. A lot has happened since you left home. You should call them and tell them what's going on in your life."

Star felt his stomach lurch. He felt the fear rise in his throat and the sweat build on his forehead. Ten long years of wondering. Would they talk to him after all this time? What could he say that would erase their anger at him? In spite of Tracy's good will, this wasn't the first time he had considered calling his parents to tell them that he was okay, but fear always stopped him. And he wondered if they would even talk to him. What if they hung up on him? Or told him to go to hell? How would he deal with that rejection?

"I'm afraid."

Tracy reached out and took hold of his hand. "I'll be right by your side when you make the call. And it about time I called my family as well. It's been a long time. Too long. I've been away just as long as you have and perhaps it's time to mend some fences. You make your call and I'll make mine. We'll do it together, how's that?"

He tried to smile, but it came out more of a grimace. "I'll try, but if they hang up on me, don't be too surprised."

"And you won't know unless you make that call."

He walked over to the phone and picked up the receiver. "Here goes nothing."

#

Bill Seavers lay in bed and looked over at his wife. Her hair was a mess, blonde hair sticking up every which way, and yet she was the most beautiful woman he had ever seen. Why had he been so dense? If he had only talked to his wife, he could have been enjoying much more in life besides the pleasure of building a fine piece of furniture. Here he was, with his high school sweetheart, resting up from another round, and thinking of how much one little word did to enhance his life. He shook his head. Why was he so stupid? He reached over and brushed a lock of hair from her face and inadvertently woke her. She opened her eyes and smiled.

"What are you looking at?" she asked.

"You. I was just thinking how beautiful you look there."

"With this hair? And no makeup? Are you kidding me?'

He brushed back her hair and let his hand linger on the side of her face. "Absolutely not. I was thinking about my stupidity in not talking to you earlier. We could have been doing this for months."

"I certainly gave you enough signs that I was interested."

"But I read them wrong. I overheard you talking to Tracy once when you didn't think I was around and I swear you said that you wanted another child, and all I could think of was how much it was going to cost. The baby would impact our lives. We'd have to have the baby in a crib here in our room, then when the child got older, would have to share a room with one of the other two, and I don't know. It seemed like a lot more than I was willing to take on."

She pushed herself up onto one elbow and glared at him. "And yet you didn't talk to me about it, instead made me think that there was something wrong with me. How could you do that?"

"I'm sorry. I didn't mean to make you feel bad. I'll admit it, I was only thinking of myself, and then when you started wearing those tight clothes that showed off nearly everything, I, well, I don't know what I thought, but it wasn't good."

She lay back in bed. "At least you finally came to your senses. Look, I don't know what you think you heard, but Tracy and I were talking about the difficulty of childbirth. She's the one that wants another child, said that having one wasn't enough, and that she was going to talk to Star about maybe having another. It had nothing to do with us."

He blew out his air. "That would have been nice to know about two months ago."

"All you had to do was ask."

He turned his head and looked at his beautiful wife. "So no more children?"

"Two's plenty. You don't want any more, do something about it, or use condoms, I don't care, just don't stop loving me, okay?"

He reached over and hugged her. "I think the kids are still asleep. Ready for more?"

Just then, there was pounding on the door. "Mom, Cindy's hitting me."

"Am not. You big baby. Don't listen to him, mom. He started it."

"Did not, you big meanie."

Mary Seavers looked over at her husband, then leaned up and kissed him on the lips. "It'll have to wait, honey. In the future, don't shut me out, okay?"

He lay back on the bed, with his arms crossed behind his head and smiled, watching his wife walk across the bedroom in her nightie. "I love you, honey."

She turned and returned the smile. "I love you too. Are you hungry? It looks like I'm making breakfast."

Seavers nodded. "Famished."

#

Ben Steele drove over the crest of the hill, with the entire village of West Harbor falling down below them under a warm October sun. He felt great, having two incriminating facts at his disposal. There was the very real possibility that the guilty party would deny all allegations, but a court trial, with the defendant on the witness stand and a competent district attorney hammering away should bring a confession out of the suspect. Steele hoped it wouldn't come to that. He was certain that he had the goods, and that by the end of the morning, they would have their killer in custody. He looked over at Walker.

"You don't seem convinced, Kevin. What's the problem?"

"It wasn't Jones," said Walker, pushing his fedora up to the top of his head. "I knew that the fingerprint didn't match, but I still feel that he was the guy. Somehow he wiped off his own prints and made sure the other one stayed. Don't ask me how he did it, I just know that he did. He's a stone cold killer, boss, and that ain't no piece of fiction. And to tell you the truth, I'm just a little disappointed that we're not picking him up. Sweat him out and he'll confess."

"He didn't do it," said Steele. "Sorry to burst your bubble, but the facts don't lie."

"Facts can be altered to fit the crime, if you ask me."

"Not this time," said Steele. "We've got our killer, why can't you be happy about that?"

"It just doesn't seem right, that's all. I feel bad for this. And I didn't see it coming. Sorry, boss, I'll shut up now."

Steele drove down the hill, passed Louella Chamber's house and took the first right, then slowed to a stop in front of the nice bungalow with the tidy lawn and the white picket fence. The detectives exited the car, walked up to the gate and entered the property, then on up to the front door. Steele knocked and waited. Seconds passed, then the door opened.

"You're back," said Adam Franklin, clutching something in his right hand. "More questions?"

"Could we come in, please."

Franklin stood aside and let the detectives enter his house. The three walked into the living room and got comfortable, Franklin on the couch, Steele on the opposite chair, and Walker leaning up against the fireplace.

"What's going on? I heard that you arrested and released both Star and Young Tom, didn't you make an arrest?"

Steele saw what bothered Walker. He didn't like arresting the elderly man any more than Walker did, but the man clearly did the crime. There was no option.

"Mr. Franklin, you are under arrest for the murders of Tony Chambers and Thomas Hoffman," said Steele. He finished reading Franklin his Miranda rights.

"That's the most ridiculous I've heard. Where's your proof?"

Steele held up one hand. "We have a match with a fingerprint we found on the tire iron found behind Thomas Jones store. Your fingerprint, Mr. Franklin. You called in the alert to shift blame and make the police look close at Mr. Jones, and for many reasons, Jones looked good for the crime. But he was innocent. You killed Tony Chambers."

"Why on earth would I do that?" asked Franklin.

"You tell us," said Steele. "And you killed Thomas Hoffman as well. We got Hoffman's phone records and found that on the day of his death, he made but one call. That was to you, Mr. Franklin. My guess is that Hoffman saw you kill Chambers and wanted money, set up a meeting with you at the old school house, and you came and killed him. How am I doing so far?"

Franklin dropped his head and looked at the ring resting in his open palm. "It wasn't supposed to work out this way."

"What way was that, Mr. Franklin?"

"I didn't mean to kill Old Tom. He was rather insistent that I give him five thousand dollars, like I have that kind of money laying around. I'm on a pension, with very limited funds, but he didn't care. He said that if I didn't come up with the money, he would go to the police and tell them what he saw. Apparently, Tony and I weren't alone down on the beach last week. Was it really only a week ago? Strange. Seems like a lot longer now."

"You don't have to do this, Mr. Franklin," said Steele.

"It doesn't matter much, does it? I'll have to go to jail and face trial and humiliation, I might as well get it out in the open now. The fact of the matter was, Tony Chambers was a bully and a brute and I don't regret killing him for one second, though it was a marvel of physics that I could kill the big man. You see, he was threatening Bonnie and I just couldn't stand by and let that happen. Yes, I know that he was a lot larger, but you'd be amazed at how much damage can be caused when a blunt instrument is struck in just the right spot.

"I followed him down to the beach, taking my tire iron for self defense, just in case he got violent with me. Anyway, I told him a thing or two about manners and how one should treat one's fellow man and the brute laughed at me. Said I should go home to my mommy. Said that he didn't have time for a wimp like me. And that's when it happened. He turned his head for just one moment, and I swung that tire iron for all I was worth, thinking that I was a dead man. I figured he'd swat away the iron, then punch me in the face, but I was so mad by that time that I didn't think. I hit him in the one spot on the back of his head that made him drop like a ton of bricks. I ran over and checked for a pulse, but he was dead. I was horrified, but what could I do? I didn't mean to kill the man, it just worked out that way."

"What about Thomas Hoffman?" asked Walker.

"I met him at the school, and we argued. I told him that I wasn't going to jail over a waste of human space like Tony Chambers and he was adamant that I give him money. I pleaded with him but he was so stubborn and the more he argued, the madder I got. Then I just don't know what came over me, but I started swinging the tire iron."

"Why did you bring the tire iron to the meeting?" asked Steele.

"I honestly don't know. Oh, do you mean did I take it intending on killing Old Tom? Don't be ridiculous. I just picked it up on my way over to the school house. I'm sorry to say that I don't have a better explanation. So I killed Old Tom to shut him up. And you're right, I did call the police and try to implicate Young Tom. I feel bad about it now, but I was at my wits end."

Steele noticed the ring in Franklin's hand. "What's that for?"

Franklin looked down at the ring, then closed his fingers over it. "It's nothing now. Not important. If you will give me a couple of minutes to get ready, we can go."

"If you don't mind," said Steele. "Kevin will go with you."

The lights dimmed in Franklin's eyes and he shrugged. "Very well. Come with me, sergeant."

Fifteen minutes later, the three exited the house, with Franklin locking the door before facing the police car at the end of the walk. The detectives escorted Franklin to the car, where Walker helped him in the back seat, then slid in next to him and Steele took the wheel. Minutes later, Steele turned the car around, then headed back to Rock Port.

#

Louella Chambers watched the police load up Franklin in the back of their car from her kitchen window and wondered if this was the end of the killings. Was it possible that slight, elderly, Adam Franklin could have killed her husband? And if so, then it was probable that he killed Old Tom as well. While she was saddened by the death of Old Tom, she felt nothing but gratitude for the killing of Tony Chambers. She might have put on a bit of a show at Old Tom's wake, concerning the burial of her husband, but deep down, she was relieved that he was gone. She had a limited income, mostly coming from a government check, and would have been hard pressed to come up with living arrangements that were equal to what she had now. With her husband gone and the threat of eviction removed, she could live out the rest of her life in her own home. At least she wouldn't have to worry about paying for Tony's funeral. Her daughter had called and told her that the county would pick up the check, nothing fancy, but at no cost to Louella. Buried at the county cemetery wasn't West Harbor, but as far as Louella was concerned, Tony had stopped being a member of the community a long time. She felt bad for her community, and a little guilty for bringing Tony Chambers to West Harbor. When he left, she hoped that she would never see him again, then he showed up and the chain of events led to misery and death. How she could have prevented such actions, she had no idea, but she felt the guilt none the less.

She stared out the window at the bright sunshine and thought of how arresting Franklin would affect the community. He was a nice man, she decided, even if he did kill Old Tom, but she was sure there was a valid reason for the killing. With Franklin in custody, she could afford to look at the big picture. Surely, Old Tom said something that set Franklin off. Who was to know that Franklin could be so violent? Then she thought of Bonnie Williams and how every time Louella went to the post office to collect her mail, she spotted Franklin perched on the stool talking up the post mistress. How would this affect Bonnie? Only one way to find out.

Louella grabbed her overcoat and slid her arms into the sleeves, then walked out into the cool sunshine. It was late fall and winter would soon be upon them, but for this moment, it was all sunshine and blue skies. She walked out to the street, turned left and covered the short distance to the post office in record time. Louella spotted Bonnie in the window as she neared, then waved as she passed under the big windows facing the road. Moments later, she opened the door and went inside.

"Winter's coming," said Louella."

Bonnie turned her head and stared at Louella. "They just took Adam away."

Louella nodded. "I saw it all from my kitchen window."

"What does it mean?"

Louella stared at Bonnie. Either the woman was addled, or was refusing to see the reality of the situation. "I suspect they arrested him for the two murders."

"Adam? How can this be? He harmless, a sweet little man who was going to ask me to marry him."

Louella moved in and hugged Bonnie, something she had never done, feeling a little silly for the gesture, then quickly pulled away. "Did you want to marry him?"

"That's not the point. He was going to ask me. I've waited my whole life for someone to ask me and now that the time arrives, I find out my suitor is arrested for murder? That hardly seems fair." Bonnie stepped back around the counter and sat on her stool. "Maybe I wanted to marry him. I don't know. It's not everyday that a man proposed marriage. At least not for me. And maybe I would have married him, I don't know. I'm babbling, sorry."

Louella sat down on Franklin's perch and looked at Bonnie. "Did you love him?"

Bonnie shook her hear. "Not really. I liked him. He was a nice man, but a murderer? That wouldn't do. I couldn't marry him now."

"So what are you going to do?"

Bonnie thought for a moment, then smiled. "I'll tell you exactly what I'm going to do. I've got some vacation saved up, I believe I'll take a Mexican cruise. How about you join me? I could use the company and I'll bet you haven't have a decent vacation in years."

"I'm not sure I can afford that," said Louella thinking of her finances. "But, it sure sounds like fun."

"You think about it," said Bonnie. "But a vacation is exactly what I need. A break from this place. You stay too long in one place and the place takes you over. Adam was the only possible suitor for me in this tiny town, and I was willing to go along, but you know what? I don't believe I would have married him. Settled is what I would have done. And for a murderer at that. Don't you worry about me, Lou, I'll be fine. Say, are you busy right now?"

Louella didn't need to think long, she had all the time in the world. "My schedule's pretty open."

"How about a nice cup of tea? You sit tight and I'll throw the teakettle on the stove. Then you and I can talk about all the men we're going to meet on the cruise. What do you say?"

"That sounds real nice," said Louella.

Bonnie exited through the back door of the post office, leaving Louella alone with her thoughts. She turned and looked out the window at the village that she had called home for the past twenty years and for the first time in a long time, she had something to smile about. Perhaps, she thought, I could come up with the money. She had always wanted to go on a cruise.

Made in the USA
Charleston, SC
27 May 2012